Grace Without Grace

Stumbling into Romance

A Romantic Comedy

Grace Without Grace
Stumbling into Romance

A Romantic Comedy

Susan Tietjen

Sunbright Press

Crescent City, CA

Susan Tietjen/ Sunbright Press
Crescent City, CA

Publisher's Note: This is a work of fiction. Names, characters, places, and incidents are a product of the author's imagination. Locales and public names are sometimes used for atmospheric purposes. Any resemblance to actual people, living or dead, or to businesses, companies, events, institutions, or locales is completely coincidental.

Grace Without Grace, Stumbling into Romance/Susan Tietjen. -- 1st ed.

ISBN 978-0-9904892-3-8
LCCN 201991284

This book is dedicated to the clumsy, the awkward, and the person who is constantly plagued with bad luck—but who needs to be loved like everyone else.

For some of us, Murphy's Law reigns supreme. No matter how hard we try, it seems like misfortune is determined to defy us. A multitude of quotes, like breadcrumbs on the trail of life, imparted by someone named "Anonymous," might lead us through the heartache––or at least give us a laugh or two along the way.

"I'm not clumsy! The floor just hates me, the table and chairs are bullies, and the walls get in my way."

"It takes real skills to choke on air, fall up the stairs, and trip over nothing. I have those skills."

"Blessed our we who can laugh at ourselves, for we shall never cease to be amused."

"Falling down is part of life. Getting back up is living."

And then there are a few words of wisdom from some of our favorite friends:

"Laughter is the best medicine."
> —Bennett Cerf, probably based on the Wisdom of Solomon

"To laugh at yourself is to love yourself."
> —Mickey Mouse.

"You can't be brave if you've only had wonderful things happen to you."
> —Mary Tyler Moore

CHAPTER 1

Grace paused, unnerved by the way the skinny brunette in the tight purple skirt and orange tank top persisted in following her. Granted, Grace had attracted all kinds of trouble throughout her twenty-three years of life, but she'd never had someone stalk her.

She dodged a sticky spot at the far end of the convenience store, one she stepped in the first time through the candy section. Now her shoe made an annoying *snick* with each step. Out of the corner of her eye, while perusing KitKats and Snickers bars, she saw the purple and orange girl slowly edge around the corner and drift toward her. Was she a shoplifter? A pickpocket?

Grace scurried off to the aisle with the batteries and antifreeze. From this spot, she had a bird's-eye view of the gas pumps and her best friend, Hannah, filling her Mercedes. Her car sat behind a CHP car, but the officer was missing. He couldn't have gone far away, though. Possibly in the bathroom. Still, it gave Grace a small measure of comfort to think that if this odd girl attacked her, he might come to her rescue.

The girl in question, hair in a messy ponytail and no makeup, ambled along the walkway between the fridges and the aisles, gaping at everything as if she'd never seen it before. She avoided eye contact with Grace, which made the hair rise on the back of Grace's neck.

The door opened and Hannah stepped inside. On her heels came a woman with two young kids. The smallest one had a sippy cup in his hand and, laughing, banged it on the shelves, threw it on the floor, and picked it up again before scurrying around the corner.

Having volunteered to pay for their drinks before they separated, Hannah made her way to the soda machines. Grace decided to grab a couple frozen burritos to prevent starvation on the final hour of their long drive north.

After that, she returned to the candy aisle. She'd made up her mind. Peanut M&M's. And if she hurried, she could avoid the creepy person in purple and toss the burritos in the microwave.

Unfortunate that Murphy, the 'if it can go wrong, it will go wrong' guy, had different ideas. Bad luck was Grace's middle name, and it came in so many forms she'd grown up one step away from paranoid. She grabbed a bag of Peanut M&M's and gasped when someone tried to snatch the candy out of her hand. Purple Girl! A tug of war ensued, Grace's eyes bulging when the girl swore at her.

"Mine. They're mine," the girl snarled. "You took the ones in my favorite colors, and you can't have them."

Favorite colors? Weren't M&M's all the same colors? This girl was nuts! There were a dozen bags still in the box on the shelf. Yes, Grace should have let go and picked one of those, but her mind was as frozen as the fingers holding the ice-cold burritos. She jerked the bag away and took off toward the fridge at the end of the aisle, jumping over the sticky spot and turning the bend like a racehorse. Over her shoulder, she saw the girl coming after her.

"Thief!" the girl screamed. "She stole from me! And she's trying to shoplift!"

In the overhead mirror, the tattooed, multi-pierced, spike-haired clerk waved at someone. Grace dearly hoped it was the cop, because Hannah was doing nothing but standing there with their drinks in hand, paralyzed by shock.

With Purple Girl on Grace's heels, Grace took another lap past the candy. Again, a steeplechaser's leap took her over the sticky spot. She rounded the corner, cringing at the screeches emanating from the purple-clad nutcase dogging her heels. The girl pushed Grace, and Grace floundered all over the aisle as she tried to stay upright. Flipping around to face her attacker, she prepared to punch the girl if she had no other choice—then realized her hands were full. Purple Girl grabbed the M&M's again and tugged hard, tearing the corner off. M&M's scattered like marbles across the dusty floor and under the chip display by the glass door.

Fury robbed Grace of common sense, and she shoved the girl, but after the nutcase stumbled back, she came after Grace with a murderous look in her eye.

"Thief!" the girl screamed again, swinging a doubled fist at Grace.

Grace ducked and backpedaled, praying for a way out of this mess, but her heart took a nosedive when her right foot went out from under her. Shock swept through her when she realized the toddler had spilled some of his juice, and she was on her way down. She dropped the burritos, windmilled her arms, and crashed into the shelves to her right. Boxes of donuts and packages of bear claws and brownies tumbled to the floor, and she landed on her backside on top of them with an "oof". The girl came at her again, but Grace grabbed one of the burritos and aimed it at her.

Purple Girl screeched, turning on her heel and running as Grace launched the burrito. The girl dodged someone as she rounded the corner, and time froze as Grace watched the cylinder of pseudo-Mexican fare sailing through the air, missing the girl, and clocking that certain someone—*the cop*—in the forehead.

Grace screamed, too, the sound muffled behind hands shaking with terror as the furious officer whipped out his gun and pointed it at her.

Hannah rushed to Grace's aid, drinks still in hand, but skidded to a halt the second the weapon cleared its holster. Grace heard the door close as the nutcase escaped, followed by the woman and her children. Silence reigned.

Tears coursed their way toward Grace's chin. She'd won. Her left hand clutched what was left of a bag of Peanut M&M's. But she was going to jail. She'd just assaulted a law-enforcement officer.

"Get up nice and slow," the cop said, his jaw set tight with anger.

"Okay, okay," she said, slipping twice in the juice as she did her best to obey. She moaned, wondering if she'd broken anything beyond the shelf she hit and the packages of baked goods.

The clerk appeared behind Hannah and stabbed a finger at Grace. "She was tryin' to steal."

"Grace doesn't steal," Hannah said, defying the clerk to disagree with her. "The weirdo in purple started it."

Slowly, the officer returned his weapon to its holster. He had a small goose egg above his right eye, which he touched gingerly.

"Sorry," Grace said. "I missed her."

"Yeah," he said. "I get it. Name and address."

"Grace Evans," she replied. "We're from Los Gatos, two-and-a-half-hours south of here, near San Jose—"

"I know where Los Gatos is. I assume you're traveling through?"

"I promise," she said, hoping he just wanted her to go away. She dearly wanted to comply.

"Are you with her?" he said to Hannah in the same terse tone.

She nodded. "Yes, Officer. Hannah Fleming. We're headed to my uncle's cabin in Secret Lake Village, near Ukiah—"

"I know where that is, too." Whatever Hannah said seemed to catch the officer's attention. Grace suspected it had a lot to do with the Fleming name. They were well-known in Northern California. They were well-known in lots of places. Turning to the clerk, he said, "Mario, show me your footage."

Mario gave Grace a dirty look but returned to the counter.

The aisle was a mess. Sticky juice dirtied by Grace's shoes and soaked into her khaki capris. Flattened food and crushed boxes scattered all over. Donut crumbs smashed on her rump. A shelf bent at an odd angle, dangling from its brackets. Grace brushed off the crumbs and took a mincing step toward Hannah, a hand pressed to her aching lower back.

Officer Tran, so his name badge said, herded Grace and Hannah toward the counter, where Grace set down the scrunched Peanut M&M's bag.

"You're gonna arrest her, right?" Mario said to the cop, glaring at Grace as she pulled a handful of napkins from the dispenser and did her best to fix her pants. Mostly, the napkins crumbled all over them and the floor.

"Don't jump to conclusions," Officer Tran said. "I've seen that girl in here before. Something seemed more off about her than usual."

"Kooky Kathy? She lives somewhere 'round here. Comes in at least once a week, but, honestly, I ain't never seen her do nothin' like this before. She only gets upset if she sees anyone doin' somethin' wrong, so I'm guessin' blondie here was stealin' like Kathy said."

"I wasn't—" Grace went speechless when Tran gave her the shut-it look.

Mario finally ran the video, and sure enough, the scene played out in living black and white, Grace the innocent victim and Purple Girl—Kooky Kathy—in all her insane glory.

Tran glared at Mario. "If I'd arrested an innocent person, you wouldn't be my favorite guy today."

Mario had the decency to appear embarrassed. Grace almost felt sorry for him. Besides feeling stupid, he had to face the job of cleaning up the mess she made. Well, that she and Kooky Kathy made.

"Here," Tran said, offering Grace the deflated candy bag. "Don't worry about the donuts and things. Mario will have to write that off as a loss." He stared Mario down when the clerk tried to protest.

Grace accepted it automatically but raised a brow at realizing it only had one M&M in it. "Uh," she murmured, realizing this also meant the officer was letting her go. "You're—you're not arresting me?"

A wry smile twisted his mouth to one side. "It was an accident, Grace Evans. This 'Kooky Kathy' is probably off her meds."

"Uh, thanks," she said, more grateful than he could imagine. She eyed the package again and then set it on the counter. What was she supposed to do with one M&M?

"You can have it," Mario sneered.

"That's okay," Grace declined, taking a step back. Hannah handed Grace her soda, pulled a ten-dollar bill out of her pocket and tossed it on the counter for their drinks. Without waiting for change, she pushed Grace out the door. They hurried to the car, Grace still shaking and praying the clerk would do what Officer Tran said he should do.

Hannah was shaking, too, but she burst into laughter the minute they climbed into her Mercedes. After dropping her cup into the drink holder, she pulled away from the gas pump saying, "It's not even noon yet, Grace. I'd hoped we get at least a day into our trip before Murphy struck."

"Uhm, no, if you recall, you forgot your bathing suit—something you never do—and had to go back for it before you picked me up. Which made us an hour late hitting the road. Which, of course, put us here in time to run into Kooky Kathy."

"Good point. Your bad-luck vibes spread far and wide, my friend. I should be used to it after so many years." She smothered another laugh. "But this one is pretty radical, even for you. I mean, having a cop point a gun at you? Maybe you shouldn't have thrown a frozen burrito at him."

"I didn't. I threw it at a shrieking, punching M&Ms thief."

"I know. It's just not…"

"Not too smart. I know. And now we're late for work."

Hannah sobered. "Yeah, we are. I texted Aunt Sharon while I was putting gas in the car. They've already left for the airport, but the kids are teenagers. They'll be fine until we arrive."

"They're probably the best-behaved teenagers on the planet. Kyle's what, seventeen now? And the twins are fourteen. They'd be fine if we didn't show up until tomorrow."

"Most likely, but Aunt Sharon wouldn't be happy. At least we're on our way. Shall we carry on with what we were discussing before we stopped for gas?"

Hannah was so excited about their plans, she'd already put Grace's near-miss incident aside, which annoyed Grace. She wanted to make a snarky comment, like "No, I'd rather see if my 'bad-luck vibes' can wreck your aunt and uncle's silver anniversary cruise to Alaska. Maybe cause the boat to hit an iceberg and sink."

For the last two months—in addition to the last two-and-a-half hours of their drive—Hannah had talked about little else but this trip, except for maybe her boyfriend. Grace wasn't exactly tired of it, but she didn't look forward to marinating in it for another hour. She sighed. She needed to consider the bright side. At least she was admiring the landscape from the front seat of Hannah's car instead of whatever might pass for a jail cell around here.

Hannah jabbered on for a while, with Grace offering an occasional grunt or a nod, then added, "I'm so glad I took the summer off from school this year. I've been pushing so hard for so long, I was starting to freak out."

"Must be nice," Grace said, stretching her sore back. "I've been sick of school for a long time."

Hannah mewed with compassion. "I know. I wish things weren't so difficult for you. Are you sure you're okay with taking two weeks off from college and your job to do this?"

Grace laughed. "Are you kidding? I can hardly wait. Remember, I'm only taking one class this summer, and it's mostly online anyway. My professor's cool with it, as long as my assignments aren't late. As for my job at the pet store, I haven't had a vacation in two years and my boss all but shoved me out the door. She doesn't offer vacation pay, but it doesn't matter since your Aunt Sharon is paying us more to 'babysit' her sainted children than the store pays me to sell birds and clean fish tanks."

"She's really generous. What about your mom? How is she?"

Grace sighed. "Passable, for someone in her slippers. At least I got to spend a couple of days with her before we left. She actually got up and had breakfast with me this morning."

Trudy Evans' poor health had eluded diagnosis until after Grace's youngest sibling was born. There were days she couldn't sleep and others she couldn't get out of bed, but either way, she was constantly weak and tired. A good day was something to treasure. Hannah appreciated it almost as much as Grace.

"That's awesome! And you'll have a couple more days with her before you head back to our apartment. Don't forget to text her a lot of pictures while we're at the lake. She's never been to the cabin, but she loves to see what you're doing."

"She does," Grace said. "Although the pictures will *not* convince her it's a cabin. I mean, you haven't convinced me it's a cabin." The comment stirred up the bantering that was almost as old as they were.

"It's a vacation home in the woods," Hannah said, chuckling. "That's qualification enough, right?"

"Not in my book, but I look forward to it anyway."

"Maybe you can find some cute guys to flirt with," Hannah teased. "There should be lots to pick from over the July 4th weekend."

Grace made another face. "I'll pass. My soulmate is none other than Murphy. He's as jealous as they come. He always makes things go wrong for the guys I meet and destroys any relationship I ever come close to having."

"I wish you could get a restraining order against him."

"Me, too. Let me know when you figure out how."

"I still think it'd do you good to do a bit of flirting."

"Nope. Aunt Sharon demands no less than responsible caretakers for her babies. Girls ogling guys don't make responsible caretakers. Besides, the guys are always more interested in you than me." Grace considered herself cute enough, but she'd never hold a candle to Hannah's top-model gorgeousness.

"Not true. Besides, I'm taken."

"Yeah, I know." Grace wrestled with the smidgeon of jealousy that pinched her, and not just because of her best friend's love interest. The entire Fleming family owned things like expensive cars and boats and cabins in the woods and took trips all over the world. A world Grace knew she didn't fit into. She wasn't sure what Hannah got out of their relationship, but Grace treasured moments such as this: incomparable companionship, a ton of fun, and being whisked away to a mountain resort in a Mercedes. She only wondered how long it would last with Hannah's boyfriend, Damien, now in the picture.

Grace pointed out a familiar landmark ahead that meant they weren't far from Ukiah: a cluster of redwood trees on their right, at the edge of the Mendocino National Forest. There were few of them this far south, and they towered over the pines, firs and other trees around them. Behind them rose the beautiful Mayacamas Mountain Range, and somewhere, tucked within that forest, lay Secret Lake and the village bearing its name, Secret Lake Village. The lake was small and privately owned, and most of the "vacation" homes surrounding it belonged to wealthy absentee owners. If they didn't vacation here or rent their homes out during the holidays, the places remained unoccupied. The real residents, the ones who worked and lived in Secret Lake Village year-round, consisted of a couple thousand people at best, and most, like Grace, were rather average people.

"We're almost there!" Hannah crowed as she exited the 101, glowing with excitement. "Hang on!"

A little faster than she needed to, Hannah took a couple of left and right turns on narrow two-lane roads, zoomed up Sunset Road on the west side of the lake, and found the Flemings' dirt-and-gravel driveway. Speeding around its curves, she finally delivered them into the front yard, part of an expanse of manicured lawns encircling a huge home in the midst of the forest.

Grace gave a sigh of relief when they stopped, glad they'd survived and glad to see the house was still as beautiful as ever. Hannah's father had given Hannah the additional garage-door controller for the cabin's three-car-garage, and when Hannah pressed the button, Grace felt as if she was being welcomed home.

Still, she couldn't help snickering the way she always did when they arrived.

"Yeah, I know," Hannah said, rolling her beautiful, light brown eyes and flipping an errant strawberry curl over her shoulder. "No one in their right mind would call it a cabin, but it is built from logs."

"Nuh-uh," Grace said, probably for the millionth time. Only now she knew how to argue the point. "It's a facade. Like fake brickwork. It's a castle pretending to be a cabin. Sticking it in a forest doesn't turn it into what it isn't."

"Yeah, well, I've never seen you complain."

"Complain? What's to complain about? Gorgeous, upscale glamour? A private dock? A twenty-six-foot, twelve-passenger patio boat tied to said dock at our beck and call?"

"Absolutely nothing to be ashamed of," Hannah quipped.

"Absolutely not. You Flemings have earned everything you own. I'm glad I'm allowed to come along for the ride, even if I had to be paid to do it."

"You know you're always welcome," Hannah reminded her, her smile softening.

Grace paused, brows furrowed. "Hey, your aunt and uncle left their Escalade for the kids and us, like they said they would, but where'd the red Beamer come from?"

Hannah took a deep breath, eyed the car in the right-hand bay, then leaned forward and eyed it some more. "Uh, I... I'm not sure. Does it matter?"

She had a tone in her voice that bordered on cagey, which caught Grace's attention. Hannah was holding something back, and Grace didn't like it.

"Do you think maybe it's Kyle's?" she suggested. "He has his driver's license and parents lucky enough to be able to buy him a car that nice."

"Uh, yeah, maybe," Hannah murmured.

"Are you okay?" Grace asked. Hannah bobbed her head but didn't meet Grace's gaze. "Earth to Hannah. It's time to park this puppy."

Hannah nodded again and steered the Mercedes inside, closing the garage door behind them before they got out. It left them in the dark for a moment. Tired from the drive, they sat there and took it all in. The tick-tick of the car's cooling engine serenaded their arrival.

"I'm hungry," Hannah said at last, popping the trunk. "I doubt the kids were considerate enough to make lunch for us, but let's put our stuff away and find out."

Grace donned her backpack, grabbed her suitcase from the trunk, and headed toward the four concrete steps at the foot of the mudroom door. All was fine until she realized the front bumper of the BMW almost touched the steps. Maneuvering her suitcase around it would take some finagling. Worse, the garage was pretty dark. Hannah and Grace couldn't see each other very well, and considering Grace's propensity for accidents, she feared they were on a collision course. Murphy was breathing down her neck.

She hurried around old boxes and narrow shelves, past the tall freezer near the steps. Right foot, left foot, right foot. She took the last step with her left foot when her shoe caught on something. A snow shovel? A snow shovel near the mudroom door in late June? The terror of impending disaster screamed through her veins.

She stumbled as her shoe broke free. Thrown off balance, she bashed her right shin into the car's bumper. Rather than fall, she bounded up the first three steps and crashed the right side of her head against the door. She paused, saying a prayer of thanksgiving that at least the door stopped her headlong flight—until said door was jerked open, sending her flailing before she looked up to see the most handsome guy in the world staring down at her.

Somehow, she managed to regain her balance, but her brains were still spinning.

"Hi," she said in shock, wondering what in the world this Adonis must be thinking about this totally uncoordinated freak using her head as a door knocker.

"Hi," he said, his dazzling shamrock-green eyes blinking in disbelief.

Then—

"Ricky!" Hannah shrieked.

No! Hannah was about to mow Grace down. Grace either had to bail off the steps to get out of her way or bulldoze the guy in front of her to make sure Hannah didn't kill her.

Praise all the powers that be, Ricky-guy grabbed Grace's backpack strap and yanked it—and her—into the mudroom. The centrifugal force catapulted her behind him, with Grace grateful the bag's strap at least wasn't wrapped around her neck.

Wide-eyed, open-mouthed, and quite frankly amazed at her survival, Grace watched Hannah leap up the last step, toss her own bags to the floor, throw her always graceful arms around Rick and hug him so tight Grace thought she'd snap his neck.

No, wait, so not true. She couldn't break this guy's neck if she tried. He was so built—as in pro-athlete built—his army-green tee was stretched to its limits, and a pair of beige cargo shorts revealed incredible calf muscles.

Oh, my heck. Ricky? *Rick?* As in Hannah's older brother, Richard Fleming?

The floor seemed to tilt, and for a moment, Grace thought she'd be sick. This couldn't be happening. The red car! It was Rick's. That's why Hannah acted so funny. Could anything be more horrible than this? She suddenly regretted not being arrested for burrito-battering a police officer. A nice jail cell would be better than being within a mile of Richard Fleming.

Grace forced herself to breathe before she fainted. The last time she saw Rick was five years ago, when his next older brother, Sean, embarrassed her in a way she would never forgive. Scott—the oldest brother—Sean, and Rick had made a hobby of teasing and picking on Grace most of her life, but That Night had been over the top. The only thing that salvaged her friendship with Hannah was Hannah's agreement to keep all three of her brothers away from Grace forever. She wasn't even to talk about them or tell them about Grace or Grace's life forevermore. Murphy's misfortune was one problem. Torment by handsome humans was another—and the Fleming boys were expert tormentors.

And unbelievably handsome.

"You look awesome," Hannah praised Rick. "You've been working out again."

Grace hated that Hannah was right. He did look awesome. More awesome than he had five years ago when he was two years out of high school. She truly didn't recognize him. If he'd been anyone other than Rick Fleming, Grace would have drooled. She snapped her mouth shut to be sure she didn't.

Rick grinned and shook his head. "It's only been a month, Sis, but I have to say you're beyond fabulous yourself. Summer always has agreed with you. Now, what did you say your boyfriend's name was?"

"Not telling."

"If you don't want to brag about him, he's got to be a jerk."

"He's not a jerk. He's just super busy. He's pre-med and works part-time in the ER near campus."

"Wow," Rick said, obviously impressed. "That's the most you've ever told me about him. You glad you took the summer off? It puts your career another semester away."

"Ditch the guilt trip. I'm only twenty-three and on my way to my master's degree."

Rick chuckled. "You always were ahead of everyone else in your class. I remember you as a kid setting up a classroom in our den, complete with a mini-chalkboard, your school books, and Dad's old encyclopedias. You loved lecturing all of your friends, especially Grace Evans."

Hannah's eyes bulged from her head, and she glanced at Grace and back at Rick. She knew this was a volatile situation. It may not be Hannah's fault Rick was here, but it was against the "rules."

Rick was still talking and ended with "I don't know if you still see... uh, your old friend, but I'll bet you were a good influence on her." He reached out to ruffle her hair the way he used to when she was a girl, but Hannah ducked away.

"Whoa, watch the two-hundred-dollar locks, Bro," she said. "My hairdresser would personally flay you alive if you ruffled my hair like I was a dog." She glanced at Grace again before asking him, "So, what are you doing here, and where are the kids?"

He jabbed a thumb behind him. "They're up in the loft playing games. Aunt Sharon and Uncle Luke were thrilled I was here so their precious offspring wouldn't be left alone until you arrived. Bad form to show up late."

"Yeah, like they don't leave them on a regular basis to go shopping or out to dinner—"

"Yes, and to work, and to business meetings... I know. But what if something had gone wrong because you were late and you didn't come at all? The kids can't be abandoned here for ten days."

"Yeah, I know, and thankfully we arrived safe and sound. But you didn't answer my question—why are *you* here?"

He shrugged. "I'll fill you in after I take your bags upstairs."

He glanced at Grace, paused as if her presence—or something about her—didn't quite make sense to him, then gave her a nod and grabbed their luggage. As if they weighed nothing, he strode past her and headed out of the mudroom.

Grace glared at Hannah.

Her best friend raised her hands in self-defense. "I had no idea he'd be here. Honest," she hissed.

"Well, he has to leave, right? I'm not staying if he does, and you know it."

Hannah sighed in frustration. "Let's find out what's going on first."

And with that, she followed in Rick's footsteps.

CHAPTER 2

Rick was hustling to the loft almost before the two women left the mudroom. Grace was torn between wanting to yell at him to not take her heavy bag upstairs and being glad she didn't have to drag it up there herself.

The minute they entered the short hall from the mudroom, her thoughts scattered. She was here. In this incredible house. Five thousand square feet of high-end living space. Cabin or not, who wouldn't love it?

The hall branched left to the downstairs bathroom and the laundry room, and to the right, it opened up into a huge state-of-the-art kitchen and over-sized breakfast nook. Grace sighed at seeing the kitchen. She longed to get her hands on it. She might be a bookworm and a bit of a recluse, but cooking, particularly for others, was her favorite hobby.

The breakfast nook sat near the French doors, which opened onto the covered patio in the backyard. There was also a formal dining area near the front door with a table big enough for twelve. Grace's second-favorite place was the living room. Its vaulted, open-beam ceiling maintained the cabin theme, along with a rock fireplace, wood floors, area rugs, and artisan furniture, all so perfect it looked more like a movie set than a home.

A grand staircase faced the entryway, and beyond it ran another hallway to the master suite. Grace had never seen them, but the spacious master bedroom and bathroom and Uncle Luke's office/library were supposedly to die for. Grace knew Uncle Luke was some kind of Silicon Valley computer programming guru and Aunt Sharon a corporate attorney, but she couldn't imagine the price tag on this place. The basement was even equipped with a gym. And a racquetball court. Insane.

The staircase was another matter, even if it was awe-inspiring. The balustrades resembled something an artistic mountain man had chipped out of small tree trunks, purposely but beautifully imperfect, and then dipped in shellac before bolting them together. The whole place always smelled like freshly cut pine.

Grace stared at the loft, dreading whatever required some element of coordination, like ladders or staircases. She had no choice, of course, whether it was to settle in for the week or retrieve her bag and leave. The other four bedrooms were up there, two pairs sharing spacious Jack-and-Jill bathrooms on either side of the enormous loft. Hannah and Grace normally used the guest room that shared the bathroom with the twins. It held two double beds, with room to spare, plus two large dressers and a palatial closet Grace couldn't imagine ever having enough clothes and shoes to fill.

Hannah avoided Grace's gaze and tackled the stairs without her.

Okay, Grace, take a big breath and relax—or at least try to concentrate. She wasn't sure about doing both at the same time. She had to force herself to use the balustrade to make the climb, even though the wood, incredibly smooth and cool under her hand, seemed much too exquisite to touch. Unfortunately, her backpack was almost as heavy as her suitcase, and with her strained back, she had no choice.

The kids were, indeed, playing video games. Rick had opened the guest room door, the second one on the right, and placed their suitcases against the wall by the door. He glanced around in amazement.

"This place hasn't hardly changed since we were kids, has it?" he asked Hannah. "Whenever I come here, I wonder how a house this old can look so brand-spanking new. Aunt Sharon's cleaning crew always does a terrific job. Not a speck of dust anywhere."

Hannah snorted. "They have no choice. Employees who don't perform…"

"Don't stay employees. Yeah, believe me, I know first-hand. But still." He glanced at his watch. "Hey, it's beyond lunchtime. I made more than enough tuna sandwiches for everyone. They're in the fridge. I'll have the kids take a break, and we'll head down if you're hungry."

"Starving," Hannah said, but Grace felt ill at the thought. Eat food Rick made? Eat in Rick's presence? What was Hannah thinking? What was with Rick? Didn't he recognize her? He knew she wanted nothing to do with him.

Rick put his fingers to his lips and blew a whistle that should have shattered windows. Three heads spun as if they'd been yanked toward him. One of them had the sense to pause the game, and after that, pandemonium reigned. All three kids leaped up and bounded over to greet Hannah.

"Hannah! You're here!" said one twin, the first to give their cousin a big hug. Cherise? No, it was Charlotte. She had a tiny dimple on her chin. Both redheads like Hannah, the girls loved being identical. Same shoulder-length hairstyles, similar clothes—often matching. Their church-going parents forbade tattoos and lip rings, and their makeup was still minimal, but parental edicts couldn't change the fact the girls were growing up and starting to buck the system. Cherise was often snotty, but Grace supposed it was Charlotte, the smooth-talker, who'd gotten their mom to let them dye the ends of their hair purple.

Questions flowed machine-gun fashion from the girls, now almost as tall as Hannah, who, as usual, fielded them with skill. They apparently had all kinds of things they wanted to do, but they knew they had to have her permission first.

Kyle waited his turn to give his cousin a teen-boy hug that welcomed her without displaying too much affection. Grace thought he could have passed for another of Hannah's brothers, his head blessed with the same gorgeous thatch of dark chestnut-colored hair as Rick's. His eyes, however, were dark brown, unlike Rick's amazing shade of green. Of course, Kyle wasn't as broad-shouldered as Rick yet, and might not be as tall.

Kyle's eyes brightened when he saw Grace. He loved to tease her almost as much as Hannah's brothers—only he wasn't mean about it—and she saw his wheels turning. What smart remark would come out of his mouth first?

"Hey, kids, Hannah brought a friend," Rick noted, turning toward Grace. "Forgive my rudeness. I should have asked your name—"

"What?" Kyle said, his eyebrows plowing into each other.

"Gracie!" The twins hollered, suddenly noticing her and immediately coming to wrap long girly arms around her neck.

"Gracie?" Rick said.

"What's with you, dude?" Kyle said. "You know Grace. How could you forget her? You guys were always mean to her."

Stone silence took hold of the loft. Rick's gaze met Grace's, his shock almost tangible. He blinked twice, as if trying to match the Grace of yesteryear to the Grace of today and make sense of it.

"Grace? Evans?"

Grace made herself take a breath to avoid fainting. Her silence had him running his fingers through his hair, pushing it back from his brow in shock.

"Wow. I-I didn't recognize you. It's been—"

"Five years," she said.

"Yeah. Man, have you changed!"

"She let her hair grow long," Hannah offered.

"Yeah, I see that," Rick said, although his quick but polite perusal of her entire figure told Grace he was admiring more than her hair. "It's... amazing. It makes your eyes stand out. They're so..."

"Blue?" Hannah narrowed her eyes at him, probably wondering what cat had got his tongue.

"I meant, well, beautiful, even prettier than I remembered, but yeah, they are blue. Like, what, cornflower blue? Right, Hannah? That's what Mom called them."

"Yeah, she did," Hannah agreed.

"I remember," Grace said, the bitterness seeping into her voice. "I heard her say it when I was sitting on the kitchen island waiting for her to put a Band-Aid on my knee. I managed—with a little help from Sean—to trip over one of your inline skates and skin it."

"Yeah, you were always tripping over something," he said. Then his eyes widened and his cheeks drained of most of their color, proof he realized he said the wrong thing.

Kyle and the twins muttered at him, making sure he knew they knew it, too. Grace thought Hannah looked ready to faint.

As for Grace, she wanted to punch him—but she'd probably only hurt herself—and scream at him for all the years he and his brothers made her feel small and ugly and stupid, though it would only make her seem petty.

She also couldn't help the part of her that, despite it all, wanted to lean into him and wrap her arms around him and see if he felt as sensational as he looked.

Of course, that was never going to happen. The very thought made her angry with herself.

"Hannah, I need your car," she said, not taking her eyes off his.

"What? Why? Where do you want to go?"

"Home. I'll come back for you in ten days," Grace told her, finally tearing her gaze away from Rick to stare at her lifelong friend. "On July seventh, to be clear. I'll do an oil change and put gas in the car to make up for the extra miles."

"But—"

"I had no idea *he* would be here. If I had, I wouldn't have come."

"That's not fair," Hannah snapped. "I didn't know he'd be here, either."

"You recognized his car," Grace said through clenched teeth, "but you didn't admit it. And you know better than anyone I'm not spending one night under the same roof as Ricky the Rude."

"Excuse me?" Rick said with resentment.

Hannah's eyes shimmered with tears. "I'm sorry, Rick, you can't stay. Aunt Sharon hired us to take care of the kids, and we're here to enjoy as close to a vacation as we've had in years. We've had this planned for a long time."

Rick looked as confused as ever as he cocked a brow at Grace. "I-I didn't mean anything unkind by what I said."

"I need my suitcase." Grace pushed her way between the kids and Hannah and stalked into what should have been her bedroom for the next ten days. With her backpack on her back, reaching the suitcase was awkward, and she was angry. Not a delightful mix. She couldn't get a hold of the handle and knocked the suitcase over twice. When she did grab it and headed toward the door, Rick was standing in the doorway, looking as powerless as she felt.

"Please don't go because of me," he said, as if he honestly wanted her to stay. Which made her angrier. He had no right to talk to her, let alone stop her.

"I could say the same for you. Please don't go because of me. Enjoy your visit." She pushed past him.

"Grace," Hannah pleaded.

The bag flipped upside down as Grace struggled to drag it to the stairs. She seriously considered letting it roll downstairs to the front door. Unfortunately, there were expensive vases and fine furniture scattered around down there and, no doubt, she'd break something. Like her, Murphy never took a vacation.

"Kyle, will you help me, please?" she asked, focusing on him and him only. She didn't want to see Hannah's disappointment or Rick's consternation. Or worse, his possible glee that he'd gotten to her again.

"No," the young man said, refusing to take the bag and glaring at Rick. "Cousin, you need to set things straight. We all tease her. She even makes fun of herself. I don't know, maybe she has an undiagnosed nerve disease or something and can't help dropping and tripping over stuff, but she's as cool as they come and you're not gonna spoil our vacation with your attitude."

"What attitude?" Rick protested.

"You're sweet, Kyle," Grace said. "But I'm not staying, with or without your help."

She turned the suitcase over and grabbed the handle, clutched the railing with her other hand and said a litany of prayers as she descended the first two steps. She carefully tugged the suitcase behind her, flinching when it rammed into her bad knee, the combined weight of both bags threatening to topple her. The next time was worse, and when the bag bumped her, she flailed, horrified when she realized she was about to go headfirst down the stairs.

"Grace!" Rick said sharply, and in an instant, he was thundering after her, like he was back on the football field as Saratoga High's star wide receiver. He grabbed her by the wrist and—to her relief—stopped the fall. Before she could protest, he scooped up the suitcase and delivered both of them back to the loft, looking as confused as she did when he set her free.

"Sorry. I, uh… didn't think about where I was going, I just wanted to keep you from falling. I don't know what you girls packed in your bags, but they're downright *heavy*. I don't even know how you got them in your car."

Grace breathed hard, amazed she managed to stay on her feet. She didn't think she'd ever gone up stairs so fast in her life. Down stairs was another matter, but she refused to think about that. She ought to be grateful—was grateful—but she hated owing Rick. In fact, if anything, he owed her this one, and ten more rescues just like it. She rubbed her wrist where his powerful grip stung her skin.

He raised his hands—as if to promise he wouldn't touch her again. "Look, I have a legitimate reason for being here," he told both women. "I'm having trouble with my car again, and two more trips to the shop haven't fixed it. Uncle Luke gave me some ideas for doing it myself, and you know his garage. He has all the tools I need."

"You don't have tools at home?" Grace didn't buy it.

"Not like he does. But I have another problem." He started to speak, then paused, focusing on Hannah as if afraid to meet Grace's gaze.

"What?" Hannah urged, her insistence suggesting that while she didn't want to be mean to her brother, she didn't want to choose between him and Grace, either. If his excuse wasn't good enough, he'd have to leave.

But what if it was?

"It's Maria," he said in a quiet voice.

Hannah's gaze dropped to the floor.

Grace didn't know if Rick was married since Hannah had honored her wishes to never talk to her about her brothers. She didn't see a ring on Rick's finger, so maybe this Maria was his girlfriend, but Grace almost felt sorry for her. Did Rick play games with her heart, too?

"Problems in paradise, huh?" She said with full-fledged bitterness.

"No way," he replied. "An old high school football buddy, Mac Larson—you might remember him—introduced Maria to me. Anyway, Maria and I only went out a few times, and… I'm not sure how I feel about her."

"Really?" Hannah said with surprise. "I thought she was nice."

"She is."

"And hot."

Rick's cheeks reddened, and he stared at the ceiling like he hoped his prayers were being heard upstairs. "She's beautiful, but she's way too clingy for the short time I've known her."

"So, you ran away from her rather than confronting her? That's relatively spineless of you, but I suppose I shouldn't be surprised." Grace was almost disappointed to learn Rick hadn't changed one bit. Whether it was in defending Grace from his brothers or sticking to his commitments, he wasn't always the star he appeared to be on the football field.

"If you met her, you'd understand," he replied with his own indignation. "Besides, I can't leave. I've already pulled out a number of car parts. It would take me at least a day to put it back together, even if I didn't fix anything. Either way, it's Friday and I can't get it to an auto shop until Monday."

The pause felt crammed with uncertainty. "Understood," Grace said at last. "Hannah, please let me have your keys. I can't do this."

Hannah wilted with disappointment. She couldn't make Grace stay, and considering the history between Grace and Rick, she understood her best friend's objections. Still, she couldn't help the hurt that swam in her eyes, which had Grace next to tears herself.

Murphy had really done a number on Grace—on all of them—this time.

Hannah sighed, pulled her keys from her pocket, and handed them to Grace. The silent request was clear. She wished her best friend would reconsider.

Grace turned to Kyle, who collected her suitcase with resignation. He wasn't as graceful as Rick as he headed downstairs, but he did it without tripping. Grace followed him into the garage, where he'd already opened the garage door. After she popped the trunk on the Benz, Kyle tossed the bag inside while she rummaged through her backpack for her I. D. wallet. She always kept it near her when she drove.

"Oh, for crying out loud. Murphy, knock it off!" she hissed when she couldn't find it.

Rummaging turned into dumping the entire contents of the backpack onto the garage floor. One at a time, she put each item back, until it was all repacked—with no sign of her wallet.

Kyle stared at her, no doubt wondering if she'd lost her mind. He had no idea what she was looking for, so he couldn't tattle on her. She should jump into the car and leave anyway, right?

That would be the worst mistake in the world, she told herself. *Murphy would* love *to make me pay for it.* She'd likely wind up in Officer Tran's jail cell after all.

"What's wrong?" Kyle asked.

If Grace were a betting person, she'd think Kyle was hoping she changed her mind. They did have a lot of stuff planned, and although he wanted to go off with friends who'd also be here this week, he still hoped to be a part of some of what Hannah and Grace did with the girls. Besides, he always disapproved of the way Rick and his brothers treated Grace. Maybe he had delusions of being her champion.

She took a big breath and stretched her sore spine before admitting the truth. "It appears I left my driver's license at home."

His face screwed up in confusion. "Uh, like, you can't drive?"

"Not legally."

The frowny face morphed into a happy one. "So, you have to stay? You'll be able to cook for us after all?"

Grace laughed. Was that why he wanted her to stay? Maybe her cooking wasn't restaurant best, but it was certainly better than Hannah's.

"Yeah, I guess I have no choice. I have to hang around."

He gave a loud cheer, grabbed her bag, and lugged it back inside. Grace trailed him, far less exuberantly. The others had drifted downstairs and stood near the bottom step as if they weren't certain what to do with themselves.

"Guess what, guys? Grace left her driver's license at home. She can't leave!" Kyle crowed.

The announcement brightened all their faces, but Grace was the most disarmed by Rick's expression. It was as if someone had answered his prayers.

"I truly hate Murphy," Grace murmured to Hannah, who threw her arms around Grace's neck.

"I know, but I kind of appreciate him right now," she said into Grace's ear. "I'd never make you stay, but I'm glad you will. It wouldn't be the same without you."

"But he has to behave," Grace said, pulling away to lock eyes with Rick. "And I'm not joking. We could all leave this place in the SUV and head to your parents' house if we need to. If your brother gives me any trouble—"

"I wouldn't do that, Grace," he insisted. "We're not children anymore. I know when I'm not wanted, and I'll do what I planned to do: work on my car, make my own meals, take care of myself. I even brought a little work from home to do on my laptop. I won't bother you."

"He means it, Gracie," Hannah begged. "Let's just have a nice time, okay?"

Yeah, easy for you to say. She wasn't reliving what happened between Grace and Rick five years ago. The hurt had been so dreadful, it nearly tore her in half. She'd had a burning, heartbreaking crush on this guy since she was fifteen—actually a good part of her life. She never felt worthy, but she always tried to be his friend. Scott and Sean were jerks, almost as hard on Rick as they were on Hannah and Grace. Grace had a difficult time believing they came from the same family, but at one time, she saw something good in Rick.

Then the world fell apart. She put her faith in Rick and he'd betrayed her, proving guys weren't trustworthy. As if trying to prove the point, Murphy made a mess out of most of her dates ever since. Being a bachelorette was far safer for her.

Rick studied her, his compassion out of place in Grace's memories.

"Every kid makes mistakes," he pointed out. "The worst you can do is let past injuries hurt your todays, which could ruin your tomorrows."

Grace felt a lump form in her throat. She loved the heavenly sandalwood-and-citrus cologne Rick wore. She wanted to breathe him in, and still hated herself for it. She agreed with him, but those past injuries had ruined all her dreams—and there was no way to salvage them.

"I think you mentioned tuna sandwiches," she muttered, wanting more than anything to get everyone's eyes off her.

"Yeah," Rick said, nodding. "Let me take your bags back upstairs. The rest of you, head to the kitchen. I'm wasting away from hunger, and my car is calling me from the garage."

CHAPTER 3

Rick had forgotten how much teenagers ate—especially seventeen-year-old boys like Kyle. The kids put together a small banquet by not only inhaling the sandwiches he made—Kyle ate three of them—but they scrounged anything in the fridge and in every cabinet that might possibly be considered food.

"Your tuna sandwiches are the best, Bro," Hannah said, licking the drippings off her fingers. "You know I've never been too fond of tuna, but you could make me change my mind."

Rick grinned at his sister. Was she trying to point out one of his redeeming qualities to Grace? He doubted it mattered, but he loved her for trying. She was the only other person on earth who knew how he felt—had felt all these years—about Grace.

"What do you think, Grace?" she asked. "Pretty good, huh?"

Grace paused mid-chew. He remembered making tuna sandwiches for all of them when they were kids and knew she loved them. Still, she'd browsed the stuffed refrigerator, probably looking for food he hadn't touched, before finally giving in and eating one of them.

"Yeah, it's okay," she said from her chair at the other end of the table, as far from him as she could sit. And then her gaze met Rick's. She must have realized how unkind she sounded because she cleared her throat and added, "It's even better to have it ready for us after the long drive. Thanks."

Still, she made a face, like thanking him was outright painful.

As for him, it felt good to have her offer her gratitude. "You're most welcome. So, tell me, guys, how is this vacation of yours going to work?"

Hannah replied, "Grace and I have a list of possibilities, and the kids have their own. We're going to sit down and put them together tonight."

"I'll be gone a lot," Kyle said. "I have a bunch of things to do with the guys."

"They can join us," Hannah suggested.

Rick knew she disliked the idea of a seventeen-year-old having too much freedom while she was in charge.

Kyle shrugged. "Maybe for some of it. I know they'll want to play Xbox and play racquetball, and we absolutely have to take the boat out."

"Every morning, if the weather cooperates," Hannah replied.

"I get to drive it," the boy insisted, grinning from ear to ear.

"We'll see," Hannah insisted. "But don't forget, whether they want to or not, it's the law in California we all wear lifejackets on the boat. When we're in a cove or near a beach, you guys can swim without them, but not on the main lake."

"It's a private lake," Kyle complained. "We don't have to use the jackets."

"Boats pulling skiers are dangerous. I'm in charge, and laws keep us safe. If it's good enough for Clearlake, it's good enough for Secret Lake. Besides, your parents insisted before allowing me the boat key."

The boy groaned and rolled his eyes but knew he'd lost the fight.

"So, Gracie, are you still doing the cooking?" Cherise asked, her eyes twinkling.

"That was the plan," Grace said, nibbling on a green olive.

"You still like to cook, huh?" Rick asked, casual but attentive. She'd experimented in their kitchen for as long as he could remember, and he always enjoyed sneaking a bite here and there.

"She's the best," Kyle said. "I love it when she helps your mom cook. She always leaves something for all of us."

"What?" Rick looked to Hannah for input.

"She still does it, as long as you boys aren't coming around," Hannah said, shaking a potato chip at him. "Any exceptional meals you and Scott and Sean were fortunate enough to scarf while we were growing up happened when Grace put Mom through cooking lessons. Mom watched them—watched being the operative word. I don't think she wanted to learn. She just loved having Grace cook for us."

Curiosity had Rick rummaging through a dozen years of memories, trying to make sense of it. "So, what have I eaten that I thought Mom cooked but didn't?"

Hannah chuckled and then listed so many dishes, including his favorite dessert, he couldn't believe it. Everything from shrimp alfredo to lemon loaf cake.

"Seriously? Those were all yours, Grace? Man, I remember thinking Mom had finally gotten it right."

"Not in this lifetime," Hannah said with a smirk.

"That stinks. I can fry an egg, make a tuna sandwich, and open a can of soup. I guess I won't starve to death, but…"

His dangling sentence was filled with hope, but Grace didn't seem the least bit affected by it. She concentrated on her plate, obviously not willing to invite him to dinner.

"Maybe she'll let you have some leftovers," Charlotte murmured, the discomfort on her face suggesting pity for Rick while not wanting to offend Grace.

"Grace is only making our dinners," Hannah pointed out. "We're all on our own for the rest."

"Except for tomorrow and Sunday morning's breakfasts," Grace interjected. "After that, it's root, hog, or die."

"Root hogs or what?" Rick said with a puckered face. "What does that mean?"

"Root. Hog. Or die. An Evans tradition," Hannah explained. "You scrounge for yourself, whether it's from scratch or with leftovers, but it's all first-come, first-served."

"Fair enough," Rick said, his brow furrowing. "Now tell me why I made lunch today?"

"You didn't know the rules?" Charlotte said, throwing a celery stick at him. Kyle and Cherise laughed.

"And you're trying to make nice," Cherise reminded him, her brows raised in a challenge.

"Absolutely," Rick agreed. "But I have a few rules of my own. Dishes are a mutual responsibility. You clean up any messes you make, I clean up mine."

"And whenever you open your mouth, you behave yourself," Hannah reminded him.

"I wouldn't do anything less," Rick replied, taking his plate to the sink.

They all joined Rick in quickly cleaning the kitchen, although Grace tried to stay as far away from him as she could. It wasn't easy, even in a kitchen this big.

"So, I'm still curious about what you guys are thinking about doing." Rick dried his muscular hands on a dish towel and tossed it to Kyle to hang up. "You're taking the boat out in the mornings and what else?"

Hannah gave him a warning look. "Don't you have a car to fix? We need to unpack our suitcases, and I think Grace and I made an appointment to watch *Avatar* with the kids today."

The kids grinned and jostled against each other in amusement, but Rick wasn't laughing. Grace wondered if he was only curious, or if he was unhappy at missing out on everything while he was here... because of her. She refused to consider the latter. It served him right.

Ideas spilled out from almost everyone except Grace, who kept her opinions to herself. Suggestions included picnics, hikes, a one-night campout at nearby Mt. Haylee campground—though not if Grace had anything to say about it—lots of games, one day in town, and, of course, the July 4th celebration.

"But the Fourth of July isn't all that's happening," Cherise reminded everyone. "It's also Secret Lake Village's one-hundred-year birthday. They're having vendors and contests, including needlework, carving, and artwork."

"I heard about it," Rick said. "A centennial celebration, huh? Sounds like it might be fun."

"Maybe," Cherise said, huffing. "We all have entries for the contests, but I need to stay in touch with my girlfriends at home and... uh, well, Rachel. She's coming here, too."

"Cherise has a boyfriend," Charlotte murmured sing-song fashion, squealing when Cherise punched her shoulder.

"A boyfriend? You're only fourteen," Rick protested, which earned him raised brows and attitude.

"Fourteen and an active member of the church youth ministry, and you won't be dating or having boyfriends until you're sixteen, right?" Hannah said, wrapping an arm around the girl's neck and hugging her tight.

"Yeah, yeah, whatever. Talk to Charlotte if you think I'm a brat."

Charlotte snickered. "What are you talking about? I never sneak out to meet boys in the side yard at night."

"Cherise!" Hannah said with disappointment. "You know better. It's not just about doing what you want when you want to do it—"

"I think I'm old enough to decide what's best for me," Cherise snapped, pulling away from Hannah with her eyes narrowed angry-cat-style.

"And you're old enough to know, especially in today's upside-down world," Rick said, "it's neither spiritually nor physically safe. Even if this boy is as kind as Mother Theresa, you can't be sure all of his friends are. What if they ganged up on you?"

"Ugh! Stop!" Cherise said, sticking her fingers in her ears. "I get it. That's why I keep brass knuckles and pepper spray in my pocket."

"What? You do not!" Kyle protested, laughing.

Cherise stared at him, then broke into laughter herself. "No, I don't. Mom thinks I need some pepper spray, but I'd hate to hurt anyone with it, so…" She shrugged.

Grace couldn't stand the conversation. It brought back too many bad memories, even more than the Fleming brothers had caused.

"Play it safe, Cherise. Please," she urged. "You have no idea what it's like to have people gang up on you…" She paused, glancing at Rick and away again. "Your church has its standards for a reason. Follow them, even if it hurts. You won't ever be sorry for following the rules. Breaking them is a different matter."

"All right! All right! Now, would someone tell Charlotte not to sneak off to the mall with her friends? She leaves me to do her chores in exchange for not ratting on me."

"Woah! I sense the need for a serious discussion, girls," Hannah said, putting a stop to the conversation. "I'm not your mom, and I'm not here to offer discipline to kids who've been raised in a good home with great parents and absolutely no excuses for misbehaving. I know you're teenagers and you're feeling your oats, and I'm willing to give input if you want it, but for now? I need to kick back and relax—and you will not do those things while I'm here. Do I make myself clear?" All three teens nodded, although Kyle smirked in a way that made Grace think he didn't take her seriously.

"Ricky!" Hannah turned on her brother.

"What did I do?" he said.

"Go. Fix. Your. Car."

"Oh, right. Sorry. Sheesh. Enjoy your movie."

Grace watched Rick leave, startled by the twinge of regret in her gut. There was no doubt he felt left out, and she was responsible. When he slipped into the garage through the mudroom door, she felt a moment of relief, but then, against her wishes, she also felt as if someone had taken her sunshine away.

Music came on in the garage, the happy tune making the sadness flee. She wanted to dance. Not that she would. Not if she wanted furniture, decorations, and wall-hangings to remain unharmed. But she wanted to.

"Wow, Gracie," Kyle said, his young, handsome face impish. "We actually got through lunch without you spilling anything."

Charlotte chimed in with "And all the plates and glasses made it into the dishwasher—"

"Yeah, yuck it up, you guys," Grace said. "Wouldn't you be sad if my bad-luck vibes suddenly tossed your underwear all over the front lawn?"

"You wouldn't!" Charlotte chortled.

"Not me," Grace insisted. "But Murphy might."

"And maybe with a smidgeon of help from me," Hannah said firmly. "Do you think Murphy would like some help, Grace?"

Grace snorted laughter when she saw the look of horror on the teens' faces.

Kyle raised a hand and said, "Got the message. No more teasing about clumsiness."

"For the duration of this vacation," Grace insisted.

"For the duration," the girls said in unison.

Hannah grinned her approval. "Now, that wasn't painful, was it? Shall we head upstairs?"

The girls screeched and Kyle growled as they bounded out of the room and up to the loft. Grace, for her part, really, truly counted the steps on her way to be sure she didn't miss any. She only tripped once, near the top. She couldn't say why. She didn't know. Perhaps she was trying too hard, but she didn't dare not give it her all.

She excused herself for a few minutes to change out of her now dry but totally grimy capris and wipe the sticky juice off her legs. She may be stuck here with Richard Fleming, but she needed to get all evidence of Kooky Kathy out of her life once and for all.

The big-screen TV—so huge Grace wondered if it had once hung at Oracle Park—filled most of the far wall, so wide it took two enormous, custom-made, slightly rounded couches to put enough seating in front of it. Plenty of room to spread out—unless the Flemings had a lot of company, and then they had a pile of beanbag chairs stuffed in a closet to the left of the TV.

Beside the closet was a small kitchenette, complete with a wet bar, an apartment fridge full of sodas and juices, a countertop microwave, a cabinet filled with lots of snacks—most of them actually fairly nutritious—and a basket of microwave popcorn. They all opted for ice-cold bottles of water right now and sat down to *Avatar*.

Grace had seen it more times than she could count. She and her siblings, Danny and Chloe, loved it when they were kids. Unfortunately, today, her only thoughts were about Rick, and those thoughts traveled two different roads.

The first was the image of Grace in Hannah's car, license in hand, driving as far and as fast as possible to get away from him. The other one led downstairs and out to the garage to watch him doing something ultra-masculine like taking apart a car. Muscles bunched as he removed nuts and bolts; fingers nimble as he handled equipment, made his repairs, and put it all back together again, his mind engaged on whatever workings he saw inside an automobile.

A BMW. A red BMW. Grace was pretty sure it wasn't a new model, but it appeared to be in far too good a condition to have problems. It screamed wealthy-man-car from hood to dual exhaust. Not exactly a muscle car, but nothing the average person could afford.

What did Rick do to afford such an awesome car? He said he brought some work with him from home. Whatever he did, he did it well. She actually hoped he liked his job, which surprised her. She was supposed to wish him a long and miserable life.

But that wasn't the real her. In her other life, away from the Rick Flemings of the world, she enjoyed seeing people happy. So many years of her mother's suffering had taught her life was far too often painful and unhappy, and if Grace had the ability to brighten anyone's days, she should.

If only she could wipe away the last confrontation she had with Rick half a decade ago. If only it hadn't cut so deeply it damaged her trust in men. She had no doubt her life would be different, even if Rick and she didn't have a future.

"You okay?" Hannah said, resting a hand on Grace's wrist.

"Yeah. Why?"

"You seem worried about something."

"Nope," she replied. She didn't want to talk about it.

Hannah let out a breath. "I honestly didn't know Rick was coming. And I think he means it. He's not here to cause trouble—I mean, he didn't know you'd be here, either. He just has a few dilemmas to sort out."

"Yeah," Grace said again, nodding. "We all do. Don't sweat it. I'll do my best to avoid him. And if I can't, I'll get along with him as long as he does the same."

Hannah's smile was tentative. "Thanks. We're going to have a great time. And I'm sure he'll only be here a few days anyway."

A few days? Grace couldn't imagine sharing the next few days with him. Who knew how much he could do or say to hurt her. Who knew how much it would take to break her heart the rest of the way?

Rick stood, hands on hips, glaring at the BMW. Getting away from Maria drew Rick to the lake in part, but his major goal really was to work on this bad girl. Again.

A lot of people believe BMWs are one step away from perfection, but here was proof of the fallacy. This "previously owned" 2008 E65 sedan had incredibly low mileage, and Rick thought he was being frugal buying it. His father taught Rick and his siblings that paying cash for used cars, particularly pricey ones, avoided the worst of the depreciation and the debt. After all, the Flemings' wealth hadn't come by accident. It came through hard work and wise money management. Rick thought the car would be perfect. Unfortunately, it had proved more than a problem-child from minute one.

Rick's job paid well. Extremely well. Having earned some notable scholarships and having his dad's support, he had no student loan debt. He shared Sean's apartment until he saved enough to buy a house. Still, to cough up hard cash for a Beamer—which was supposed to be in super shape—only to have it come with a grocery list of breakdowns and repairs, was totally wrong. Apparently, Rick hadn't done enough research. This particular year and model had a sullied reputation.

Rick opened the garage door to let in light and air, then backed the car out a little to make it easier to get around but stay out of the hot sun. Grabbing Uncle Luke's extravagant portable lift, he set it under the car and raised the entire vehicle nearly two feet off the ground. It couldn't get much better without digging a repair pit.

Rubbing his neck, he surveyed the shiny tools and spotless workbench, which looked more like a display in a top-end speed shop than a garage. He knew Uncle Luke used these tools, but his uncle wasn't here that often and was a stickler about putting them away in their original condition. It was almost annoying. Rick would probably spend more time cleaning the tools than he would fixing the car. He blew out a breath, grabbed what he needed along with the creeper, and went to work. Idling rough was one thing; stalling, or not being able to get the car above thirty-five miles an hour? Intolerable.

The radio helped calm Rick's frustration, but without warning, his thoughts turned to Grace Evans.

Aunt Sharon had been hesitant about Rick's coming here but didn't say why. She did mention Hannah was bringing a friend but not who. Rick didn't know Grace and Hannah were still close because his sister never mentioned their relationship after the split between Grace and him. Sharon was adamant he wasn't to interfere with Hannah and the kids, but he'd never do that. He did bring his swimsuit and wanted some time on the boat over the next few days, but even if he got the car fixed, he hadn't planned to stay more than four or five days anyway.

That was until Rick realized Hannah's friend was Grace. It was almost too stunning to assimilate. He hadn't thought he'd ever see her again. Ever since the night they parted, Grace had insisted through Hannah that he never contact her again, and he had no hope of ever talking to her—really talking to her—the way he'd wanted to do. Now, maybe, just maybe, the right time had come. He only knew he had to be careful. Grace was still touchy about him—not that he blamed her—but, in a way, it wasn't fair. If only she'd given him the chance to explain himself before their world fell to pieces.

Rick dropped a wrench which smacked him in the face, but when he tried to pick it up, it skittered across the garage floor. He lay there on the creeper, chagrined that the first thought that jumped into his mind was how Murphy followed Grace wherever she went. It wasn't a kind idea, although he didn't mean it unkindly. In fact, he saw a lot less evidence of her clumsiness today. Still, while no one had a patent on being a klutz, he remembered clearly how what happened occasionally to most people escalated to bizarre levels around Grace.

He shook his head as he tossed the thought aside and grabbed the wrench. He had work to do, and neither Grace Evans nor Murphy were going to get in his way.

He disassembled the suspicious parts, examined them, thumbed through the Chilton's manual he'd also paid a small fortune for, and groaned. He'd already tried everything it suggested. What more could he do?

Frustrated, he tossed it all aside and worked on the maintenance list first: fluids, spark plugs, filters, wiper blades. He also suspected a squeak he heard was a defective belt. He'd bought every kind available to be sure he had what he needed whenever he tracked down the culprit.

He grinned when he remembered the last time he and his dad tackled this monster. Mom glowered at him and said, "You're as silly as your father. You have the money to take it to the shop. Why do you want to do it yourself?"

"*She*, Mom. Cars are 'shes' to a guy. Like a boat. I've paid a shop for the repairs twice, and they still haven't fixed her."

Mom gave Rick that look, the one that said, if they hadn't succeeded, what made him think he could? Answer? He was a Fleming. The Flemings were driven to succeed and he had to try. Besides, he'd worked on enough cars to know he could duct tape it back together and limp it to another shop if he failed.

He worked until it was about time for dinner. He was starving. His tuna sandwich was nothing but a fond memory. He wondered what Grace was cooking tonight. The idea that she was the source of some of the best home-cooking he'd ever eaten drove him to finish, wash his hands in the garage sink, and head for the house—even if he wasn't invited.

Oh, man, it smelled great when he stepped into the mudroom. He needed to shower and—

A blood-curdling scream rent the air, and he charged toward the kitchen, wondering who was being stabbed to death!

⸺ ❦ ⸺

"Okay, Kyle, Charlotte, it's time to set the table," Grace said, whisking the measuring cup of water and flour to make sure there were no lumps. That accomplished, she added a ladleful of the hot stew broth from the pot simmering on the stove—the six-burner, propane-powered, professional grade, stainless steel Wolf stove—

stirred it well again, and then slowly added it back to the pricey Tramontina pot. The ladle tapped against the sides of the pot as she blended the ingredients while it gradually thickened.

"It smells marvelous," Hannah said, looking over Grace's shoulder.

"It's lamb stew. It's not like you haven't eaten if before. It's peasant food in some parts of the world. It's really more of a wintertime comfort-food."

"Yeah, but you know my mom hates lamb. She never makes it, peasant or otherwise, and I'll eat it any time of the year."

"Which is why I picked it," Grace said, grinning. "I hope everyone enjoys it."

Hannah sighed. "Yeah, I wish you'd come live with me wherever I go. I need my own personal chef."

"Well, bestie, you can't have me. For one thing, you couldn't afford me on a teacher's salary, and for another, I love to cook and I love to eat, but I'm not into the prima-donna-chef number. Are the rolls done?"

Hannah gasped. "No! I forgot to put them in!"

Grace's shoulders slumped. At least stew was hard to overcook, and if she left it on low it wouldn't get cold while the rolls baked. She pulled the oven open and Hannah gave her the full baking sheet. After Grace put it inside, she went to set the timer.

"Ahhhh!!!" Cherise let loose a chilling scream, dropping something into the sink and grabbing her hand.

Terrified the girl had chopped off a finger, Grace raced to her side along with Hannah.

"Let me see," Rick said, coming up behind Grace.

Grace jumped, not expecting his sudden appearance, but she joined him and Hannah in crowding Cherise. There was an awful lot of blood in the sink, along with a partially peeled carrot, but no body parts.

"You okay, Sis?" Charlotte insisted, she and Kyle leaning over Hannah's shoulder.

"I don't know!" Cherise whimpered. "I hate this potato peeler. It's one of Mom's designer brands and its sharper than a Samurai sword."

Rick pried her fingers loose to get a good look at it.

"A potato peeler?" Grace said, realizing the damage could only be so bad.

"It *hurts*," Cherise insisted, hissing when Rick made her rinse it off to see it better.

"Must be quite a peeler. It gouged you pretty good, but I don't think it needs stitches," he reassured her.

"I agree," Hannah said, and Grace, having applied more Band-Aids than she could count, tore off a paper towel, handed it to Cherise, and headed her toward the downstairs medicine cabinet. "We'll finish the salad," she told her.

Rick must have washed up at the sink in the garage. His hands were clean, though he still had smudges of grease on his forehead and beside his nose. The mechanic-shop scent drifted off him, oddly pleasant, and Grace caught herself breathing deeply, as she'd wanted to before, taking in as much of it—and him—as she could.

"Ewww," Hannah said, wrinkling her nose and backing away from Rick. "You stink. You have to eat at the bar. The dining chairs are upholstered. Like, as in white fabric? Aunt Sharon would kill you if you sat on them wearing those clothes."

Rick blew a breath between pursed lips in irritation. "Don't worry about it. I planned to take a sandwich up to my room, hop into the shower, and go over some work accounts while I eat."

Grace wasn't immune to Hannah's glance in her direction. It would upset her to see her brother left out. More than that, Grace had made enough for an army, and it was wrong for her to deny him the same meal the rest of the family was eating.

If only she didn't want to scream at the thought of being at the table with him again.

A look from Hannah reminded her that she survived lunch. What was another meal?

"Forget the shower. Change your clothes, and hurry," Grace said to Rick, avoiding his gaze. "It's almost ready, and I don't want it to burn."

"What?" He sounded confused.

"Grace?" Hannah asked. "Are you sure?"

Grace raised a brow, warning her friend not to make a big deal out of it. "He made our lunch. I guess I owe him dinner."

Rick cleared his throat, catching Grace's gaze. "Thanks, Grace. You don't have to do that."

"Yeah, well, your sister and your cousins would like your company." She turned to address Cherise's mess and finish the salad she'd abandoned, far too aware of Rick jogging off toward the staircase.

The green salad and dressings, fruit salad, and stew were soon on the table. Cherise took her chair with a wounded-bird-look on her face, but everyone fussed over her and teased her until she started giggling. When Rick joined them, Grace caught her breath. He looked devastatingly handsome in a clean pair of jeans and an emerald green tee that brought out his eyes. His hair was delightfully mussed and still damp from the super-quick shower he must have taken. For an instant, she missed the manly streaks of the grease, but the powerful scents of shampoo, deodorant, and heavenly cologne more than made up for it.

Rick glanced at each of them and said, "Who's going to say…" He paused, then let out a small rasp of laughter and cleared his throat. "Who's going to bless the food?"

"I'd love to say *grace*," Grace replied over-sweetly. "Shall we?"

They all bowed their heads as Grace prayed. Her family wasn't much into religion, but Hannah's was devout, and Grace had learned to appreciate the good side of religious observance through her friend. The Fleming teens had never known it any other way, so Hannah and Grace at least had to respect Aunt Sharon's and Uncle Luke's wishes.

After she said "amen," Rick sniffed the air. "Is something on fire?"

Grace thought it was another tasteless joke—until she smelled it, too!

"No!" she cried. The rolls! She forgot to set the timer! She jumped up from the table, hoping to rescue what was likely incinerated by now. She swung around… and knocked her glass of water over. When she grabbed for it—which yanked her sore back—she managed to smack it to the floor, where it shattered into a million pieces.

"Oops," Kyle said from his chair beside with hers.

Grace gritted her teeth against uttering expletives religious ears oughtn't to hear and dropped her napkin into the middle of the water puddle dripping its way onto the floor. She hurried to turn off the stove and remove the pan of decimated, smoking mounds of ash. Okay, they weren't that bad, but they certainly weren't edible. She dumped them into the sink before turning on the cold water. Oh, man, what a way to ruin a meal. *Good going, Grace.*

Before Grace knew what was happening, Rick went for a handful of paper towels and the dustpan, while Kyle wiped up the water on the table. It was all cleaned up before she had time to assess how much damage she'd done.

"It's good you hadn't gotten your stew yet," Rick said with sympathy. "Your soup bowl is full of water."

"Yeah, I see that," Grace grumbled, emptying it in the sink and drying it. "I suppose I've met the requirement for proving I'm Grace Evans."

Rick's eyes caught hers, a mixture of mirth and sadness radiating from them.

"Is that who you are? Nice to meet you, Grace. Thank you for inviting me to dinner. It smells fabulous." He took a bite of the stew and paused. He chewed thoughtfully and then faster, his eyes lighting up with appreciation. "Wow. This is terrific. I don't think I've ever had beef stew quite like it. It's even got peas in it. That's different. Awesome different."

Hannah burst into laughter, and the tension in the room seemed to dissipate. "It's not *beef* stew, nerd—it's *lamb* stew."

"Lamb? I've never eaten lamb in my life."

"Because Mom can't stand it, remember? But Gracie's family does, and she makes lots of dishes with it."

"I'm glad I'm here to enjoy it. Thank you, Grace."

Grace didn't know what to say, other than: "You're welcome. I just wish I hadn't burned the rolls."

"That's my fault," Hannah muttered. "I forgot to bake them in the first place."

Grace shrugged. Accidents happened. More than their fair share around her, but that was the way it was.

Still, she couldn't help sneaking a look at Rick as he savored her stew. That alone was its own kind of compliment. He didn't appear to care about the rolls, and what about helping to clean up her disaster? He'd done it kindly and without blame. It made her wonder if she'd misjudged him.

CHAPTER 4

After the meal, they gathered at the table to toss around ideas for their vacation. The kids also gave Grace a list of what they hoped she'd cook for dinner. Rick hung around, giving his stamp of approval on all of it, despite his insistence he wasn't staying that long.

"Okay, so," Charlotte said, counting fingers as she spoke. "Tomorrow, we'll take the boat out in the morning and drive around the lake. After that, Kyle wants to run off with his friends, and Cherise and I want to play with Uncle Luke's archery equipment."

"You've got it," Hannah said, checking her notes on her iPad.

"Then we can do what we want until dinner," the girl continued. "Maybe play a game?"

"Yeah, but Sunday will be the pits," Cherise complained, dragging her fingers through her hair and checking for split ends.

"It always is," Kyle said, bumping her shoulder. "It's called 'a day of rest.'"

"Yeah, more like a day of wretched boredom. Eat breakfast. Go to church. Come home. Eat lunch. Hang around and read or something. Eat dinner. And if we aren't dead yet, go to bed."

"Get over it, Cherise," Hannah insisted, chuckling. "We're obeying your parents' wishes, end of subject."

Cherise narrowed her eyes in anger and Grace smothered laughter. Leave it to Hannah when she was in her mother-hen mode to put an end to bellyaching.

"On Monday," Hannah continued, "we'll go boating most of the day. If we're lucky, we'll catch some fish. If not, it doesn't matter because we'll take a picnic lunch and the floatation devices and can just go have fun."

Kyle shook his head. "Jeff's folks have a ski boat, and Ethan and I are going out with them."

Hannah pursed her lips in objection. "Your folks' patio boat is powerful enough to pull skiers, and you know there are water skis of all sizes in the equipment room behind the garage. Your dad always has stuff here for you and for guests."

"I know, but Dad said I can, and I'm not hanging around my goofy sisters if I don't have to."

"All right, but you stay in touch on your cell phone," she insisted.

"No problem."

Grace could tell from the boy's cheesy grin that he knew he'd won a fight which had never been one. In a way, she was glad for him take off, rather than having an ongoing battle. It would make for a nice girls' day.

Unless Rick was still hanging around and wanted to come.

"I want to drive our boat," Charlotte grumbled, earning a snort from Rick.

"I don't know about that, Pipsqueak," he said.

"Cherise is Pipsqueak," she corrected primly. "I'm Short Stuff."

"Oh, excuse me for forgetting, Short Squeak."

Charlotte stuck her tongue out at him but Cherise laughed.

The discussion carried on, plans presented, arranged, and rearranged, with Rick giving occasional input mostly intended to curb the kids' arguing with his sister. Grace was relieved that two of the girls' friends were also coming to their Secret Lake homes. Aunt Sharon had given permission for them to have fun at each other's homes with appropriate adult supervision.

It took more effort than she'd expected to make everyone happy, although Grace gave little input. Her job was to cook. Anything the Flemings decided to do that included her was a perk—especially if Rick left her alone.

She wondered, not for the first time, what it would be like to have all the opportunities the Flemings enjoyed. Her dad made good money. After all, they lived in Silicon Valley, same as the Flemings did, but most of his income was spent on Mom's titanic medical bills. Each penny in their house was counted, and Grace had always felt one step away from poor.

Kyle jumped up from the table as soon as they were finished, said he was off to see how Jeff was doing, and headed out the front door. Grace glanced at Hannah wide-eyed when she heard what sounded like a motorcycle engine starting up outside. Hannah shrugged her shoulders.

"He's seventeen. I can't believe Aunt Sharon let him have a bike, but Uncle Luke once had one and loved it. You probably didn't notice it at the side of the garage."

"No, I was paying attention to the red BMW inside the garage. Motorcycles are dangerous," Grace responded, shuddering at the thought.

"They are," Rick agreed, stifling a smirk. "But, believe me, Uncle Luke has good reasons. They're less expensive to run than a car, need constant upkeep—which is forcing Kyle to learn mechanical skills—and in wintertime are colder than a deep freeze, which motivates most guys to work hard for a car as soon as they can get one."

"So, I suppose we won't see much of Kyle while we're here," Hannah concluded.

"Probably not. He's growing up. But remember, it's one less mouth to feed and a lot less sibling rivalry."

"You guys are boring. I'm headed out to the dock to see if I can get ahold of Rachel," Cherise said, high-tailing it out the French doors and through the patio, phone in hand.

"Me, too," Charlotte said. "Well, I don't want to talk to Rachel, but I want to see if Skylar and her sister have made it here yet. Her folks were on the edge of changing their minds about coming. My life will be over if she doesn't come."

Hannah shared a look of exasperation with Grace and Rick. "I swear I was never so dramatic when I was their age."

"Yeah, trust me, you were," Rick said, laughing when Hannah shoved his arm.

"I'm gone," he said, hands uplifted to ward her off. "The garage awaits."

"Have fun," she said.

As for Grace, she was glad for the quiet which descended over the room.

"We're on our own," Hannah said. "Would you mind if I check in with Damien for a bit?"

"Nope," Grace said. "The patio beckons me. I've homework to do."

Collecting her laptop from upstairs, she ventured outside and settled on one of the chaise lounges to study. It was gorgeous out here: beautiful, professional landscaping; a beautiful view of the distant forested mountains; and in the far distance, an even more beautiful glimpse of the lake. If only she didn't find herself constantly distracted by thoughts about Rick. What was he doing right now? Was he under the car? At the workbench doing something complicated with tools and car parts? Getting a bit more grease on his forehead and nose?

At least he wasn't teasing her. She was glad for that, even if guilt for making him feel unwelcome nibbled at her conscience.

Later, finished with their phone calls and bored once again, the twins wandered inside. Rick drifted in shortly after, saying he was done for the night, and before Grace knew it, the Flemings challenged each other to a Monopoly game.

Grace snagged her phone. Monopoly? She hated Monopoly, particularly with the Flemings. The entire clan was ruthless. The only thing worse would have been having Kyle there. He'd learned how to do ruthless better than any of them, even Sean.

"Have fun, guys," she said, heading for the living room. Hannah's call to Damien had taken forever, and now Grace decided it was her turn to make a call.

"You don't want to join us?" Rick asked with reservation. He knew perfectly well she hated Monopoly.

"Yeah. I'd love to make a fool out of myself while getting scalped. I'll save myself the embarrassment."

She pulled her iPhone from her pocket, checked the bars, and was reassured—as usual—that the reception was fantastic. This place amazed her. Despite being surrounded by a forest, having a dock to the lake not five feet downhill from the back of the cabin, and being part of a community sparsely spread around the lake, they still had all the conveniences of town living, including electricity, satellite service, indoor toilets, and the internet. It was perfect.

She hoped Mom was having a good night. It would be nice to hear her voice, but to Grace's disappointment, the call went to voicemail. She left a message but didn't expect a response. When her mother didn't answer this early in the evening, it usually meant she'd gone to bed—which suggested she wasn't feeling great.

It was chilly, with night coming on. Despite the area having hot summer days, the elevation presented nights that were cool or sometimes downright cold, even at the end of June or into July.

Grace pushed the button on the gas fireplace and watched as the fire flashed up and around the fake wood inside. Immediately the warmth swept outward, filling the room. So much nicer to bask here than be roasted in there by the Monopoly gang.

Cradling her phone in her hands, Grace knelt on the thick bear rug in front of the fireplace—fake bear, but a really quality one—and let the flames mesmerize her. Laughter drifted from the table in the kitchen. They were having fun. She was glad for their sake, but she wished she could have gone home. She didn't belong here. If only she hadn't forgotten her license.

Sighing, she kicked off her sneakers and sat cross-legged on the rug. A book sounded awesome compared to Monopoly, and she pulled up the one she was reading on her phone. Unfortunately, she found it next to impossible to get into it, distracted by the laughter, cat-calling, razzing, and whatever else carried on in the Fleming part of the world.

Grace's back protested at her position sitting on the floor, reminding her all too painfully of her confrontation with Kooky Kathy. Had that happened only this morning?

She decided to lie down with her backside to the fire and enjoy the chance to unwind.

Rick felt bad when Grace left. She'd always hated Monopoly. He remembered it only too well, and he didn't blame her. She was a good sport—an amazingly good sport considering the way misfortune plagued her—but they showed her no mercy in the game and celebrated when she was broke. No, she was right to do her own thing. Only now, he ached to ditch the game and join her in the living room, despite knowing he was as welcome as a leper.

He watched the wheeling-and-dealing tycoons Monopoly turned his sister and cousins into and decided it was more proof of the Fleming genes. They all had the need to win.

He quickly moved ahead of the others, but his heart wasn't in it. A headache was nipping at his temples and urging him to offer it as a passable excuse to get out of the game. He didn't want Hannah to guess his intentions—even he wasn't sure about them—so he did his best to play poorly for the next twenty minutes. Then he tossed his pieces down and stood.

"Here, guys. Figure out a way to split up what's left of my hand. I have a headache. Think I'll go upstairs and rest for a while."

"Leave Grace alone," Hannah snapped, her brown eyes rounded with tension.

"I promise," he said.

The cool air in the living room raised goosebumps on his arms when he first walked in, despite Grace's having lit the fireplace. He came to a halt when he saw her curled up in front of it, sound asleep. He should go upstairs. He shouldn't stand there, staring at her.

His heart melted. Gosh, she looked wonderful. She didn't think so when she was younger, although he never understood why. He could only guess it was a combination of the way some of the kids at school treated her and the ornery comments his brothers sometimes made.

It upset him. He'd always liked Grace, which had been a problem when he was younger. Like most boys, he didn't want to admit it. But more than that, he hadn't wanted to draw Sean and Scott's attention any more than Grace did. They loved to make fun of everyone, having earned a reputation for sometimes being bullies on the playground. Rick knew firsthand. They were harder on him than anyone else, and those kids didn't have to take it at home.

If he'd learned earlier to confront them, his life might have turned out completely differently than it had, but ultimately, he knew none of what happened five years ago would have happened if not for Sean.

Grace mewed and her eyelids twitched. She was dreaming. He perched on a chair far enough from her that she wouldn't consider him a perv if she caught him, but he couldn't make himself leave.

His gaze trailed over her features, admiring how she had done nothing but get better. Her slender body, with curves in all the right places, was only a part of the gorgeous package. Oval face, pert nose, and full, delicious lips; fair, flawless skin; thick, pale blond hair. Mostly he loved her bright blue eyes rimmed with pale lashes.

Grace had had a rough life for as long as he could remember. No doubt Trudy Evans still struggled with her health. Grace's dad was likely as submerged in work as ever to provide for his ailing wife. But how were Grace's brother and sister? His calculations left a hole in his gut. Danny and Chloe were both grown now, maybe even living on their own. Time had gotten away from him. What a fool he'd been to let his brothers rob him of the life he could have had.

Grace sensed she was walking in a dream, but she was still filled with excitement as she rounded the corner and hurried toward Hannah's house.

She slowed when she came across Rick playing catch on the front lawn with Scott and Sean. The two older boys called her names and told her to get lost. Rick glanced back and forth between them—worried or amused? She couldn't tell.

Grace wished Hannah was waiting outside for her like she usually did. Because she wasn't, Grace knew she should leave, but she steeled herself against the names Scott called her. She wasn't about to chicken out. She'd put food in the slow cooker that morning for the Evans' dinner, Mom felt good that day, Danny was helping Chloe with her homework, and now Hannah and Grace could tackle the science project they had for school.

Sean laughed and Grace twitched, wondering why her hand hurt. She looked down, tears in her eyes so thick they blinded her. But she remembered. Scott had thrown a baseball at her, simply to be ornery, and while he insisted it was an accident, the ball hit her. Hard.

The scene melted, the sky turned dark, and Mom's car sat at the curb in front of the Flemings' house. She and Marilyn Fleming were checking Grace's hand. It was swollen and bruised, but it wasn't broken.

"This has to stop, Marilyn," Mom insisted. "Your boys are generally good kids, but they aren't nice to Grace. She's clumsy enough. They don't need to try to hurt her if it's their goal, so I don't get what's going on here."

"I don't understand it, either," Marilyn insisted, tears choking her voice. "My husband will lay into Scott again tonight when he gets home, but I don't know what else to do."

"This is the third time this year one of them hurt her, but the bruises don't bother me nearly as much as the emotional upset. Grace is scared of her own shadow."

"Oh, Gracie, I'm so sorry," Marilyn said. "I can't stand bullies, and I can't stand having my sons act this way."

"I'm taking her home. I'm not convinced she's safe here," Mom said.

"But, Mom," Grace protested, panicking. "Our project—"

"I'll go home with you, Gracie. Okay, Mom?" Hannah insisted.

"Of course, honey." To Grace's mother, Marilyn said, "I'll come to get her after Jack gets home. Boys, head to your rooms. You're grounded until your dad says you're not, and you might be over twenty-one before that happens. Now."

Scott brooding, Sean angry, they headed up the walkway to the house. Rick stared at Grace, regret in his eyes, which made her feel guilty. His lips moved, but she wasn't sure what he said—maybe an apology? Then he was gone, and the dream fell apart.

Grace shifted in her sleep, aware in the deepest part of her mind Mom hadn't let her set foot in the Fleming house again until the boys apologized, two weeks later. She wasn't sure Scott and Sean meant it, but she remembered how upset Rick was. He truly felt bad.

She also remembered he wasn't the one who threw the ball.

Grace shifted, moaning, and flexed her left hand a few times. Rick's thoughts immediately jumped to the night when Scott threw the baseball at her. Later, before their dad arrived and when the three boys could talk, Rick berated Scott.

"Hey, I didn't mean to hurt her. I was... goofing around," Scott countered. His jaw was set in a way that proved, while he knew he shouldn't have done it, he didn't feel all that bad about it.

"Most people would dodge the ball," Sean pointed out, popping a stick of gum into his mouth and chomping on it. "Ordinary people would at least duck. Graceless Grace just stood there. Kind of stupid if you ask me."

"You're a jerk," Rick snarled. "She's a girl. She doesn't play baseball. She wasn't watching you and didn't see it coming. You threw it right at her, Scott. Why would anyone purposely throw a baseball at a girl who spends half her nights each week in ballet with our sister? Have you noticed how fragile her—Hannah's—hands are?" He gulped. He didn't need his brothers knowing he'd noticed Grace's hands. Hands so small and delicate and... elegant? The boys had been forced to attend Hannah's recitals all their lives, and while he knew his sister was a truly special girl, he'd always thought Grace outshone all the other ballerinas, including Hannah. Legs, hands, the arch of her back; her harmony with the music. Her movements spoke to him in ways that, as a guy, he couldn't explain. She was almost perfect, never clumsy, in complete contrast with the rest of her life— except possibly cooking, and even then, she had her moments. Dance transported her away from whatever misfortune this world seemed determined to inflict on her.

When Hannah quit dancing, had Grace stopped, too? He'd never thought to ask.

"Yeah, what about her hands?" Sean said, his eyes hooded in annoyance.

"It would be easy to break them," Rick insisted, swallowing hard when Scott came nose to nose with him.

"But I didn't, so what do you care? What are you, a wuss? Wanna save the Bad Luck Girl?"

Rick stared back, as brave as he dared get. Scott was a junior varsity football player, and he was full of himself. His goal on the field was to pound anybody who got near the quarterback, and the drive spilled over into his personal life.

"Maybe you should go kiss her and make it better," Scott said, a sarcastic smile twisting his mouth.

"Drop dead, Scott," Rick said, heading off to his room and slamming and locking the door.

Grace's face puckered as if she wanted to cry, hurtling Rick's thoughts back to the present. Was she having a nightmare? He felt guilty just watching her. He should leave before she woke up and caught him.

Grace flinched, awareness sending her nerve endings on high alert. She wasn't alone.

She jerked awake and found Rick eyeing her as he rose from a chair not far from her. She sat up fast enough it tweaked her back and made her grunt. Right about now, she wanted to go back and punch Kooky Kathy.

"You okay?" Rick asked with concern.

He seemed sincere, but he probably also felt awkward at being caught anywhere near her. Good. He should. "Yeah, I twisted my back this morning. Long story."

He nodded, stuffing his hands into his jeans pockets and taking a couple of steps back. "Sorry. I, uh… ditched the game. I have a headache and was headed upstairs to catch up on those accounts on my laptop, but, uhm…" He gestured toward the fireplace. "It was so nice and warm here I couldn't help…."

Grace couldn't help the annoyance his expression triggered inside her. A dumb excuse for breaking his agreement to avoid her, let alone watching her while she slept.

"It's crazy to need a fire in late June, isn't it?" he said weakly.

Grace merely stared at him, wondering why she never had the guts to do that when they were younger. It made him even more uncomfortable. Fantastic. He deserved that too.

The dream filtered back into her thoughts, of her settling into bed that night after Mom wrapped her hand and wrist in an Ace bandage and packed it in ice. Scott and Sean were buffoons, too in love with themselves to realize their popularity came from their good looks and their father's money.

But it wasn't Rick who threw the ball.

Why did she have such a hard time forgiving him for something he didn't do?

Immediately her memories jerked her back to five years ago, the last time she saw Rick, the awful remarks Sean said to her while Rick did nothing to protect her. She'd stormed out of the Flemings' home and given Hannah her ultimatum. She not only meant every word, she had a right to make such a threat.

"Sorry about the Monopoly thing," he said, his gorgeous green eyes fastened on the flickering fire. "You never did like it. I don't blame you. I swear my brothers behaved as if they had real money in their hands."

"You were as merciless as they were, and you know it. For that matter, the entire Fleming clan, Hannah included, has carried the torch. Is your car done?"

She flinched when she saw the hurt marring Rick's handsome face. *Mean, Grace, mean,* she scolded herself. When had she allowed herself to become as bad as the people who made her life miserable? She ran her fingers through her hair, knowing it was probably a mess from lying down, but mostly it came from wanting an excuse to avoid looking at him.

"I haven't even removed all the parts yet," he replied, the hurt turning into resentment. "I'll need the weekend, but don't worry. As soon as I can get it all done, I'll get out of here. I don't want to rain on your parade."

He turned and hurried upstairs, leaving Grace's eyes stinging with tears. Which, in turn, triggered the ache in her heart she thought she buried years ago. It was one thing to stay away from Rick; it was another to purposely hurt him to do it.

———

Rick dropped onto his bed, staring at the ceiling and wishing he was anywhere but here. He looked at his hands, hands now those of a twenty-five-year-old man. They were stained in a few places with car grease, thick from working out, and scarred across both palms from the accident. *The* accident. His badge of shame.

He wondered how differently life would have gone five long years ago if he'd taken Sean's dare to kiss Grace. Would she have hated him more for doing it than not doing it? Would she have accused him of using her for a thrill instead of showing her how he truly felt? He feared both as much as he feared showing his feelings to Sean. Still, was there something—anything—he could have done that would have changed that awful night?

Grace's clumsiness annoyed Scott and gave Sean another reason to tease her, which upset Rick. Everybody had clumsy moments. Even clumsy days. After all, he smacked himself in the face with a wrench this afternoon and had to chase the wrench across the garage floor before he snagged it. He was the klutz, not Grace.

He sighed, wondering if what Hannah often told him was right. Sometimes angels came along and, in the strangest ways, guided God's children in the right direction. Coming here had been a last-minute decision, the thought jumping into his head out of the middle of nowhere. But maybe this week might turn out to be a gift from Heaven. If he could get past Grace Evans' defenses, he might be able to earn her forgiveness, even if he wasn't able to find a way into her heart.

———

Grace rose and gazed out the window into the backyard. They'd eaten early and there was plenty of daylight left. It seemed so inviting, despite the drop in temperature. The peace and the silence outdoors drew her.

She ignored Hannah and the twins when she drifted through the kitchen and out the French doors to the patio, where pine and fir trees scented the air. She rubbed her arms against the chill as she wandered around the yard, admiring the beautiful flowers while engrossed in another comparison between Hannah's family and her own.

Like this place, a second home to the Flemings, there was so much her parents couldn't afford. Of course, most people didn't have what the Flemings had. Silicon Valley was an aberration, not the norm. She even admired Hannah's parents and her aunt and uncle. They were strong, dynamic people, deeply religious, grateful for all they had, and placed teaching their children good morals above costly possessions. Still, they had enough money they couldn't avoid spoiling them, too.

Grace's family might not be as close as Rick's seemed to be, but they were kind people. Mom's health problems, too long unexplained, weren't diagnosed until Grace ten years old, leaving Grace to all but raise Danny and Chloe. Dad's efforts to take care of Mom and provide for all of them consumed him. There was never any blame, just hard work and concern. She missed Dad a lot and sometimes resented Mom for being so frail, but she also knew they were doing the best they could. How could she ask for more than that?

Grace drew a deep breath, rubbing her arms again. Maybe she didn't have a right to ask for more, but she wanted more.

A lovely yellow tea rose caught her attention. She tried to lean over and smell it, but the bud was too low. She raised it toward her nose and then cringed when a thorn pricked her finger. She jumped back and pushed the fingertip into her mouth, wrinkling her nose at the coppery flavor.

"Get a life, Murphy," she groused. "You drew enough blood from Cherise. You don't need mine, too. Isn't it enough I'm so blasted clumsy?"

The voices of the past whispered in her head in response. Not only the Fleming boys' wisecracks and name-calling, but those of far too many kids in school. Even her younger brother made fun of her.

"Graceless Grace, did you fall down again?" "Grace Without Grace, what did you trip over now?" "Mom, Ungraceful Grace knocked over three glasses and broke them." Worst of all, Sean loved to sneer at her, "What's for an encore, Grace?"

No, the worst of all was Murphy. If Grace could drop it, break it, trip over it, lose it, spill it, burn it, or do it wrong, she did. Murphy cast his spell without a word. His way of taunting her was to make her do it again and again.

She abandoned the flowerbeds and headed to the rear of the property. At the edge, a narrow gate opened onto a short set of stairs which led to the Flemings' private dock. From here, she had a breathtaking view of the lake and the mountains on the other side.

The Flemings' party boat sat gently bobbing against the bumper pads that protected both it and the dock. Laughter bubbled out of her at the thought of getting into the boat this week. She'd done it tons of times, so it wasn't like she was afraid. She only knew each day would offer a handful of tales to write about in her journal. As long as she didn't drown herself or anyone else, she supposed it would be fine.

She finally drifted back inside, where the girls were putting away the game and Hannah was grinning at the trouncing she'd given them.

"It was a quick game because I'm such a tycoon," she said, flipping her hair with her hand in her I'm-so-hot way.

"Then take me to Hawaii for our next vacation," Grace said. "Where Rick won't be."

Hannah froze, her eyes rounded in surprise. "Wow. Where did that come from?"

Grace winced. *Mean, Grace, mean,* she scolded herself again. She explained what happened earlier and Hannah groaned.

"He promised he wouldn't bother you."

Grace thought before answering this time. "He didn't, exactly. It was a little creepy, waking up and finding him sitting there, looking at me."

"I'll talk to him—"

"No, let it go. I think I'm making too much of it. He said he'd been drawn by the fire, and I was, too, so… just let it go."

"It's Friday night," Charlotte interrupted. "Our friends won't be here until tomorrow. We brought lots of old movies from home and we're popping popcorn and watching them all night. You guys in?"

"Sure," Hannah said.

"As long as you pop the popcorn and carry it upstairs," Grace muttered, "because I'm not touching anything I can burn or spill." She loved popcorn, although she rarely ate it because she wanted to devour every greasy, salty, yummy morsel until she herself popped.

"I'll do it," Cherise said. "I want the real thing, though, not the microwave stuff. It tastes better, and I can put a gallon of butter and a pound of salt on it. Char, you get the movie ready and grab sodas for us from the fridge upstairs."

Charlotte agreed and took off. Hannah threw her arm around Grace's shoulders and steered her toward the staircase.

"The hardest part for you is believing you can climb the stairs without counting the steps. Have some faith, girl!"

"Yeah, if I don't count, I'll probably fall and break a leg."

Hannah laughed, but Grace tried not to count and tripped twice, proving she was nuts to take the risk.

CHAPTER 5

They started with one of Grace's favorite movies, the sci-fi *The 5th Wave*. For the next two hours, they were immersed in it. Grace didn't realize, until they turned on the lights and made trips to the bathroom in between movies, Rick had joined them. Granted, he was on the other couch, alone and quiet, but he was still in the same room as Grace.

He avoided her gaze, which in its own way troubled her. The cabin belonged to his aunt and uncle, and he had more right to it than she did. As long as he didn't bother her, she shouldn't have anything to whine about. But now, with him so far away and looking so lonely, she felt bad for behaving so unkindly toward him.

Hannah must have had similar sympathies because when she returned to her place, she waved her brother over to join her. "You're not sitting there all alone," she insisted. To the twins she said, "Girls, move over. Let him sit between us."

To Grace, she offered an olive branch, whispering, "He won't say a word to you. Okay?"

Grace gave a shrug of submission, thinking it might ease some of her guilt without pushing her dreaded anxiety buttons.

Rick hesitated, but when Grace didn't complain, he complied. Grace's heart rate rose a notch with him this much closer, but not because she was upset by him. No, she wondered what it would be like to sit next to him.

It was difficult to push those thoughts aside when the lights dropped and the second movie began to roll. Then her stomach dropped when she realized which flick the kids had picked. She didn't care for horror, but she utterly despised *The Ring*. To her, it wasn't terrifying, it was totally evil, and she had no idea why the twins liked it enough to watch it over and over again.

She sunk down in her seat, propped her huge bowl of popcorn between her knees, and made a point of hiding behind it each time the scary parts came. And closing her eyes. That helped, too. Not enough, but it helped. Except she kept thinking about sitting next to Rick. She imagined him holding her and protecting her.

Which sort of worked… until it didn't. When the worst part came, with the girl climbing out of the well, dripping, matted hair in her face and a mad, murderous look in her eyes, Grace squealed and threw her hands over her face.

Time froze as she realized she couldn't keep the popcorn bowl between her knees without at least one hand. She gasped as it popped into the air, watching in slow motion as it shot upward. She tried to grab it, but it bounced off her fingertips, skyrocketed to her left, did a perfect one-eighty, and landed upside down in Rick's lap, dumping every buttery piece on him—minus a handful that splattered Hannah.

Hannah gasped; Cherise barked laughter. Charlotte paused the movie, and Hannah called Alexa to turn on the lights. The mess didn't look any better in bright light than it did in the near-dark.

"Oh, my gosh," Grace said, wanting to drop dead. "I'm so sorry. I'm such an idiot." She ran to the bathroom and retrieved the trash can and a handful of towels. "You need to wash your pants now or they're going to stain."

Rick sat, arms akimbo, staring at the mess strewn all over him and on the couch. It was as if the bowl was another version of the evil girl in the well. His eyes sought hers, filled with shock, and then Cherise started laughing at Rick like a hyena.

"Wow, man, you're such a good catch you didn't even have to use your hands."

Grace's cheeks set on fire. Good grief, why did she always have to ruin everything? One night. Couldn't she be a normal person watching an awful movie for just one night?

Hannah's grin was the best of the best, but it came from a little sister seeing her big brother decimated. She was eating it up.

"I'm so, so sorry," Grace said again, grabbing her popcorn bowl and tossing it into the trash can. She'd wash it later. She began gathering popcorn from Rick's legs but paused, mortified she was touching him. A glance at him told her that he appreciated her help, but what did she do with the feelings warring inside her? She wasn't supposed to crave being close to him anymore.

Hannah added her own offerings to the pile, but when all that was left was located where Grace had no intentions of putting her hands, she wiped her fingers on one of the towels and set the trash can in front of him.

"Uhm, you'll have to do the rest," she said.

His gaze twitched with a peculiar blend of bewilderment and mirth. Mirth? He thought this was funny, too?

He shed himself of most of the popcorn and then rose to stand over the can and shake off the rest, clearing his throat far too frequently. Grace dropped to her knees and gathered what fell on the wood floor, as Hannah collected what remained on the couch.

"I'm off to change clothes," Rick said, laughing as if someone had told a side-splitting joke. "I've never seen anyone do anything like that in my life. It was right out of a movie."

He ran off, a few stray kernels fluttering off of him. Grace snagged those, too, and set the can near the top of the stairs to take down later. Thankfully Hannah's clothes seemed unscathed.

Grace washed the grease off the couch, eternally grateful Aunt Sharon had the foresight to have both pieces of furniture made from some kind of pricey stain-resistant Naugahyde.

Rick was back in a flash, redressed and looking more handsome than ever, his soiled clothes in his arms. Grace reached for them, but he held them away from her, grabbed the trash can of errant popcorn, and bounded down the stairs.

Grace wanted to throttle Hannah for grinning from ear to ear. Instead, she shook her head and followed Rick, going much slower, of course, and hanging onto the banister. If there was anything she was good at, beyond cooking, it was laundry. She'd messed up enough of it in her life she knew how to get almost any stain out of almost anything. She needed to make sure he did it right.

"I can do laundry, Grace," Rick said when she joined him in the washroom. "You need to check out your own clothes." He pointed at the stain on her blouse—one of her favorites—and she gave a tiny mew of dismay. Dang.

"You have something on under that? We could add it to mine."

"Yeah. An Under-Tee." She unbuttoned the blouse, treated it, and tossed it into the washer. Rick added his treated clothes to hers, added the laundry products, and set it to wash.

Embarrassment caught up with her, and she leaned back against the dryer, her arms wrapped tight around her middle.

"Ah, come on," Rick said. "It was an accident." He choked on laughter again. "A really crazy, wild, amazing accident, but it was an accident. Maybe if I'd been sitting the way you were and done what you did, it would have happened to me, too."

"No," she insisted. "No one else does anything the way I do it."

He chuckled again but still tried to hold back. "Accidents happen, but I'll admit your delivery is... different. Which means you're unique. Nothing wrong with that."

She pressed her hands to her face and shook her head. Why in the world was the guy who always made her feel stupid trying to make her feel better? It refused to register in her brain.

She felt him lean close and peeked between her fingers to see what he was up to. Oh, my gosh, he smelled so good. Sandalwood and citrus again. His finely chiseled face, his strong jaw and high brow... calendar-model perfect.

"Grace?" he said, thumb and finger pulling one of her fingers away from her face. "You don't need to hide. I'm not upset. If you are, I'm sorry. Please, don't cry."

Cry? Cry? Her fingers found the tears on her cheeks and brushed them away, as embarrassed by them as she was by the popcorn. She didn't realize she was crying. "I'm so tired of spilling things. And I'm a wuss. I hate scary movies."

Rick chuckled again, only this time it was heartier. "Me, too. Can't stand them. Scott and Sean used to hold me down and make me watch them, which gave me nightmares for a week. I was grateful to get a place of my own and put an end to it."

"That's awful," Grace said, having no difficulty imagining Rick's brothers acting that way but not able to imagine Rick being a victim. "You have your own place?"

"Yeah. A house in good old Los Gatos, not far from my folks' place. Where I can watch blockbuster action movies," he said. "Or comedies. I had a gut ache from watching this movie, but I was totally entertained by the bowl-flipping thing you did. If you'd do it the next time they pick a scary movie, it would be great."

Grace wanted to groan. She even considered being offended. Instead, seeing the sparkle in his eyes and the way his tanned cheeks flushed, she found herself smiling instead.

"Maybe I should take up knife juggling."

Rick responded with a belly laugh, which made her legs almost melt. She remembered his laughter from their teen years, the laughter she'd always loved.

"Please," he sputtered, "don't. Even if you were good at it, I don't think I'd want to place my bets against Murphy."

Her smile faded. "I know. He's definitely got it out for me. I'm assuming he'll do his best to ruin the rest of my life the way he did the first part of it."

Rick's humor evaporated. "Only if you let him—it, Grace," he said. "As I said, we all have our moments, and I refuse to let the bad things in life ruin the good ones. Are you going back upstairs?"

Grace bowed her head, partly annoyed he'd cut off the discussion so abruptly, but also glad to be done with it. "I can't stand that movie. I think I'll go grab my jacket and take a walk to the dock."

"You won't have long. It's well into dusk."

She nodded. She needed some more fresh air. He shifted from one foot to the other and back in discomfiture. "Would you mind me tagging along? No conversation needed. I'd love to stretch my legs."

Grace's heart did a few flips in her chest, and light-headedness assailed her. Was this happening? Was she actually standing here in Luke and Sharon Fleming's laundry room in the Flemings' not-cabin cabin with Rick Fleming? Had he, for real, asked if he could join her on a stroll to the dock?

Was she crazy? Why in the world did she want to consort with the enemy?

Maybe because of the movie? Maybe because it would be nice to not be alone, the way she was always alone, except when she was with Hannah? There wouldn't be any popcorn to toss. Or glasses to break. Maybe she wouldn't even fall off the dock and drown.

"I think you're crazy," she said, brow furrowed in disbelief. "I don't know anyone in their right mind who'd want to be around me on a dock on the lake at dusk."

Rick threw hands out to his sides. "Then I'm not in my right mind because I have no fear of you or Murphy."

"Yeah, we'll see how you feel—if you survive the adventure."

"So I can come along?"

Grace shrugged. "It's your neck."

"I'm not taking anything for granted. I made a promise to behave myself."

They stared at each other, his eyes fastened on hers, his handsome face open, his stance relaxed. Friendly. The way Grace remembered him before the fateful night that destroyed her faith in him.

"Okay," she said, barely above a whisper. She hoped she wouldn't regret it.

"Great. Let me tell Hannah what we're doing." He pulled his phone from his pocket and texted her. His sister told them to have fun.

She'd better, Grace thought. *She knows we both hate that horrid movie.*

Grace rescued her popcorn bowl from the trashcan and went to wash it, while Rick emptied the trash in the garage. Both goals accomplished, he set the empty can by the staircase to take up later, then waited on the patio for Grace to get her jacket.

Grace had thought the walkway to the gate, which bisected the lawn into north and south halves—each big enough to be small pastures, was pretty wide. With Rick beside her, it suddenly wasn't. The stairs to the dock were even worse. Rick let her go ahead so she had plenty of room to maneuver.

"Never get tired of this place," Rick said, stuffing his hands into his pants pockets as they strolled, side-by-side, on the short walkway which joined the dock. The dock didn't have handrails, which always bothered Grace. She came to a stop.

"On second thought, I think I'd be better off admiring the view from here," she said, wrinkling her nose.

"Nah, I'll keep you safe."

"Ha!" she chortled. "I saw how that worked with my popcorn attack."

Rick laughed in response. "It was a surprise attack, and I'm willing to take the risk. Do you need to hang onto me?"

No, that she couldn't do. It bothered her to have him offer, even if he was simply being a gentleman. She shook her head, screwed up her courage, and set off along the length of the wooden dock. She didn't realize she'd stopped breathing until she reached the end. Glad to have Rick walk a little behind her, she sucked in a few deep breaths before sitting, her back toward the boat, and forced her hammering heart to calm down.

Rick joined her, putting a comfortable distance between them, his feet dangling above the surface of the water. His legs were long, his shoulders wide, his pose strong yet relaxed.

Grace forced herself to pay attention to the enchanting view of the lake as it took a right-hand bend before them, disappearing around a corner filled with sky-high pines and an occasional stand of redwoods. In the near distance, three mallard hens were herding their dozens of ducklings to the opposite shore for the night. Grace grinned at how cute they looked.

Rick chuckled. "Ever wonder what it's like to be a duck?"

"Doesn't everyone wonder what it's like to be an animal?"

"I suppose. I wonder if any animals are bright enough to wonder what it's like to be human."

Grace met his gaze, her brow wrinkled. "Is this Richard Fleming trying to be philosophical?"

"What, you don't think I can?"

She lifted her shoulders, now both somewhat amused and annoyed. "Maybe I've always wondered if you knew what it was like to be human."

His silence drew her eyes to his again. She could see the hurt lying under the surface. It made her swallow hard.

Hurting him had become a reflex.

"I'm sorry, Grace. I'm sorry you feel that way. That my brothers and I made you feel that way when we were young. I've never had the chance to apologize. Hannah wouldn't let me. She forbade me to talk to you. Anywhere. Ever. I would have, you know. Apologized."

Grace felt the panic filling her lungs. It rose slowly, like a thick, hot, traitorous sludge, threatening to drown her. "Please. Please, don't," she said, waving him away. "I can't do this right now." She didn't want his apology. It would mean she'd have to forgive him, and she wasn't sure she could ever do that.

Rick flinched and looked away, thankful the serenity of the lake held sway.

He'd blown it. He pushed too hard, too soon. This was the closest he'd come to fixing what got broken five years ago, and he feared he'd never get another opportunity.

Even worse, he was stranded here for several more days and didn't want to make it unbearable for either of them.

Out of the corner of his eye, he contemplated Grace and was reminded of everything she once meant to him and of everything he'd lost. He found himself rubbing the palms of his hands together, more aware than ever of the coarse skin across his scars. He needed to button his lips and leave her alone. Those scars had come at a great price. He blasted Sean that night, determined to protect Grace, and she didn't even know. The results had been terrible and had taken some time for the two brothers to work out, but he had to accept he might never be able to work things out with her.

The bugs buzzed around the lake, the distant hum of crickets and the cadence of frogs joining in. Twilight rimmed the mountain ridge to the west a rosy gold, offsetting the silhouettes of the trees. Grace pulled back her sleeve and checked her watch. Hannah made fun of her high-school graduation present, even if it was a really nice Eco-Drive. Hannah used her phone and didn't even wear a watch, but Grace had always liked her watch better. Her life had been ruled by time: her need to rise early in the mornings, to help Mom, to be at school or doctor's or dentist's appointments or sports activities for Mom or Danny or Chloe. Now, seeing how close it was to sunset, she realized she was foolish to come here this late in the day. Darkness was Murphy's right-hand man, and the thought made her restless.

The nip of a mosquito decided it. She slapped it, cringing when she smashed it on her cheek. "Yuck. I forgot the bug spray. I'm going back," she said.

Heart racing, she squirmed around and got her knees under her to try to stand without falling into the lake. Rick rose effortlessly, but seeing her discomfort, extended a hand. She didn't want to take it but was grateful when he helped her get to her feet. He made no move to let go and guided her down the dock toward the stairs, now draped in shadows. Unsettled by his touch, she let go as soon as they stepped onto firm land.

Rick hooked his thumbs into his jeans' pockets and, eyes twinkling, paused and asked, "So, what's with Hannah and her boyfriend? I don't get why she won't tell the family anything about him."

Grace shook her head, mounted the stairs, and heaved a silent sigh of relief for making it into the yard unscathed. When Rick joined her, she turned and replied bluntly, "Hannah's in love and doesn't want you guys to ruin it." He flinched, proving she'd struck another nerve. "Damien's a great guy. In all fairness, I wish he'd propose, but he's too tied up with school and work to take on more responsibility. It's killing Hannah. She just wants to be with him."

"Damien, huh? She's never even told me his name. I don't want to hassle him. I want to meet him. After all, he may be my future brother-in-law and the father of my sister's children."

"And he'd better measure up, right?"

"I only want to know he's good to her."

"Beyond. He treats her like royalty. He goes to church with us in San Jose, and they belong to one of those wait-until-you're-married groups."

"Really?" Rick searched her face as if wondered what she believed. "Don't you think that's good?"

"I think people who set their own boundaries are good people if they live them, and hypocrites if they find excuses not to."

"Wow. Don't hold back, Grace Evans."

"You asked, Richard Fleming. I have a problem with people who profess religious piety and then hurt other people like it doesn't matter."

The silence between them felt heavy as they approached the covered patio.

"We were kids, Grace, remember?" he said at last. "That's why children need parents. *Lord of the Flies*, right? They not only don't know how to behave, they have no idea what it means to be a hypocrite. Most of us learn; those who don't… pay a heavy price. I wish people didn't get hurt through the process, but I think that's part of life, too. Don't you?"

Did he need her approval? Was he trying to make excuses? Was he trying to force her to forgive him?

Grace let out a long, slow breath, trying not to see bad where good might be intended. After all, she was supposed to forgive. Didn't their minister frequently focus his sermons on the topic? Even Grace's mother believed it was an important part of a person's character. Grace just hadn't found a way to do it. If what the Fleming boys and the kids in school did to her wasn't enough, all the other humiliations were. She called it Murphy on some days, bad luck on others, but sometimes she felt as if God had it out for her. How did someone make peace with that?

"I think Hannah just wants to make her own decisions, like everyone else," she replied. "She's the baby in your family and the only girl. She needs everyone to let go and trust her. You should. She's made very few mistakes in her life, and none of them terrible. Maybe the biggest chance she's taken is keeping me in her life, but I'm selfish. She's my best friend, and I don't want to lose her. Besides being far too patient with me, she's an awesome person."

"She is," Rick said, nodding. He opened the French door and waved her inside. "Thanks. I'm grateful for the insight. I'm, uh, going to go take our clothes and then head off to bed. Good night, Grace. I hope you have fun here."

He was gone before she could think of a response. She turned and climbed the steps, counting them as she went, avoiding the movie on her way to her bedroom. She pulled open her drawer and took out her nightshirt before it dawned on her that she'd again been unnecessarily rude to Rick. She gave him permission to accompany her to the lake, and he'd been a gentleman the whole time. It was as if the minute Rick came back into her life, she turned into a person she didn't recognize. A person she didn't like.

It brought tears to her eyes, but she wasn't sure whether they were spawned by guilt or anger. All she knew was it made her think *she* needed to apologize to the guy who broke her heart.

<hr>

Rick tossed his clothes into the dryer but checked Grace's blouse for drying instructions. Pulling a hanger from the small basket Aunt Sharon kept on the folding counter, he hung it up to dry.

He took his time climbing the stairs, cringing as he caught a flash of the movie before heading into his room. He propped himself up on his bed and turned on his laptop, checking the two most important accounts he needed to keep an eye on while he was here. They looked great, or at least he thought they did. He had difficulty focusing.

His thoughts were a jumble of past memories and present challenges, peppered by the sadness he felt about the way he and his brothers had treated Grace when they were younger.

He felt Grace's resentment, like sandpaper against his skin. She had no idea he harbored the same feeling toward his brothers, particularly Sean.

His fingers hovered over the keys, and then he opened his pictures, scrolling through thousands of memories. He stopped and studied a few of those with Grace in them. They brought back the feelings he had for her. She was so cute. No, beautiful.

He flipped further back in time, coming across Hannah's baby pictures. The Fleming siblings were each two years apart, and six-year-old Scott adored Hannah from the moment she was born. There he was, holding her in his arms and looking tenderly at her sleepy-eyed face. He was quick to tackle anyone who would even think of hurting his baby sister. So why was he so insensitive to Grace's feelings? Rick never understood it.

Next, he scrolled forward, pausing to browse through the girls' ballet performances and Hannah's piano recitals—which Grace always attended—and T-Ball and softball games, which made Rick cringe. Grace was always covered in dust and mud. She sometimes managed to hit the ball, but she rarely got around the bases without falling down or tripping over the other players. And that was if people didn't push or knock her down on purpose. Why were some kids mean to others? Why were some children marked as targets?

Halloween. A few pictures reminded Rick of why eighth grade made him come close to disliking the holiday. Sean and Scott chose costumes which scared half the neighborhood to death. Here was a photo of Grace standing in front of Hannah, who was so scared she was sobbing. Until he was older, Rick didn't understand why Grace wouldn't stand up for herself. Yet, here she was, refusing to let monsters get to Hannah without a battle. Now, it dawned on him fighting for herself wasn't nearly as important to her as doing it for someone she loved.

Now, he was humbled by Grace's loyalty to Hannah.

Mom and Dad disapproved of the turn the three boys' behavior took as Scott headed into his junior year in high school, a handsome, popular jock. Popularity went to his head and he used it to get girls, cut classes, teach his brothers to be disrespectful to adults and take them to parties even he shouldn't have attended. He bucked the parents when they caught wind of a few of his exploits, but when he and Sean were almost arrested at a party that got out of hand, Mom and Dad laid down the law. Thankfully, it worked its magic by the time Scott headed off to college.

Sean was a different matter. When they were little, he and Rick were close. They shared the same games and toys, many of the same friends, and as they grew older loved the same sports. Scott planned their pranks and pressured his brothers to help execute them. Somehow, they got away with far too many. Sean resented Hannah and especially Grace, because they took Rick's attention away from him and the fun they had.

Rick zoomed in on a few more photos. They were proof of Sean making Grace's life miserable. In these pictures Scott had taken, the girls were at the table trying to eat a snack and do homework, and Sean was squirting ketchup on their papers and in Grace's hair. What upset Rick was seeing himself in the background laughing. How could he have thought it was funny?

Mom caught him in the act. Hannah tattled, complaining Sean made the girls fix their lunches, do their laundry, and take off their dirty socks for them. The tongue-lashing they received that day grabbed Rick's attention. Seeing the truth made him choose to adopt his parents' faith, perhaps every bit as tenaciously as Hannah had, and he made the decision to behave more responsibly, even when it was hard. He only wished he'd made Grace aware of the change.

Flipping to a group of more current Christmas pictures, he smiled at one of Scott and Julia. Rick liked Scott's wife. Disagreements with Scott dwindled when his brother grew up and finally married. Julia was a strong Christian woman and the perfect partner for his brother. But after Scott left home, Sean got really full of himself. The camaraderie between him and Rick became strained. He still wanted to pull pranks on people, especially Grace, and he loved to take risks Rick didn't. Driving too fast, staying out too late the night before a game, being late to school because of it. Sean still had great grades and felt justified, and it annoyed him when Rick started getting rides to school with friends to avoid Sean.

It grew worse when Sean saw Rick's growing friendship with Grace, the way he'd hang around the house when Grace was there, how he fit in with her and Hannah in a way Sean couldn't. Rick never understood Sean's jealousy, and well… after that night…

He sat back from the computer and rubbed his rough palms back and forth on his jeans again, a habit he hadn't quite overcome. People shouldn't be unkind to each other, but there were things that should never happen between family.

Rick let out a soft breath at the thought. He was grateful he and Sean had managed to repair their relationship, and Sean was busy trying to be a better man. Too often he still didn't have a filter, and he'd lost a number of girlfriends over it. Now he had a steady one in

Lisa, a woman who loved his crazy sense of humor, although she set her limits—and Sean respected them.

Why hadn't he respected Grace's?

The last group of pictures Rick opened were of Hannah's graduation, five years ago. Because it was Grace's graduation, too, his parents hadn't allowed Rick and Sean to attend. Rick still felt the sting of it. His mother took these pictures of the girls and sent them to him, with the understanding he was never to show them to Hannah. He wasn't supposed to know anything about Grace.

In these photos, Grace looked proud of herself, but he didn't miss the evidence she'd also been crying.

<hr />

It was dark, but Grace still *heard* the grin in Hannah's voice as she grilled her about the stroll to the dock with Rick.

"I tolerated him, he tolerated me, and nobody drowned," she finally snapped, exasperated. "What is this? Hannah trying to play matchmaker? Not interested, girl. Knock it off."

Hurt silence was followed by the sound of Hannah bunching her pillow and flopping onto her back.

"How's Damien? You guys were on the phone for an hour."

That was all it took to turn Hannah's focus away from Grace and onto her ever-dramatic aspirations about the love of her life. Damien was one step away from perfect but always one step out of her reach. Which turned dreaming into frustration, which turned into hard facts, which turned into dreaming in a never-ending cycle of talk talk talk.

Grace was floored when Hannah fell asleep not much after one o'clock. She didn't remember that ever happening.

Grace wished she could go to sleep. She tossed and turned as the day's events rolled through her mind: their long trip, having a gun in her face, finding Rick not nearly as awful as she remembered but every bit as luscious—and dredging up a past she'd done her best to forget. Finding out, even half a decade after they parted on such terrible terms, he still hadn't married.

Thankful Hannah was a heavy sleeper, Grace pulled out her laptop to look at her homework. Among her assignments was a paper due on *Inferno*. Unfortunately, Dante had a hard time competing with the memories of sitting on the dock with Richard Fleming.

The twins stayed up for a while after Hannah fell asleep, but Grace felt the softness of the night fall over the house when they finally shut off the TV and went to bed. It left her even more alone, with lots of time to avoid studying. When she finally closed the computer and turned out the light, all she could think about was surviving three more days around the man she swore she'd never talk to again.

CHAPTER 6

The Flemings were normally early risers, like Grace, but Hannah had made a solemn promise to the twins that they could sleep in this morning, even if they didn't take the boat out until later. Too bad Grace didn't know how to sleep in.

The house was quiet when she slipped into the kitchen. She wondered if Kyle had come home last night. He and Rick apparently planned to play racquetball before the group took off with the boat, but at present, the door to the basement was closed, with no sounds echoing from downstairs.

Grace had wanted to exercise in the mornings. Her back felt better, and for a brief moment, she toyed with the idea of using the treadmill. In the next instant, the image of her breaking into a sweat in front of Rick, or falling and breaking a leg, or worse, breaking the Flemings' treadmill, made her realize the insanity of even considering it.

No, it was a marvelous gift just to be alone in the kitchen. The pale light of dawn, combined with the smell of the Keurig coffee, had her humming with pleasure. She sipped her coffee as she toyed with her homework.

The assignment still eluded her. She decided to FaceTime her mother instead. Maybe she was up early this morning.

"Hey, Mom," Grace said, seeing Trudy Evans dressed and neat.

"Good morning, Sweet Cheeks," Mom replied, her own cheeks unusually rosy today. "How's the village?"

"It's survived me thus far."

She chuckled. "Good for it. How was the drive?"

In perspective, hilarious, and they shared laughter over Kooky Kathy and the shock of Grace being on the business end of a gun.

"Wow. That's awful, sweetie. I'm sure he wouldn't have pulled the trigger," her mother said, sobering. "You scared him, you know, but they're trained to know when to shoot and when not to shoot."

"I know, but I wish he'd chased down Kooky Kathy and scared her, too. She deserved it."

"What she truly needs is help, Grace. Now, what about the cabin? Is it as spectacular as ever?"

"Yep, and the kids have grown so much. Kyle's one step away from being a man. He was my champion yesterday."

"You needed a champion? Well, I guess you would. Good old Murphy."

"No. It's not Murphy, it's…" Uh-oh. She shouldn't have said anything. Grace bit her lip.

Mom's smile slipped. "What's wrong?"

"Uhm, nothing's wrong, just unexpected." Grace described their arrival, and Mom roared when Grace described falling up the steps, banging her head against a door, and being rescued by the Adonis who slung her behind him into the mudroom.

"A handsome backpack slinger. How exciting," her mother said, which made them both laugh.

"Yeah, the slinger is the problem. It's… Rick Fleming."

The longer pause turned cold. The Fleming boys' behavior had strained the friendship between Trudy and Marilyn over the years.

"It's okay, Mom," Grace reassured her. "Believe it or not, Rick apologized to me. It's been five years, you know. He's twenty-five now."

Her mom looked flustered. "Oh, dear, how time gets away from me. I suppose he's married and has a family by now."

Grace shook her head. "I don't know why and I don't really care, but he's still single."

Mom's mouth twisted into a wry smile. "Sounds familiar, Gracie. Looks like it hasn't done much for either of you."

"Rick's probably just picky. You know why I'm not in a relationship."

Mom sighed. "I understand, honey, but you shouldn't let Murphy control you."

"Bad luck and clumsiness do control me, Mom," Grace grumbled. "It's not like I haven't tried. Dumping soda on my date? Sinking his boat? It doesn't exactly win friends, let alone proposals. Neither does getting flat tires, breaking a guy's favorite trophy, throwing up on him—"

"Oh, sweetie, I understand." Her mom tried to stop her.

"As long I don't lose him, set him on fire, or get him shot by a cop, life might turn out sweet. Or how about last night?" She related the tale of the sailing popcorn bucket in detail. Not that sitting near Rick constituted a date, but dumping popcorn on him was definitely an example of Grace Evans' gracelessness.

"Gracie, stop it," her mom insisted, not able to resist laughing at the soaring popcorn. "Somewhere out there is a man who will have good-luck vibes radiating out of him, and a forgiving heart, too."

"Yeah, he's located at the North Pole, somewhere between Santa Claus and the Aurora Borealis. Hey, Mom, I think I hear the others getting up. I'll let you go. I need to get breakfast started."

"What? They can't make their own breakfast?"

"Yes, but I offered to make two fun, special breakfasts, today and tomorrow. I like to cook, remember? But I want a vacation, too, so starting Monday morning, breakfasts are—"

"Root, hog, or die. Ha! You go for it, baby. You teach those Flemings an Evans thing or two."

"I will, Mom. Bye."

The house was as silent now as before. No one had come downstairs. Grace just couldn't deal with her mother anymore. She touched a nerve. One Grace tried to keep tucked away, out of reach of everything, including her heart. She dearly wanted to find a terrific man to share her life with. She wanted babies and memories and fun Christmases and summer vacations, even if they were only in her own backyard.

But her history with guys was abysmal, and she couldn't see it ever changing. Even if she found someone, she had no doubt Murphy would mess up the relationship with spectacular efficiency.

The mudroom door flew open, and Grace jumped. Alternative rock played quietly on the other side of the door before it closed and Rick ambled into the kitchen. He'd cleaned his hands, but new bits of grease stained his cheeks. He paused, probably not sure he was welcome.

"Uh, good morning."

"Morning," Grace replied, shifting in her chair.

"I, uh, I came to get a coffee."

Grace nodded, not sure if he was asking her permission. Not that he needed it.

"Can I make you a cup?" he asked.

Grace's cheeks warmed at his unexpected kindness. She raised her cup, the one he couldn't see from there, in response. "Mocha Nut Fudge," she replied. She wasn't a big coffee lover because of the bitter aftertaste, but she loved the chocolate creaminess of a latte.

He smiled in appreciation. "One of my favorites." He examined Aunt Sharon's lavish collection, murmuring about which flavor to choose. "Aha. I found a Crème Brûlée. Although I wish I had a real Starbuck's Caramel Crème Brûlée right now."

Yeah, so would I, if I could afford it, Grace wanted to snipe— although she'd never say it out loud because it sounded shallow. Life was hard; that was all there was to it. And while she enjoyed an occasional splurge, she mostly drank good old-fashioned water. If she wanted her ancient beater-car, her part of Dad's family cell-phone plan, her Kindle, and her computer, all with Wi-Fi and/or cell service, and everything she needed for school, she had to cut expenses somewhere. Barista coffee wasn't exactly cheap.

Rick leaned against the island, keeping his distance from Grace. Sipping quietly, he appeared to be doing his best to avoid even looking in her direction.

After several minutes, curiosity seemed to get the best of him. "Tackling homework?"

Grace shrugged. "Trying to. It's not going so great."

"Because I'm bothering you?"

No. Yes. Not his presence so much as his existence. Grace again wished she'd gone home.

"I'm bored," she admitted at last, putting away the assignment and closing the computer. "I don't know why. It's one of my favorite classes."

"Which class?" Rick asked.

"English Lit. I love literature. All kinds of literature."

But it wasn't working, and she knew it wasn't the class or the assignment.

"Literature?" He made a face. "I guess you were a bit of a bookworm, but I remember you and Hannah taking T-ball and ballet together. My sister landed the scientific gene, but for some reason, I thought you were more athletic than bookish."

Grace stared at him askance. Him remembering her dancing was amazing enough. That he knew her history and considered her athletic was laughable. But the fact he'd been right about her past, just not the way he knew it, made her sad.

"Hannah is a born scientist," she said. "She says she wants to use her master's in microbiology to teach, but I think she's more a crusader. She wants to save people from everything from cancer to MS to the common cold."

Grace was talking too much, and she was talking to Rick Fleming. She needed to shut up. But she couldn't leave it there. At least she had to add, "I want to hand the beauty of quality writing to future generations. I won't graduate as soon as Hannah, but I'm on the road to my master's, too, and hope to teach literature at the college level."

As for why she stopped dancing? She had no intentions of discussing it.

"Why won't you graduate when Hannah does? You've gone to school together forever."

Grace's laugh was less than amused. "Uh, yeah, but I don't have Daddy Warbucks for a father, so I can't take as many classes each semester as Hannah does. You know my dad works hard to pay the bills and take care of mom, and he also wants to help Chloe and Danny. That doesn't leave much for my tuition."

"Hannah thought you were the smartest girl in school. Said you got straight A's. You should have gotten a ton of scholarships."

"I'm not all that smart—I just work twice as hard as everyone else, mostly because everything I do goes wrong. Lost homework assignments, computer glitches, broken-down printers, term papers with missing pages. You name it, it's happened. I keep triple copies of everything and turn my assignments in early to be sure I have time to fix the headaches, and I guess it makes me look like a good student."

"Wow. That must truly—"

"Suck. Yeah." The conversation felt too gloomy and Grace wanted to end it. "How's the car repair going?"

He huffed laughter, getting the hint he needed to get back to it but not rising to the bait. "If you're bored enough, I'd love an extra pair of hands to help."

Her brows rose to the top of her head. "You're joking. You wouldn't let me near Uncle Luke's tools or your precious Beamer."

He smiled drolly, his gaze fastened on hers. "All you have to do is hold or hand tools to me as I need them. It spares me having to get out from under the car over and over again."

"I would think a lapful of popcorn from two seats away would put you on high alert."

"What can I say? I'm a slow learner. Your help would get the job done sooner and get me out of here faster."

Before Grace could decide how she felt about the offer, feet thundered downstairs, announcing the arrival of the twins, sleepy-eyed but full of energy.

"Where's breakfast?" Charlotte mewed, and Cherise scowled at Grace's failure to have food on the table already.

Grace gave a silly smile. "My purpose for being here has arrived. I've got work to do."

"Yeah, I'll get out of your way," he grumbled, grabbing his mug and wishing the girls a good morning before heading toward the garage.

"Can I help?" Charlotte asked Grace.

"What are we having?" Cherise added, flopping down at the table and looking anything but helpful.

"Eggs and French toast," Grace replied, but she wished she'd asked what Rick would like to have.

"Yum!" Charlotte immediately pulled the eggs from the fridge, and Grace thanked her as she set about cracking a dozen of them into a huge measuring cup.

"Did Kyle come in last night?" she asked Cherise.

"Yeah, about two o'clock."

"Hmmm," Grace said, wondering how the morning conversation would go between Hannah and Kyle. It was way beyond his curfew, unless he'd gotten permission ahead of time—which Grace seriously doubted. Meanwhile, he'd always been a big eater and would probably make his way to the breakfast table regardless of his lack of sleep.

It wasn't long before apple juice, fluffy scrambled eggs, and piping hot French toast were on the table. Cherise paged Hannah on her phone, and Charlotte alerted Kyle. Hannah arrived dressed for the day, but Kyle came bleary-eyed and hair smashed every which way. He and Hannah exchanged a few curt words, complete with dire warnings if the boy disobeyed the rules again, and then the door opened from the garage.

"Thanks for the invite," Rick told Cherise, eyeing the food with enthusiasm. She had apparently paged him, too.

Grace glanced at Cherise, who lifted a brow at her, almost daring Grace to get after her for it. Her message was loud and clear: she loved cousin Rick and didn't want him left out.

"Wow, nothing got burned or broken this morning," Kyle muttered as he took a seat next to Rick. His cheeks turned bright red when Hannah cleared her throat, reminding him of his agreement.

"Sorry," he murmured to Grace, but she had no doubt it would happen again. It was ingrained into everyone who knew her. She'd have to move to a foreign country to get away from it. She was at least grateful she hadn't over-salted anything, put too much or too little cinnamon into the French toast, or knocked over the syrup. She did find a bit of eggshell in her own eggs—*yuck*—but she didn't crack them and considered breakfast a complete success.

"Okay, so today's agenda reminder," Hannah announced, pulling her phone from the hip pocket of her designer jeans. "Fun on the lake, come back and play with Uncle Luke's bows and arrows, have lunch, and then enjoy some personal time. Does it still sound like fun?"

The kids agreed, but Rick sat ruminating, probably wanting to get back to his car.

"And for dinner?" Hannah asked.

"Pizza!" Kyle said. "Pepperoni for sure."

"And more," Grace added, chuckling. Pepperoni was the status quo, but she had a lot of other pizza toppings she liked as well, if not better.

"You make pizza from scratch, too?" Rick blinked in amazement.

"Another dish you've eaten without knowing it," Hannah said. "When Grace stayed at our place on a Friday night, we'd get started early, make the pizzas before you guys came in from your games or dates or whatever, and you had no idea." She glanced at Grace with a wink. "And if you continue to behave yourself, maybe Grace will leave a few pieces for you."

His voice laced with annoyance, Rick said, "Don't bother. I have to go into town for a few things. I'll bring something home."

"No," Grace said, the unfairness jabbing her conscience. "There will be more than enough."

She wouldn't deny she was still bothered by having to share the table with him, but he'd been more than kind so far. She could do better than be vindictive.

"So, what flavor of ice cream are we making tonight?" Charlotte asked, her eyes dancing.

"Tonight?" Grace said. "Homemade ice cream on top of pizza? We might need a box of Tums, too."

The kids laughed and tossed around ideas, settling on mint chocolate chip.

"But Aunt Sharon only left us one package of chips," Hannah noted. "Which means we don't have enough for the cookies you want to make next week. We'll have to put it on the shopping list for later."

"I really do need to run to the store," Rick said. "I'll grab the chips, too. Anything else? Don't think too crazy. Remember, it's Secret Lake Village after all. Marty's Market has an amazing inventory for a small town, but it is a small town."

"I want some barbecue potato chips," Kyle said. "Mom left regular, but I prefer the barbecue flavor."

"I forgot my face scrub," Charlotte said, naming brand, bottle color, and amount. Cherise interrupted, adding demands of her own.

"Whoa," Hannah said, hands upraised, rescuing a perplexed Rick. "I think our morning boat ride needs to take second place on our list. Rick isn't used to buying those things, girls. What do you say to us all going into town?"

Even Grace thought it sounded better, and after they threw themselves together, Rick grabbed the keys for the Escalade and they headed for the vehicle.

Kyle claimed shotgun and the girls giggled as they settled into the back, leaving Hannah and Grace right behind Rick. Grace's gaze met his in the rearview mirror as he fastened his seatbelt, but she averted it quickly, trying not to notice he hadn't shaved that morning and looked way too sexy.

<hr />

Grace's avoidance amused Rick, particularly since he'd caught her watching him more than once since she arrived—and he was old enough to know she liked what she saw.

Before he let sleep overtake him last night, he allowed himself to reconsider the list of crazy coincidences that brought all of them to the cabin at this time. Which led to a bit of soul-searching and the need to turn to a higher power for guidance. Prayer had always filled him with a strength he knew wasn't his own.

Before going home, he needed to explain to Grace what happened that night. At least it would feel like his apology meant something, if not to her, then to him.

They drove into town and down historical Main Street to Marty's, the traffic making it an ordeal to find a parking place. The holiday was heating up, along with the temperature. It was supposed be a scorcher today.

The store's parking lot was full, and Rick drove slowly looking for a spot, past the town's park that surrounded the recreation hall and small pool, the building next door that was a combination sheriff office/fire department, and a larger variety of businesses than anyone would think this small town could support. The redeeming quality was that Ukiah's townsfolk frequented the village's unique businesses as much as the village residents visited Ukiah. That, and the tidy sums the wealthy homeowners paid Secret Lake citizens to care for their properties, kept the town in business.

A loop back to Marty's rewarded them with a lucky space in the store's parking lot after all. The kids hurried inside to find what they wanted, leaving Rick to walk with Hannah and Grace.

"They know Aunt Sharon left me money to take care of whatever they need," Hannah grumbled. "I'm scared we'll be taking half the store home with us."

"A good parent knows when to say no," Rick quipped, casting a cheesy grin at his sister. "We don't have enough room in the SUV for even a quarter of the store, so it shouldn't be too difficult to set some limits. Unless the kids want to walk back."

"You be the bad guy this time," she replied. "Kyle already hates me for getting after him for staying out so late."

"Let's make it a team effort. I'll toss stuff out of the carts, and you explain why they can't have it."

Grace chuckled at the suggestion. "I think I might be safer as a spectator, which I'm uniquely qualified to do."

"Let's just hope Kooky Kathy isn't here today," Hannah muttered, bumping Grace's shoulder and making her laugh.

"Kooky Kathy?" Rick asked.

"Inside joke, Bro," Hannah said, and the two girls snorted more laughter. Rick's frown had Hannah spilling the story, which shocked Rick. Lunatics, cops, and firearms? Wow.

Grace and Hannah grabbed a cart and went one way while Rick headed another. They'd agreed ahead of time everyone would report to Hannah when they were done, and she, in turn, would let everyone know when they were ready to meet at the checkstand.

The store was the largest non-residential building in town besides the recreation hall, and Rick jockeyed around more people than he'd seen in Marty's in a long time, collecting items for his car from the generous auto department and some food from the grocery area. He had no idea how long his luck with sharing the meals Grace prepared would hold out, and while Aunt Sharon was marvelous at having the cabin's freezer and cupboards loaded, she bought for her family's tastes, not his.

"Hey, look who's here!" a male voice said, catching Rick's attention.

"Hey, Marty. How's business?" Rick shook hands with the business owner, a man he'd known and loved a good part of his life. Marty was a broad-shouldered black man with a cheerful happy-face grin and eyes sunken into his face. Rick had never seen him with a beard before, so he did a double-take at the goatee sprouting on his chin like a patch of dehydrated gray grass.

"Fantastic. The Centennial has attracted people from all over California, Nevada, and Oregon."

"Wow. Totally crazy. I assume not everyone's here yet. I mean, it's busy, but I'm sure it'll get busier closer to the Fourth."

"It will, but our two motels and the three B&B's are already full, and Ukiah's packed. I heard all the highway-side motels from Willits up north to Cloverdale down south are full clear through the July Fourth weekend. The hefty use fee for the lake hasn't discouraged the boaters one bit, either, which means the lake will soon be filled to the max."

They exchanged a few more pleasantries, and then Rick headed toward the checkstand to wait for the others. The lines were long, and he found Grace standing to one side, reading a *People* magazine, her expression perplexed. She glanced up when he arrived, and his heart sank when her cheeks flushed and she glanced around for the rest of their group. What did she think he was going to do to her in a store full of people?

"Oh, my, my, my, I can't believe who's in town."

Rick whipped around at the sound of a familiar voice, eyes widening at the woman staring at him from the closest line. She tossed her light brown hair behind her shoulder, her hips swaying like she was moving to music.

"Uhm, hey, Hazel. How are you?"

"I'm simply peachy, Rick. You here for the celebration?"

"No, my sister is. She's taking care of my cousins." He paused, nodding at Grace. "Along with my sister's best friend." He gestured toward her. "This is Grace Evans. Grace, this is Hazel De Niro. I don't know if you two ever met in high school. Hazel and I graduated in the same class." He didn't miss the disappointment on Hazel's face. He hadn't introduced her as an old girlfriend. "I won't be here long. I'm working on my car."

"Hello, Grace," Hazel said.

Grace returned the greeting, but the woman's green-brown eyes slid over Grace and quickly dismissed her. To Rick, she said, "So, how's life treating you? You working? Married?"

"I work for my uncle's computer company in San Jose. Not married. What about you? Married? Kids?"

She cleared her throat. "Divorced. A little girl who's four. I'm a legal assistant in San Jose. We ought to get together sometime."

Rick had broken up with Hazel in high school for a reason. He had no interest in her. "I don't date outside my church anymore," he said. "It makes life less challenging, you know?"

Hazel's head bobbed. She glanced at Grace again. "Sure. I get that. Have a nice time." She was next in line for the cash register and turned her back on Rick as she went to unload her cart.

Awkward.

Grace's phone pinged, and she looked at the text. Rick caught a glance at it and knew his sister and cousins were headed their way.

"At last. I'm glad we can finally get out of here," he murmured.

"Oh, it is you, isn't it?" another voice said, an older woman dragging a friend from the cracker aisle toward Rick. "Rick Fleming, it's wonderful to see you."

"Mrs. Markel," Rick said, hoping he didn't sound as uncomfortable as he felt. "And Mrs. Dominguez. Good morning."

"It is a beautiful morning, isn't it?" Mrs. Markel replied. "I was talking to Valerie Chester just yesterday, at the restaurant, about how calm the weather's been."

Mrs. Chester ran The Hungry Bass, the nicer of the two restaurants in town, but was also the town gossip. Rick needed to be careful about what he said to these two old schemers, particularly since he stood next to an attractive woman. They'd probably already constructed some story in their heads.

"Well, I told her the holidays were right around the corner, and maybe we'd have the traditional visit from the Flemings. My granddaughter Cindy would love to date you, my boy. You know I've tried to get the two of you together for years."

"And my granddaughter, Luz, has had a crush on you since she met you three years ago," Mrs. Dominguez added. "They'll be here for the Fourth. We should plan a picnic."

Rick took a step back, hyper-aware of Grace staring at him. He wished he'd stayed at the cabin and let everyone else do the shopping.

"I'm sorry, ladies. I can't obligate to anything. I'm here with family, but I have to leave as soon as I get my car fixed. Got to get back to work."

"Oh, I'm sorry to hear that," Mrs. Markel said. She didn't have time to say more before Hannah arrived, the teens crowding around her, their selections piled into one cart.

"Let's go!" Kyle said. "We need to hurry back if we want any time on the lake before lunch."

Rick chose not to be a gentleman as he slipped into the line ahead of Hannah, but he didn't miss her Cheshire Cat grin. She knew he was avoiding the Matchmaker Brigade. They pounced on him all too often when he came to the village.

Rick huffed when he saw Grace and Hannah whispering to each other, and then Hannah laughed and shook her head. He turned his back on them, refusing to care what they were talking about, even though he knew it was gossip about him.

CHAPTER 7

Rick's ongoing popularity shouldn't have surprised Grace. After all, he was hunk-handsome, single, and not a felon. In today's world, that said something. Still, she couldn't help the tiny stab of jealousy when he introduced Hazel, but it was his comment about dating that planted a rock somewhere in the pit of her stomach. He didn't date outside his church? When had that happened? Certainly not in high school. Hazel was a perfect example. Grace refused to consider the disappointment storming her defenses. She wasn't a member of his church, either.

But why should that matter? She would never date him.

The stark glare of the outdoor sunlight hammered Grace, along with the skyrocketing heat. She pulled out the sunglasses she'd transported from home in her backpack, glad she hadn't forgotten them at home, as she had her driver's license. Murphy had a strange sense of humor.

They weren't far from the vehicle when Rick came to a sudden halt, causing Grace to plow into him. He turned to put a hand on her shoulder to steady her, but his surprise became hers when she saw a woman leaning against the end of the Escalade. Arms folded, a soft smile on her lips, her beauty made Grace's jaw drop. *Good grief*, she thought. *Where did the movie star come from?*

"Hey, handsome," the girl said to Rick, her long, dark hair draped over her elbows toward her waist. She was obviously Latina but had no hint of an accent.

"Maria," he replied. "What, uh, brings you here?"

"I should ask you the same thing. You didn't mention you were leaving town, but I saw you throw your bags in your car. Your mom told me what's up, so I thought I'd surprise you. This place is great. It looks like it's going to be a laugh on the Fourth."

Grace saw Rick didn't know what to say. He complained that Maria followed him around, and here she was in Secret Lake Village, proving his point.

"Maria!" Hannah said with surprise, joining Grace. "What in the world are you doing here?"

"Your mom said you and Ricky were here with your cousins, and I thought I'd come and check it out. I've never been to Secret Lake Village. I hope Ricky will show me around."

Grinning, Maria gave Hannah a hug and waved at the kids. The girls gave finger-waves back. Kyle's eyes widened as if he'd gone into shock. Grace sighed, thinking men were all alike. A beautiful woman could spin their brains into pudding.

Hannah laughed. "Stand in line. I swear half of the village wants his attention. He's only here to fix his car, then he's back to work."

"You're exaggerating, Sis," Rick said, running a hand across his jaw. "I don't think a few old ladies wanting to match me up with their granddaughters amounts to half the village." He turned to Maria. "Do you have a hotel? This place is pretty booked. Beyond the holiday, the Centennial Celebration is drawing people from all over."

Did Grace sense Rick hoped Maria didn't plan to stay?

"Yeah, I got lucky," Maria replied, but she kept glancing at Grace—and Rick's arm around her shoulders. "Someone canceled as I was walking into the third hotel I visited. I grabbed the room, of course."

Another twinge of jealousy tweaked Grace, the second one in twenty minutes, despite having no right to feel that way.

"You have anything planned for today?" Hannah asked.

Grace knew Hannah felt concerned about Maria. It was her way.

"Nothing specific. I finally found a parking place and planned to walk to a grill I saw and grab an early lunch. My phone doesn't have the best reception here. Thought I'd ask around and try to get a hold of Rick."

Grace wondered at Maria's statement about her phone. The reception here was remarkable for such an isolated community.

"We're taking our boat out when we get back to the cabin," Kyle said. "If you have your bathing suit, you should come." He pointed at the cart full of purchases. "We're going to make homemade ice cream tonight, and Grace is making pizza."

Grace's heart dropped. An infatuated teenage boy was apparently inclined to spill his guts. The idea of having Maria spend the day with them—and put on a bathing suit in front of the whole Fleming family—seemed to have the boy all but slobbering.

"Oh, you're so sweet," Maria said. "My room is in Ukiah, and I can't check into the hotel until after three o'clock, so that would be terrific. But I don't want to impose."

"You're not imposing," Hannah insisted. "Please join us."

Grace wanted to say "Yes, you are imposing. Now go home." But she would have to face why she felt that way and that wasn't happening.

"Thanks, Hannah. I'll grab my car and follow you." Maria hurried through the parking lot, her hourglass figure fabulous in an outfit Grace couldn't fathom ever wearing. How could anyone look so alluring in a Pepto-Bismol-pink sleeveless top and stone-washed jeans? Yet she did, and with style.

The Fleming clan clambered into the Escalade, and Rick headed home, brooding.

"She's nice, Rick," Hannah said, even while she avoided meeting Grace's gaze. "I feel bad for her. She likes you a lot, and she's here alone."

"I'm still not sure I'm interested," he admitted.

"What?" Kyle asked, horrified. "How could you not be interested. Man, she's a *babe*."

"There really is more to a relationship than appearances, Kyle," Rick insisted. "Believe me, some women use their bodies to get you into the worst situations. Besides, she's not only not a member of our church, she's also a bit old for you, so you might want to put your tongue back in your mouth."

Blushing furiously, the boy slid down in his seat and turned to look out the window.

Maria followed them to the cabin in a car that appeared worn and weary. Grace wondered which reflected Maria more. The car or her wardrobe.

After they put their purchases away, they changed into boating clothes. Grace was the first to arrive on the patio in her bathing suit and a casual lace cover. The suit was plain, one-piece, boring-black and delightfully affordable, but when Rick joined her, followed by Hannah and Kyle, she felt self-conscious.

Then Maria joined them, as model-gorgeous as Hannah had ever been but wearing a skimpy bikini which didn't fit in with the Flemings' more conservative lifestyle. Behaving as if she had no idea how she affected them, she tossed on a coverup, but considering it was see-through, it served little purpose. Hardly able to keep his eyes off the girl, Kyle tripped over himself while helping to get the smaller ice chest packed with ice and water bottles.

Hannah made a point of bumping Grace in the shoulder before they headed out the door to the boat. She whispered, "Sorry, Gracie. I don't think this was such a good idea. Maria's a bit much."

"I'm fine," Grace replied. "They can have each other. It keeps Rick out of my way, which means I don't have to feel guilty every time I look at him."

Hannah's lips flattened. "Says the girl who wants nothing to do with him because she was in love with him and got her heart broken. If you'd let him apologize—"

"No. Don't go there. You promised. And I wasn't in love with him."

Hannah shrugged her shoulders and nodded. "Okay. Let's go join *Maria* on the boat."

Grace made a point of joining the twins, not Maria. The girls were giggly and silly, mimicking everything Maria did. They thought she was hot, too, and there was no doubt they wanted to know her beauty secrets, but they also felt the tension between the adults.

Donning their lifejackets took some of the flair out of the fashion department, and as the boat sped around the lake, Grace had to admit it felt marvelous out here. The air, cooled by the water, was refreshing, as was the occasional spray of lake water that showered them.

"There's our favorite cove!" Kyle pointed, urging Rick to a shallow inlet where they stopped, anchored the boat, and shed the jackets. Kyle cannon-balled into the water, splashing all of them, then Hannah joined him, followed by the twins. Maria tried to cajole Rick into jumping in with her, but when he encouraged her to go first, she had no trouble performing a perfect swan dive from the side of the boat.

Grace watched Rick, who in turn watched their small gang splash, play-fight, and have a great time. When his eyes rose to meet hers, she felt the heat surge into her cheeks. How could he see someone like Maria and look at her this way? As if he couldn't get enough of Grace. As if she were truly beautiful.

"You won't melt, Grace," he said, a smile tugging at one corner of his mouth.

"What?"

"If you jump in. You won't melt."

She grimaced. "No, but I might find a way to drown myself, or drown someone else, or get eaten by a shark." Or he could embarrass her to death by laughing at her bathing suit.

He laughed at what she said. "No sharks. Not in fresh water. And we don't have cottonmouths or alligators here, either. And you're too beautiful to become fish bait, so you're safe."

Grace shook her head and dove in before Rick dared give her another compliment. The water was her way out, or so she hoped. He jumped in close behind her, and followed in a leisurely breaststroke, flipping onto his back and floating when he caught up with her. Grace couldn't help the warning look she gave him when he came too close, and she didn't miss the irksome hurt in his eyes as he left her to join the others.

They didn't stay at the lake long. With the late start on their day and the trip to town, they were soon ready for lunch. Grace was glad to get off both the boat and the dock without harm. And she only stumbled once climbing the steps to the gate.

If only her heart hadn't gotten bruised when Maria hooked her arm through Rick's and drifted into the house with him.

⁘

After lunch, they collected Uncle Luke's archery equipment from the storage room behind the garage. It included portable horse-mat backstops, a box of targets, three bows and several sets of arrows.

"I'd forgotten you like archery," Rick told Grace.

Grace grunted, checking the bow for any irregularities and the arrow fletchings for damage. "When I'm not trying to kill myself with it," she replied.

"Is this really dangerous?" Maria asked, all thumbs with the bow in her hands.

"It's a weapon," Rick pointed. "That's its purpose. Follow the rules and everyone will be fine."

"I don't know the rules. Life's more fun that way."

Rick sighed in exasperation, and Grace bit her cheek in amusement. He'd probably spend more time as Maria's private coach than he'd get shooting, which would probably annoy him.

"We only have three targets and bows," Hannah pointed out, turning to Rick. "We'll have to take turns. Maybe we should let the kids go first so you can explain the rules while they shoot."

Resigned to the inevitable, he had Kyle—more than willing to comply—demonstrated for Maria as they went through all the steps in the sport.

Maria remained all thumbs when it came to holding the bow, and the arrow kept falling to the ground. When she finally managed to hold it in place, she let go of the arrow too late after releasing the string and it flipped and landed a few feet in front of her. In a way, it made things easier on Grace. Having Rick busy elsewhere made it possible for her to concentrate on her own shooting.

Maria huffed with annoyance when she finally figured out how to shoot but again and again missed the target. The string also kept snapping the inside of her left arm, which eventually turned into an angry welt.

"I think I know what's wrong," Kyle said at last. He came to push Rick out of the way. "Can I help?"

Grace kept her grin to herself when she saw Maria's reluctance. She wanted Rick's help, but she didn't want to be rude.

"Please," Rick encouraged Kyle.

Grace would have sworn she heard Murphy giggle from her right shoulder. She wondered what her bad-luck imp was up to now. Determined not to let misfortune have the last word, she carried on, frustrated at not being able to hit the center of the target herself. She was normally quite good at this.

"You're pulling to the right and aiming too low," Rick murmured in her ear. "And if I remember correctly, this bow has a tendency to do that anyway."

Grace looked at him askance. "You know each of these bow's peculiarities that well?"

"Yep. I've played with them for years. May I?" He reached toward her but waited for her permission before wrapping his arms around her and setting the fingers of his left hand around her fingers. He pressed his left cheek to her right one and helped her grip the bowstring with his right hand

"You'll have to compensate twice over, but I think it'll work if you point it... right about there."

He let go, backed away, and left her to do the rest. She did as he suggested, and the arrow flew true, burying its face in the right-hand edge of the bullseye.

"Wow! Good shot!" Kyle crowed. Maria's mouth hung open, but when Grace took a good look at her, she saw the girl was not only surprised at her shot, she wasn't happy with Rick giving Grace a hands-on lesson.

Grace felt a competitive streak rearing its rare but ugly head. Fighting back a grin, she took another arrow, mentally repeated what Rick told her, and placed the arrow a half-inch nearer the center.

The others applauded, except for Maria, who stood shaking her head. "I'm no good at this. I think I'll go sit down." She handed her bow and quiver to Rick, who happily made use of them.

They all practiced for a while, Grace pleased she now had a feel for the bow. Every shot hit the target, and most weren't far from the bullseye or the ring around it.

With her last arrow in the set, Grace drew again, sighting carefully. She heard Hannah and Rick on either side of her, doing the same. She held her breath and let loose, shock striking her when, at the last second, the string broke!

She yelped when the string whipped her left shoulder, then gasped when her arrow managed a nearly forty-five-degree left-hand turn that knocked Rick's arrow right out of the air.

There were cries all around, Maria gasping, the twins laughing, Hannah asking how in the world it happened, and Kyle telling her she should take up exhibition shooting.

"Uh, I don't think so, Kyle," Grace said, teeth gritted against the pain. "I couldn't do that again on purpose if my life depended on it."

"Yeah, and doing it not-on-purpose might get someone killed," Rick said.

Grace flushed hot, knowing he was right. Knowing she'd done nothing to cause it, but hating he'd said it in front of everyone. She held her hand to the sharp pain on her shoulder, feeling her legs growing weak from the shock.

"The string broke," she muttered, handing the bow to Rick.

"What the heck? How did...? Man, this stinks. Are you okay?"

Hannah handed her bow to Charlotte and grabbed Grace by her good arm. "Of course, she's not okay," she snapped at Rick.

Grace gritted her teeth even tighter. The welt had turned from a sting to an entire hive of bees attacking her.

"Do you need to sit down?" Hannah asked, leading her toward the covered patio. Even Maria seemed concerned, coming to help Hannah get her to a chair.

"No, I don't want to sit down. Help me get to the bathroom. I need to see the damage."

Hannah nodded, pushed her past Maria, and hustled her through the house to the downstairs bathroom. After Grace unbuttoned her shirt and pulled it back enough to bare her shoulder, both of them hissed in dismay.

"Holy moly, Grace, this is *bad*. You have deep blisters. Several. How did that happen?"

"It's called a snap-back. It happens when something like a cord or a rope is stretched tight and breaks loose. Linesmen have to be careful when power cords threaten to break. If they do, they can whip around and literally decapitate someone."

"What? Gross! Well, you still have your head on, but you need to see a doctor."

Grace snorted. "No, I don't. They're just big, nasty blisters. What I need is some of the salve your aunt keeps here for burns, along with a pile of ice to numb them, Band-Aids to pad them, and a handful of ibuprofens to knock out the pain."

"And then you need to lie down for a while."

"Uh-uh. We need to start the pizza dough. It takes a while. And someone needs to get the ice cream maker going."

Hannah wasn't happy, but in no time at all, she put Grace back together. The lump under Grace's shirt from the icepack made her look like a sideways Quasimodo, and she hoped no one would make fun of her. She lost her sense of humor somewhere between the archery competition and the bathroom.

They managed to get the pizza dough made and set out to rise before Grace admitted she felt a little light-headed. Hannah asked the twins to man the ice cream maker, while Grace settled into one of the dinette chairs, as content as was possible under the circumstances, to watch Kyle and Rick in the yard competing with the bows and arrows. Kyle was good. Really good. No doubt Rick was better, but Grace couldn't help the softness that settled into her heart when she had the distinct impression Rick let Kyle win in the end. If he did, he did it so subtly Kyle didn't know, and the boy reveled in his success. If Kyle won fairly, then Rick lost with grace.

A smile tugged at Grace's lips at the play on words. Rick lost with grace? No, it was more like Rick had lost Grace. She shook her head and pushed the thought aside. The hard part of the moment was seeing Maria giving Kyle and Rick hugs. Although Grace didn't believe Rick could ever or even should be hers, having Maria around didn't make it any easier to swallow.

By the time they needed to assemble the five family-size pizzas, the pain medication had done its job. The twins put the finished ice cream in the freezer and helped Kyle toss another salad, Maria set the table, and Rick brought in bottles of root beer from the garage's reserve refrigerator while Hannah helped prepare the toppings. The dough and sauces were Grace's own recipes, and she was in sole charge of them.

"So, are you going to toss the crusts, Gracie?" Kyle asked, mischief in his eyes.

"I'm not sure the shoulder can handle it."

"Aww, come one. It's fun to watch."

"Yeah, especially when I miss and it lands on my head. Or the floor. You know I don't have time to make more dough if I blow it."

"Spoilsport."

"The worst kind. So back off and let me get to work, guys. I need Sharon's biggest breadboard. Are the ovens ready?"

With everything on track, Grace set to work, rolling the dough. She'd brought three pizza pans from home, knowing this would be one of their meals. It was a favorite dish for her family, too, so she owned a half dozen of them—which Hannah thought was crazy—but it made the work go faster.

With the ovens on, so many people watching, and the brisk pace of the work, the kitchen grew hot and perspiration dotted Grace's forehead. Normally, she avoided attention, but cooking put her in the zone, allowing her to ignore them. When she had four crusts done and scattered across all the countertops, she paused.

"Come on, Gracie," Kyle wheedled. "Four pizzas are enough if you blow it. Toss the last one. Have you ever watched someone toss a pizza crust, Maria?"

Grace looked between Kyle and Maria, knowing he was a love-sick puppy who had no idea this girl had no interest in him. As for Maria, her large brown eyes were wide with fascination, but the set of her chin suggested she didn't believe Grace could do it.

"I've seen it in a pizzeria," she replied. "But I've never seen an everyday person do it."

An everyday person? The way she said it sounded like Grace was a loser.

So, she did it: shaping, rolling, lifting and tossing, spinning and catching. It was something she did almost naturally.

Except when bee-sting-welts on her shoulder nearly undid her. Every time she raised both arms to catch the dough, she cringed. After several throws, she could hardly raise her left arm and had to quit. She went to drop the newly formed crust onto the board but almost missed. Trying to grab it to keep it from falling on the floor, she hit her elbow on one of the pot handles. She dropped the dough to catch the pot, but it careened to the back of the stove, crashed into another pot, which shot to the left and hit the third pot. Grace reached for all of them, wanting to stop the dominoes from falling, but she missed and hit one of the front burners with the palm of her left hand near her thumb.

She shrieked in pain, then shrieked in surprise when someone snatched her wrist and pulled her to the sink, forcing her hand under cold water. Rick apologized for grabbing her while reminding her to let the cold do its work.

"It's okay. You'll be okay," he reassured her, showing her his hands, like he'd done before, to reassure her that he'd let go.

She caught her breath, closing her eyes and leaning against the counter. The water took away the sting and felt so good.

"Gracie, I'm so sorry," Kyle apologized, coming close enough Rick needed to stick out an arm to keep him from touching her.

"It's okay, Kyle," she said, shaking her head. "It's my fault. I shouldn't have tossed the dough."

"We'll put the pizzas together, okay?" Hannah offered. She'd done enough of it with Grace she could do it blindfolded.

"What about the sauces?" Grace asked, on the edge of panic. All that work, and one moment of showing off had probably ruined everything.

"A little slopped onto the stove, but we're good."

Rick brought Grace the burn gel, but the blister needed a Band-Aid. He brought that, too. Part of her wanted to hug him for it. Another part was still annoyed he touched her without permission.

Yeah, right, Graceless, her own personal demon whispered into her ear. *Like anyone needs permission to save an imbecile on fire.* The monster was right, but it was the humiliation that mattered. Along with the frustration and self-contempt for her clumsiness.

Amazingly enough, the crust had landed in a heap at the edge of the board, and after Hannah formed it into a ball for her, Grace somehow managed to roll it out. Afterward, Charlotte, her face pale with worry, brought Grace another small icepack for the blister. Thankfully, the first three pizzas went into the ovens without further incident, and Grace excused herself.

Not to go to the bathroom, however. Humiliation was best endured in private.

She made it as far as the bathroom doorway before she leaned into the jamb and let silent tears flow. Why did she have to show off? Why did she have to be such a klutz? Why did Murphy persist in ruining everything?

Rick had no idea what possessed him. Slipping out of the kitchen to follow Grace probably wasn't a smart idea, but he couldn't help it. He was worried about her, although he hung back in case she did actually need to use the bathroom. His chest tightened when she made it to the door jamb and pressed her forehead against it, shoulders shaking from silent sobs.

She had plenty to cry about: the snap-back injury from the broken bowstring, her burned hand, her embarrassment. His palms itched at the thought of the burn. Burns were the pits.

"Grace?" he murmured, stepping up behind her, longing to comfort her, aching to make up for everything that had ever made her cry. She smelled of spring flowers and sunshine. Her hair, her cologne, her fair skin all made his heart ache. She once said she liked him. His gut told him she still did. Did crushes last that long? His had.

She stiffened at his presence.

"I'm so sorry about all of this," he said. "I'm not stalking you, I promise. I thought maybe you needed a sympathetic ear. It must frustrate the heck out of you to have so many things go wrong."

Her face was red from crying and streaked with tears. She brushed them away and sniffed, trying to pull herself together. She closed her eyes and drew in a deep breath, her face darkening. When those gorgeous, watery, blue eyes opened again, they were anything but friendly.

"I don't think you really want to offer a listening ear, Richard Fleming. You might get more than you bargained for."

His shoulders drooped, the regrets embedded like poisoned roots in his heart. "If it would make you feel better, my ears are all yours."

She took a step back. "Not now. I'm not losing it now…"

"Okay," he took a step toward her, "so how about a shoulder to cry on instead?" He lifted his hands, beckoning to her.

Shock reddened her cheeks. She stared at those hands and his face and then back at his hands. Stock still, she watched as he closed the distance. Wary? Uncertain? Wishful? What name could he give the look in her eyes?

CHAPTER 8

What was Rick doing? Grace's heart ached worse than if it had landed on the hot burner instead of her hand. The last time she let down her defenses, Rick ruined her life.

She was a senior in high school, and Rick had moved into an apartment with Sean. When he came without his brothers to visit, he behaved like he was doing now, more of a gentleman than a crazy friend. He played games with Grace and Hannah, watched TV shows with them. In the fall, he started taking them to the movies or to Cold Stone. He celebrated Thanksgiving and Christmas with them. He invited them to the company's New Year's Eve party, but after Hannah canceled, Rick took Grace anyway, sending her hope spiraling to the heavens. Spring came, and he escorted her to a dance at Berkley, to San Francisco for dinner, on a leisurely walk through Sequoia National Park on a Saturday afternoon. She never thought of them as dates. She had a hard time considering him a friend after so many years of being leery of him. She had a harder time telling her heart not to care about him because it always had, and it had never done her any good.

And then he betrayed her. Betrayed her when she was most vulnerable. How could he think they'd be friends, or more, after that?

And yet, looking into his face, she didn't see the little boy who pointed fingers and laughed at her when she got peanut butter in her hair. She didn't see the kid who fell down in hysterics after the lid popped off the salt shaker, dumping the entire container into her soup. Where was the gawky teenager who snorted his mirth when she lost control of her bike and ran into the back end of a parked car? The high-school senior who roared when she set the science lab on fire? Or the boy who thought it was hilarious when his brothers grabbed her, school books, homework papers, history project and all, and threw her into the pool?

She couldn't find that boy. What she saw now was a man with the most gorgeous green eyes filled with remorse, tinged with compassion... and colored with... what? Hope?

His arms neared her and paralyzed her like a mouse. Gently, they enveloped her and pulled her against him. Kind. Comforting. Strong.

The tears came again, painful and hot, and she wept into his chest, not with pain alone but also with relief. For those few moments, he held her up, letting her share his strength, giving her time to get her legs under her again.

When he finally let go, he stepped into the bathroom and grabbed a handful of tissues. She mobbed her face and blew her nose, certain she looked like a train wreck. Then she saw the mess she left on Rick's shirt and winced. Even worse, she tried to dry it for him and succeeded in making the same mess she had of Mario's napkins.

"It's okay," he said, chuckling, and pressing her hand against his chest to stop her. "I won't melt."

"I'm sorry."

"Don't be. You didn't do anything wrong."

He was so close, leaning over her. His gaze traveled over her face from her eyes to her nose to her mouth. It settled there long enough to send trails of heat up her face. When he sought her gaze again, his eyes were filled with admiration.

He touched her cheek, removing a wisp of tissue as his excuse, but letting his fingertips linger. He lifted her chin, and for a long, breathless, terrifying moment, Grace thought he might kiss her.

"Grace!" Hannah called. "Are you okay?"

The spell shattered and Grace stepped back, horrified she'd nearly fallen into the trap.

She spun toward the mirror, dubbed her train-wreck of a face a traitor, and did her best to straighten her hair and clothes.

"I'll be there in a minute, Hannah," she called back, sliding past Rick and heading toward the kitchen, hoping he'd stay behind for a moment. She had no appetite for razzing from anyone in the Fleming family.

Instead she heard the garage door close as she entered the kitchen and knew Rick had decided to get back to work on his car.

Hannah turned to greet her, her hands gripping Grace's arms when she saw the look on her face. "You've been crying. Does it hurt that much?"

"Life hurts, Hannah," Grace said, giving one of Hannah's hands a squeeze. "How are the pizzas doing?"

"The first three are out, the last two are in, and we're almost set to go."

Grace sighed. What a relief to not to have to micro-manage everything like she did when she was a girl.

"Have you seen Rick? I don't know where he went," Hannah said, her face puckered into a frown.

"I heard the garage door close," Grace replied, turning to grab a few fingerfuls of grated mozzarella cheese from the bowl and eat it with her back to Hannah.

"Oh. I thought maybe…" She paused, but Grace ignored her. "Uhm, so Kyle, will you text him? Let him know dinner's on in five?"

Kyle complied, then filled the glasses with ice before pouring the root beer. Grace was glad for his help. Her hands were shaking, and she'd die of thirst before she poured even so much as a thimble of water right now.

The counter held the cooling pizzas, which Hannah had already sliced. Maria surveyed everyone silently as she moved with them to the island. When the timer went off and the other two pizzas were removed and cut, Rick joined them, avoiding both Maria and Grace—for which Grace told herself she should be glad. They took the time to bless the food, Kyle handed Maria a plate, and they began the buffet line Grace and Hannah preferred for this meal.

"This looks wonderful," Maria murmured, glancing back and forth between Grace and Rick.

"I claim the pepperoni," Kyle said, pushing Cherise aside and snagging two pieces.

"Everybody gets some," she insisted, slapping his arm.

"You don't need to fight over it," Charlotte said, her face puckered in disapproval. "My favorite is Hawaiian. I put extra pineapple on it, which is going to taste *so good*."

"Oh, man," Rick said, eyeing the one that seemed to have everything imaginable on it. "A combo, right?"

"Yep, Bro, made especially for you," Hannah said, taking a bite out of her slice of plain cheese pizza.

"Fantastic. Hey, what's this one? It looks anemic." He made a face, which had Grace wanting to take back his pizza.

"No complaints," Hannah insisted, glancing at Grace. Hannah could see she wasn't pleased. "If you don't want it, don't eat it."

"But what is it? It's white."

"Ooooh, that's my second favorite," Charlotte said. "It's chicken alfredo."

"What?" he laughed. "Yuck. That sounds awful. Who would put chicken alfredo on a pizza?"

"Ricky, hush your mouth," Hannah said sharply, her eyes snapping toward Grace's. He didn't get the hint.

"Seriously! It sounds terrible."

"You should try it," Charlotte said, waving her slice under his nose. "You'll like it."

"It might kill me," he said. The room went deathly silent and he froze. His eyes slowly raised to meet Grace's. The color left his face, and she knew in that instant he'd been teasing—the way he always had with Grace.

"I'm sorry. I was truly goofing around, Grace. I really haven't ever eaten it, and it does sound weird, but I wasn't trying..." He paused, pulled a piece off the pan and took a bite out of it.

Grace watched as he chewed. He paused and then chewed again, first curiously, and then with enthusiasm.

"Man, this is *good*!" he said. "It reminds me of, uhm, something, what?"

"Chicken alfredo, goofball," Kyle said, braying laughter.

"You know, like, shrimp alfredo is your top pick whenever we go to Olive Garden?" Hannah prompted, her tone suggesting he should have trusted her. He would have avoided offending Grace, but now it was too late.

Rick muttered another apology. "I think I'll go eat on the patio. After that I'll get back to my car. I've let too much get in the way today."

Kyle and Maria joined him, and Grace felt a slow burn build inside her when the woman stroked Rick's arm and talked to him like she'd been his girlfriend for years. Even worse, Rick laughed at something she said, and he didn't object when she tore off a piece of her pizza and stuffed it into his mouth. Which man was the real Rick? The one who almost kissed Grace? Or this one, apparently encouraging Maria to flirt with him?

"You need to get off your feet, Grace," Hannah suggested.

Grace joined her and the twins at the table, her back to the patio. The girls watched her every move, and she wondered what they were thinking. Then she realized she might not want to know.

Rick finished eating, helped with the cleanup, and took the compacted trash out to the garage. Once he tossed it into the can, he stopped to catch his breath. He had no intention of going back inside, not even for homemade ice cream, not only because he couldn't be around Grace right now, but he wanted to avoid Maria, too. He was safe here. Maria wouldn't set foot in a garage in the outfit she put back on after they returned from the lake.

Maria was beautiful, no doubt about it. He'd rarely been drawn to other women the way he was to her. If only she weren't so aggressive. He preferred strong women, but he didn't want to feel tethered like a black widow's lunch. His childhood had been immersed in his church, and his activity in his Youth Ministry helped him set the standards for his life. Maria fell outside those standards. The bikini, too many of her too-personal questions, her suggestive flirting all bothered him. Still, he had to admit she was enchanting. What man wouldn't be fascinated by her?

His thoughts skittered away from Maria and toward Grace. He wanted to help her, to hold her, to comfort her. Why did that seem more appealing right now than whatever it was Maria offered him?

He caught a whiff of the petroleum distillates filling the garage and let the scent calm him. He loved that smell. Gas, oil, car tires. They reminded him of all the years he and his dad spent monkeying around under the hood; of Scott teaching him tricks he shared with Sean.

A memory sent a quick shock through him. A week ago, Scott visited Rick's house with his wife and their little girl, Cindy. Cindy was an adorable tyrant, a towheaded whirlwind that kept Rick's oldest brother and his wife on their toes. Cindy loved the garage. There were all kinds of things she wasn't supposed to get into out there.

After they left, a moment of daydreaming allowed him to think how fun it would be to have a child of his own to share the garage with. Strange that he imagined his child having Grace's smile.

In her other life, the one without Rick Fleming, Grace wasn't vindictive. In hindsight, she realized her antagonism toward Rick was more spite than grievance, and she feared what it was doing to her.

If only she knew what to do about it.

"Rick promised he'd play Xbox with me," Kyle grumbled, heading to the garage as he checked his phone, wondering what was keeping his cousin. He certainly understood being so caught up in a car he'd forget about video games, but how could he turn down mint chocolate chip ice cream?

Grace expected the seventeen-year-old to ditch this boring party any minute for his friends. Hannah was getting fidgety, too, but Grace attributed that to Maria. The girl bombarded them with far too many questions, most seemingly harmless and inane, but too many of them personal ones about Rick. He should be the one to tell her about his daily habits, his favorite flavor of ice cream, or exactly what he did for a living. Otherwise, it was none of her business.

Finally, Maria checked her phone and came to her feet, stretching like a cat. "Gosh, it's late. I'd best get checked in to my hotel. What do you have planned for tomorrow?"

"We're going to church," Charlotte replied.

"Oh, yay," Cherise muttered, twirling her finger over her head.

"That's a good thing," Maria said, earning an eye-roll from Cherise. "You know the churches here?"

Hannah tried to kick Charlotte's foot to stop her, but the name spilled out of her mouth too quickly. Charlotte glanced at Hannah in surprise, wondering what she did wrong.

Maria grinned, obviously delighted by the information. "That's wonderful. I love to go to church. My family is mostly Catholic, but I think everyone has to search for their own religious satisfaction. Right? So, I'll see you all tomorrow."

Hannah jumped to her feet and escorted the woman out the front door, locked it, and then turned and stared at Grace for a moment before saying, "I think she's nice, but... I hope my brother doesn't hook up with her."

Charlotte asked, "Why not? She's beautiful, and she knows some artists in San Francisco."

Grace's chest tightened when she remembered Charlotte loved to paint. She'd taken art classes most of her life, but she had her heart set on learning to oil paint from someone famous. Did Maria really know important people? Or was she pandering to Rick's cousin to gain her trust and get closer to Rick?

"And?" Hannah challenged Charlotte.

"She lives in San Jose, not far from the university. She said maybe Ricky would bring me to her apartment one day, and she'd take me to meet a couple of them."

"Only if your parents go along, girl," Hannah said. "We don't know Maria Del Rey from Mirella Ponce."

"Huh?" Charlotte said, confused.

The stiffness on Grace's face cracked, and she chuckled. "She's a famous gangbanger, Charlotte."

"Maria's hardly a criminal," Hannah said. "But you never know people's intentions. Rick says she's a bit too friendly for the short time he's known her. Part of the reason he's here: for a little space, so he can get some perspective on their relationship. Can I ask you guys a favor?"

"Sure," Charlotte agreed.

"Cherise?"

"Yeah, whatever. I think Maria's cool, but I don't really care."

"If she comes around again, keep personal information to yourselves. She can give all the third degrees she wants—it doesn't mean you have to answer her."

"What's a third degree?" Cherise asked.

Now Hannah rolled her eyes. "Oh, kiddo, you make me feel old. When the cops grill people under bright lights, it's called 'the third degree.' Are you two going up to use the Xbox, or are you going to let Kyle and Rick have it?"

Charlotte whooped. "Come on, Cherise. We have to get to it first. It sucks to be them."

"Language!" Hannah called as the girls raced from the room.

They'd no sooner left than Hannah's phone rang. When she answered it, she waved goodbye to Grace and rushed out the patio doors, headed for the back of the property and privacy.

Damien.

It wasn't fair. Everything in Hannah's life seemed so sainted. She didn't have to work; her scholarships and her father's financial backing helped her with school. She had a Benz, designer clothes, perfect teeth, and hair and nails done in studios Grace couldn't afford. Hannah's dad even paid for their apartment. It was a perk for Grace, of course—something her own father could never do—but was intended to make life easier for Hannah, not her.

Added to that, Hannah was deeply in love, and Damien was an incredible guy. If they didn't get married in the near future, Hannah wouldn't need to go back home after graduation. Her parents would gladly supplement her teacher's salary to make sure she had a nice place to live, something better than the small tract home Grace's parents owned. Those annoying green eyes of jealousy prodded her. What would it be like to live with such privilege? How would it feel to share it with the love of your life?

She never imagined she'd have a friend as faithful as Hannah. For that, she considered herself blessed, but she wouldn't mind a few more possessions.

Expecting the phone call to last a while, Grace forced herself upstairs, where she grabbed her laptop and settled on one of the couches to do her homework.

At least this time, her efforts paid off. Assignments finished, she took a quiz and was sure she aced it. Nothing had gone wrong. It was liberating. What she learned fascinated her, but she also felt some of the pressure from the class requirements lighten.

"What happened to Maria?"

Grace jumped. Rick had come up behind her without warning. She looked around. "What happened to Kyle?"

"He took off. Ethan called. He and Jeff are getting together at Ethan's place. Kyle's staying the night. So, what about Maria?"

Grace stared at him. What was she, his private-relationship coordinator?

"She finished grilling the twins about the Fleming family, including about going to church tomorrow, and decided it was time to leave."

"Oh. I wish the girls hadn't told her about church. The doors are open to everyone, but I kind of hope she doesn't come, even if it would be good for her. I still don't know what to think of her."

"I'm sure Kyle would love to take her off your hands."

He chuckled. "Yeah, well, I have a feeling she'd eat a kid like him alive... Hey, what happened to Hannah?"

"She's outside, on the phone."

"Damien?"

"Yeah."

"You doing homework?"

"Done. For now," she said.

"I'm sorry about the comment about the pizza. I spout those sorts of things to family and close friends all the time. It doesn't mean anything."

Grace shrugged it off. "I get it. I was being too sensitive. Life's hard enough without me looking for trouble."

She was shocked at the relief that suffused his face. He blew a puff of air through his lips and brushed his hair back from his brow, but she also saw him relaxing. She hadn't realized how tense he was.

Had she caused it? She'd been so focused on how uncomfortable he made her, she hadn't noticed.

Footsteps on the stairs preceded Hannah joining them, her face glowing with happiness. Glancing between Rick and Grace, she frowned but didn't say anything. Rick volunteered Kyle's plans, and then the twins clamored for their attention, begging Rick and Hannah to join them for a video game.

"What about Grace? We shouldn't leave her out," Charlotte said.

"We can rotate in and out," Cherise suggested.

"Nope. Remember? I don't have a death wish," Grace said. "You guys go for the jugular."

Rick's eyes sparkled with mischief. "Why play if you don't play to win?"

"My point exactly," she said, pulling up a game of Spider Solitaire on the computer. Sometimes she won, but no one made fun of her if she didn't. "You guys do your thing."

Eventually, the night wound down, the twins turned in, and Hannah and Grace settled into bed to read for a while, leaving Rick to work on his laptop in the loft.

The romance book Grace was reading was moving along, a delicious tale of long-lost love, but tonight it made her feel sad. What if this was the extent of her love life? She hadn't dated for more than a year, and only a few of those guys had been even close to serious. She didn't blame them for escaping while they could. Who wanted a girlfriend who was a danger to herself and everything you owned?

Hannah tossed her iPad aside and rolled over to stare at Grace. "You know my brother still likes you, right?"

Grace's eyes flew open. "Where the heck did that come from?"

Hannah pursed her lips. "It kills me to know how you feel about each other, but you can't forgive him for what happened."

Grace glared at her. "I can't believe you want me to like your brother. I wouldn't want you to like mine."

Hannah shuddered. "*Ewww*. Sorry. Danny's turned out pretty cute, but he is your little brother. My brothers, on the other hand, were always my idols, I guess because they're older."

"Seriously? After the way they treated us? Are you still crazy?"

Hannah laughed. "You never did understand them, Grace. Yeah, they could be jerks, but they were mostly hair-brained goof-offs. That's the reason they were so popular, not because they were major bullies and forced people to worship them—although Scott had the tendency. Dad set him straight, and he finally realized he had to get it together or hit the highway. I only wish…"

Grace pulled in a deep breath, hating the way her gut twisted with dread. She'd faced difficult truths all her life, but anything involving Hannah's brothers had been the worst for her.

"You wish I would let bygones be bygones? I've been trying, Hannah, but you weren't there. You didn't see what happened That Night."

On the rare occasions they talked about it, that was the way they referred to it. In capitals. As if That Night was some important title in a book.

"And you won't talk about That Night. It isn't fair. Maybe I could help if you'd tell me, and even if not, I'd love to give you moral support. Might be good for you, you know."

Grace groaned. "I know." She rubbed her forehead to chase away a tension headache. "It's just so hard."

Hannah flopped onto her back, her fists bunched. "Honestly, Grace, sometimes."

"Yeah, you want to pound me. I know. You can't possibly be as upset with me as I am."

"And you can't go on living this way. You need to talk to someone. If not me, then maybe a counselor."

"So now I need a shrink?" Grace's eyes narrowed. "Wow. I love you, too, my friend."

Hannah sat up, sincerity written all over her face. "What you need is honesty. With me. With yourself. With someone. You're hiding from the truth, and it's made you bitter. Can't you see that?"

Grace felt her cheeks redden, and she sat up, too, her shoulders hunched and her head bowed. Bitter? She didn't see herself that way, but what if Hannah was right? "You really want to know, don't you?"

"Yes! I've been worried about you ever since it happened. Five years, Grace—five years! And you haven't been the same since."

Grace couldn't meet Hannah's gaze, so she let her eyes follow the pattern in the Berber carpet at her feet. Before she knew it, she was painting a picture of the past that had haunted her for every one of the last five years.

CHAPTER 9

"You know your brothers teased me constantly when we were kids. I actually don't blame them. If I wasn't spilling milk, I was tripping over anything and nothing. I was pretty good at badminton, archery, and cooking, but I couldn't hit a softball if my life depended on it, and I broke one of your dad's garage windows throwing a ball. Remember?"

"Yes, but you were a gifted dancer. I don't think you had a clumsy moment the entire time we danced."

Grace sighed and rubbed her bad knee. "Until I couldn't."

Hannah gave a sad nod. "Yeah, I know. It wasn't your fault."

"No, it was Murphy's. Life did become easier for me when Scott went to college, especially after he met Julia. He didn't even notice me anymore. Sean was a different animal."

Hannah sighed. "He's always been different. He worked a lot of hours to afford his apartment and his car and his part of his college expenses, but he still found time to party."

"But you know how he was. He'd drop by, raid your folks' fridge, make a mess, eat a ton, and then throw his napkin in my face and tell *me* to clean the kitchen. He constantly called me Graceless or UnGraceful, Dropsy, Stumblebum, Flounder Face. He told tasteless jokes that were meant to hurt me."

"He's still goofy, Grace, but he's like that with everyone except Mom. He even teases Dad. But Rick was different. When he started college, he got a decent job and moved in with Sean, but they hardly ever saw each other. You know Rick was awesome when he came home to visit us."

Grace nodded, loving the memory. "All through our senior year. The movies, the ice cream, the games. I let myself trust him; be a friend to him. When you weren't able go to his boss's New Year's Eve party, I almost backed out, but he talked me into it. Made it sound exciting. The dinner was amazing, and we danced, and I didn't break or spill anything. It was wonderful, even if we had to leave early.

Remember? With him nineteen and me seventeen, we had to go when the alcohol started flowing. We celebrated the New Year's Eve at my house with my family, and he was so much fun."

"You said you had a great time. And you two started doing things together after that."

"Yeah, but I didn't think of it as dating. We were friends. The way you and I are friends. Except…" Her smile drooped.

"What?"

"If I was at your place and Scott or Sean came around, Rick withdrew. Like he didn't know me. It hurt, Hannah. I didn't understand it."

Hannah breathed deep. "Yeah, it wasn't fair. I wish he'd explained it. Remember, he was Scott and Sean's baby brother. They teased him, too. He wanted to protect you from their jokes and stupid pranks, but I think he was too busy protecting himself. Anyway, please, finish telling me about That Night."

Grace grimaced. Talking about it was like picking at a scab on a wound that never healed.

"Your folks had the barbecue, and Scott didn't come but Sean did. Rick hardly paid attention to me until after Sean left and you went inside to help your mom clean up. Then he slid over to sit next to me, and at first, I was a kind of annoyed. How does someone change faces like that? It totally rubbed me the wrong way. And then he turned on the Fleming charm. He had me so mesmerized a bomb couldn't have gotten my attention. He was flirting, I mean openly flirting, and we talked about another trip to Cold Stone."

Grace's thoughts turned inward as the memories leaked out of her.

⁓

It was a typical May evening. The day's heat had dissipated and the evening turned cool. Grace shivered, and Rick hung his light jacket around her shoulders. It was soft and smelled of him, citrus and sandalwood and the musky scent of a guy. He slipped his arm around her shoulders and pulled her close, murmuring he'd help keep her warm, sending shivers of delight up her spine instead.

She was lost in his smile and his fascinating emerald green eyes, loving his touch. They talked about everything, so easily, so naturally. When he touched her cheek with a curled finger, her skin ignited and her heart hammered in her chest. He leaned forward, angling his lips toward hers.

The patio door flew open and the moment shattered.

Sean stood there, his hazel eyes rounded in surprise. Grace gulped, wishing she was somewhere else, especially when Rick pulled away from her.

"Forgot my hat," Sean said, strolling over to pick up his 49ers duckbill from the ground by the table. He smacked it against his thigh and tossed it onto his head, fighting a grin as his gaze pinned Rick's. "So, what's this?" He pointed at Grace. "You taking a closer look at a loser?"

"Knock it off, Sean. It was funny when we were ten and twelve, but it's not funny anymore."

"Really?" Sean laughed. "She is. Did you notice UnGraceful dropped her fork twice at dinner? And she still has barbecue sauce on her chin. She's a klutz, Rick. What do you see in her?"

Embarrassed, Grace scrubbed at her chin, but it made Sean laugh harder.

"I've always wondered about you, Graceless," he said. "What's the real reason you have an interest in my brother? You're too young for anything serious, unless maybe you're planning to suck him into something that will… you know… force the relationship to another level."

Rick jumped to his feet in a fury. "Tell me why your girlfriend tolerates you? You can't be serious for a single minute, and you have no respect for other people's feelings. Get out of here!"

"Yeah?" Sean said, his handsome Fleming face spreading into a grin. "Make me."

Rick groaned and shook his head, then sat back down, grabbing his cup of soda and taking a drink.

Grace stared at him in horror. Why wasn't Rick standing up to his brother?

Sean ruffled Rick's hair and gave it a tug. "Awe, come on, baby brother. I don't wanna leave until I see you kiss Miss Fumble Fingers. It would be entertaining."

Rick cuffed Sean's hand away and glared at him, which only made Sean laugh harder. Rick snuck a look filled with regret at Grace.

Rage stormed through her. She'd had enough. She jumped to her feet and threw his jacket at him.

"What's wrong with you? With either of you? Sean, you're just plain mean. And Rick? Have you been pretending you were my friend all this time? Why? So you can humiliate me whenever the moment suits you? Well, both of you can consider it a job well done."

Rick's face drained of color and he reached for her, on the verge of saying something but not getting it out.

Grace slapped Rick's hand away. The Fleming brothers were jerks. All of them.

"I never want to see you again!" she snapped. "Any of you. Scott included. If you ever come around me, I'll stop being Hannah's friend, and I mean it. She's the best thing that ever happened to me, but I hate you so much, I'd rather lose her than be anywhere near you!"

<hr />

Grace met Hannah's gaze. "You know the rest. I was so hysterical when I ran through your house and out the front door, you had to chase me down the street in your mom's car to catch me."

"And I took you home, but you wouldn't tell me what happened. Instead, you threatened to end our friendship if I ever breathed a word to you about my brothers or told them anything about you. That's the problem, Grace. You made assumptions. If you'd talked to me about it, I'd have filled you in on what took place after you left. Rick didn't want the situation to get out of hand while you were there, which is why he didn't confront Sean. But after you left, he laid into Sean big-time. It ended in a huge fight."

Grace blinked in surprise. Rick had fought Sean over the way he treated Grace? She couldn't picture it.

"It was an all-out fistfight, Grace, and Sean pushed Rick into the barbecue. Dad accidentally left the grill on, and Rick's hands hit it. It was terrible. Both palms were blistered, except in the places where the skin pulled off and attached itself to the grill. It was so awful, he vomited and nearly passed out. We rushed him to the hospital, and Sean was mortified. He kept apologizing, over and over, saying it was his fault, that he was just goofing around and it got out of hand. That he wished it never happened. Despite the pain and misery, Rick kept stressing out about you. Said he'd hurt you worse than Sean hurt him, and he needed to do something about it."

Grace stared at Hannah, her face cold with shock. She had no idea. She'd never let Hannah tell her.

"The next morning, Sean and Rick called and said they wanted me to go with them to your house to apologize. I begged them not to go. I didn't want to lose you. Both of them took it hard. How can people find forgiveness if they can't apologize?"

Grace rubbed her forehead again, feeling light-headed herself. A part of her still didn't believe Rick could stand up to his brothers, especially about her, but it didn't change the fact her life might have turned out differently if she'd made herself listen.

"I know you won't believe it, but Sean's a different man," Hannah added. "He still has a kooky sense of humor, but he's not obnoxious about it anymore."

"You're right. I don't believe it."

Hannah leaned forward and reached for Grace's hand. "At least try to let go of your anger and resentment. Someone Above wants good things for you, and whether it's Rick or someone else, He'll make it happen if you allow it." She tugged on Grace's hand, which made Grace wince.

"Sorry. Your shoulder?"

"Yeah. It stings. I'll think about it, Hannah, but this is hard to get my head wrapped around. Let me sleep on it, okay?"

"Yeah." Hannah's head bobbed, hope shining in her eyes. "But you can do more. You know what I always tell you when life gets tough."

Grace cocked a half-smile and nodded. "Pray about it. I'm still not good at it, but I'll try."

She slipped into the bathroom and got ready for bed. She also took two acetaminophens to help the ibuprofen do its work on her myriad of aches and pains.

She'd left her laptop in the loft and decided to retrieve it before she settled down. When she found Rick still there, engrossed in a screenful of computer-geek stuff, she paused. Her cheeks flushed when she realized they hadn't closed their bedroom door and he might have overheard what she and Hannah had discussed.

Sensing her presence as she came to grab her laptop, Rick's gaze lifted to meet hers.

He *had* heard every word—she saw it in his eyes. She could also see he didn't know what to say or how to say it. Still, he set aside his computer and rose, shifting uneasily.

"I wish I could do all of it differently, too, Grace," he said. "That Night, I mean. I thought I was right, trying to get Sean to back off and go away. I'm so sorry he hurt your feelings."

Grace's face flushed, and she didn't know what to say, either. She was still so hurt, so angry. How did you let go of something that awful, even if you had some of it wrong? After all, Rick was still blaming Sean for what happened. Rick had been as responsible as his brother, if not more so, and he needed to acknowledge it.

Rick stepped closer, hovering over her, his gaze fastened to hers, as steady as it had been that night. "We were kids, Grace, remember? You'd just turned eighteen. I had my twentieth birthday a few weeks before yours. Our lives aren't scripted, like a movie. We stumble through it a good part of the time, or at least I do. I know I blew it, but I hope you'll understand someday. I cared. I really cared."

It was as if half a decade disappeared. As if they were back in the yard, right after the barbecue. Rick reached toward her, his fingertips a featherlight touch on her cheek. She flushed from the roots of her hair to her neck and shoulders. He was leaning toward her, bending down, his lips a few inches from hers.

What was she doing? She backpedaled, terrified by the way Rick's presence turned her brains into mush. She wasn't ready for this, even if it felt like she'd been waiting for it all her life.

"I... I'm going to bed," she said

"Good night, Grace," Rick said, tenderness in his voice.

She paused, then offered a genuine but cautious, "Good night."

Turning, she fled for her door. Hannah must have closed it to change her clothes. Grace reached for the handle at the exact moment the door jerked open, leaving her to stumble pell-mell into the room, slam into Hannah and knock both of them to the floor. Grace yelped in pain as one of the blisters on her shoulder popped, then she rolled away from her best friend, who lay there gasping for breath.

Rick was there in a heartbeat, the panic on his face reminding her that she would never ever be allowed to make a graceful exit from anyone anywhere.

"Are you okay?"

"Yeah, but I think Hannah's dead."

"I'm fine!" Hannah gasped. "Grace, what the heck? I open the door and you mow me down like a weed whacker. All you had to do was yell 'Back off.' Geez."

Rick and Grace stared at her for a second and then burst into laughter. Grace laughed so hard tears rolled down her cheeks. Struggling to stand, she picked up her laptop in one hand—praying she hadn't broken it—and took Hannah's right hand in the other. Rick grabbed the left one, and they pulled her to her feet. Grace supposed the way Hannah held her chest meant she had a few bruises that matched Grace's.

"Good night, ladies," Rick said, still choking on laughter. "I hope you make it downstairs safely in the morning. I understand someone is making us pancakes."

"Get out of here," Hannah snarled, but when he left them alone, she turned to Grace and they laughed even harder.

Grace swore Sunday morning came earlier than usual. She was still exhausted after a night of restless sleep. Hannah was such a heavy sleeper, she didn't even move when the alarm went off.

It gave Grace first dibs on the bathroom and the closet. She grabbed her clothes and Hannah's strappy cork wedges. The girls traded shoes and clothes all the time, so she doubted Hannah would mind.

Grace coveted them because they showed off her ex-ballerina legs without putting too much stress on her weak knee or putting her at risk of falling to her death from spiked heels. She preferred kitten heels and, in fact, mostly wore either flat-soled boots or sandals, but today, for some reason, she wanted to dress... well, *nice.*

She also wanted to run downstairs to toss a pork roast into Aunt Sharon's Instant Pot pressure cooker before making breakfast. She needed pulled pork for their tacos that night.

With dinner plans under control, she turned to the pancakes. Frustration had her gritting her teeth after she poured the first batch into the pan and saw the container of baking powder glaring at her. She'd forgotten to add it.

Which meant she had to dump the entire batch and start over. In the meantime, the sausage browned more than she wanted, and she was annoyed they were cold by the time she finished the omelets.

The good news was no one even noticed. She reheated whatever needed reheating in the microwave and backed out of the way. All they cared about was filling empty bellies. They were all dressed for church—although Hannah gave Grace a dirty look when she found her friend wearing her cork wedges.

Grace gave her a cheesy grin but was left witless at seeing Rick so handsome, clad in his Sunday best. He wore blue slacks and a gray sports jacket, a pale blue shirt, and paisley tie. His hair was freshly washed, slightly damp and cutely rumpled. Man, he was drop-dead gorgeous. As fearful as she was about taking a chance on him, she wanted to run her hands through that hair.

Breakfast over and the cooked roast stowed in the fridge for the day, they were off to church at the Flemings' favorite local parish. It wasn't until they walked through the parking lot that Grace was reminded of how women of all ages were drawn to Rick Fleming. Many who knew the Fleming family came to welcome them, paying special attention to Rick. A few gave Grace even dirtier looks than Hannah had at her shoes, and then…

Grace's heart nearly stopped when Maria appeared, gliding toward them draped in a gossamer red gown which on anyone else would have been outrageous. Maia-Mitchel-type hair, dark, thick, and falling in luscious waves over her shoulders and down her back, she was blessed with a slight widow's peak, and her skin glowed a gorgeous honey-gold. Grace wondered if the red dress belonged in a conservative church, and yet Maria wore it like it was made for her. Her lipstick matched, and her long lashes, stolen from Bambi's mom, made her so exotic, Grace felt ugly in comparison.

Maria gave Rick a million-dollar smile. How in the world could a guy resist her? How in the world could another woman compete?

"Good morning, sweetheart," Maria murmured, rising to her toes to kiss him on the cheek.

Rick took a step back and wiped the lipstick from his face. "Uh, good morning," he replied with reservation.

Maria looked wounded, and Grace found herself feeling sorry for the girl. It wasn't fun to have a guy reject you. She doubted Maria had a lot of experience with rejection, either.

"It's a beautiful day. Hello, Grace," she said. "How are you?"

Grace fished for words before replying, "Fine. Thank you."

"And Hannah, it's good to see you again. Girls. Kyle."

Hannah and the kids welcomed her, but Grace didn't miss Hannah's careful perusal of her brother and both Maria and Grace.

Maria was nothing but proper—beyond offering the kiss Rick hadn't expected. Her crush on Rick was obvious, and Grace wondered why he wasn't head over heels in love with this woman. Grace had her own reservations about Maria, of course, but she didn't know why. She had to admit her personal feelings about Rick made her anything but an impartial judge.

"It's almost time," Grace pointed out. "We'd best go inside." She headed into the church's narthex, refusing to admit her heart ached with something akin to jealousy. She reminded herself once again she had no right to feel jealous. She headed toward the water faucet, needing to calm herself before heading into the sanctuary. The water wouldn't come on, and she wrestled with the faucet handle until a stream of water spewed out and blasted her in the face. Grace gasped and jumped back sputtering when the faucet refused to turn off, soaking the front of her peach tunic. She wanted to scream.

"Oh, Grace, good heavens," Hannah muttered, hurrying her into the bathroom. Together, they managed to dry off her face without destroying her makeup, did what they could with her hair, and used the hand-dryer to shrink the water spot on her tunic.

"That's enough, Hannah," Grace insisted. "The service is about to start, and I'll draw more attention if I walk in late. Hopefully, it'll dry before the meeting ends."

Hannah sighed and tossed a handful of wet paper towels in the trash. "Okay, my friend. Let's go get preached to."

Grace wanted to have a heart-to-heart with God when she saw Rick sitting with the twins on one side and Maria and Kyle on the other. Which left the remainder of the Fleming bench for Hannah and Grace.

"Yeah, Someone Above has something in store for me," Grace muttered as they took their seats. "And He has a funny way of doing it."

Rick shifted uncomfortably on the bench, aware Maria was as close to him as she could get without sitting in his lap. Her perfume was enticing, something that reminded him of a blend of roses and lavender, and her slight but well-endowed figure wowed him.

Consider him crazy, but he still wished she hadn't come.

"Glad you're here," Kyle told Maria.

"I'm thrilled to be here," Maria replied. She was effervescent, her beauty entrancing Kyle—and every other man in the congregation.

Rick glanced at Grace and Hannah when they arrived—doing a double take at Grace. Not five minutes ago, she was lovely, but now it looked as if someone had tried to drown her.

"So, do you go to church regularly?" Kyle asked Maria.

Rick wanted to laugh. His cousin invited everyone to church.

Maria twinkled happily. "Oh, absolutely. My family roots are Catholic, but I'm open to whatever makes my life happy."

She glanced at Rick, her expression plain. She would do anything, even change religions, to be with him. It made him feel crummy. He wasn't even close to feeling like that toward her. He wondered how it felt. *No, wait,* he thought. He knew exactly how it felt. He'd felt that way about Grace—still felt that way about Grace—and if Sean hadn't destroyed everything, who knew what would have happened.

The organist stopped and the quiet conversations halted when Reverend Moore took to the pulpit, adjusting the microphone sprouting from the lectern, and welcomed them. Again, Rick glanced at Grace, wishing he could be sitting next to her instead of being stuffed between the twins—who were already shoulder-to-shoulder and hunched over on their phones—and Maria.

He insisted the girls ditch the phones, exhaled and tried to relax, and prayed the answers he needed weren't out of reach. What he didn't want to face was the reality Grace wanted nothing to do with him. If she refused to change her mind, should he consider spending more time with Maria? Maybe it wouldn't hurt to get to know her better.

<hr />

Grace and Hannah got caught in the crowd when the meeting ended and everyone headed out the door. It took a moment to find Kyle, who'd bumped into old friends in the congregation. Then the twins, giddy as kindergartners, towed two girlfriends over to join them.

"They're here! They're here!" Cherise crowed, flapping her arms crow-style.

"Hey, Rachel," Hannah said, and Grace waved at Skylar.

Skylar was a cute girl, chocolate-skinned and slender, her hair done up in dreads. "Hey, Grace," she said. "Uh, what happened? Did you fall in the lake before coming to church?"

Grace took a deep breath and let it out slowly. "No, the water faucet is possessed. I really need to talk to the Reverend about having it exorcized."

All the girls laughed.

"I want to go to Skylar's for the day," Charlotte told Hannah. "And Cherise wants to visit Rachel."

"Why can't the girls come to our place?" Hannah asked, her brows puckered with concern. "You'd all be together."

"We want to do different things," Cherise groused, "And it's no fun at our place."

Grace almost snorted. No fun? Did Rachel's parents have Disneyland in their backyard or something? What was more "fun" than the Flemings' cabin?

Hannah relented. "Be home for dinner, and I mean it. I won't let you go again for the rest of the week if you try to wheedle more out of me."

"We won't," Charlotte insisted, turning to throw her arms around Skylar in excitement. "We're going to have a blast."

Rachel, a sturdy girl with light brown hair and a lovely smile, was beaming when Cherise hooked elbows with her and headed toward her parents' car.

"Yes, you did send me flowers," Maria insisted, her voice catching Grace's attention.

"What are you talking about? I've never sent you flowers in my life."

Grace's ears perked. What in the world was going on?

"You did. Remember? After we went to dinner at the Lexington House."

Grace squirmed. It was one of the most expensive restaurants in Los Gatos. Rick took her there?

"I didn't send you flowers. Someone else must have, and you got confused. Look, Maria, I like you. You're really nice, but I need to concentrate on my car. I need to get back to work. Let's put this off until I'm back home."

Grace saw Maria getting teary, but to her credit, she smiled, sniffed, and nodded. "Okay. I'm staying for the celebration, and maybe we'll run into each, but I don't want to intrude."

The crowd drifted away and left Grace staring at the two of them. Rick seemed pained, as though someone stuck bamboo slivers under his fingernails, while Maria still appeared hopeful.

Grace glanced at Hannah, feeling even worse at finding her sympathetic. Hannah felt bad for Maria, too—but her silent message to Grace came through loud and clear. If Grace waited too long....

Rick shifted in discomfort with Grace and Hannah watching them. Maria came to touch Hannah's and Grace's hands, wished them well, and turned and drifted through the remainder of the crowd toward the parking lot.

"You okay? That was… rough," Hannah said, resting a hand on Rick's arm.

"Yeah, it was. I like her, but I don't know her well enough for her to get so intense. It's… awkward." Rick cast Grace an uncomfortable glance. "It makes me want to back away from her."

Grace should have felt relieved by his comment. Instead, she found her thoughts more focused on how would they survive the day with only the three of them in the house.

CHAPTER 10

"So, did you really not send Maria flowers?" Hannah asked, trying not to smirk, as they headed into the kitchen to scrounge up lunch.

Rick glared at her and threw open the fridge door. "Root, hog, or whatever you called it?" he asked, pulling out a Ziploc bag holding three pieces of leftover pizza. "Mine. I'm hungry, and I need to get back to my car."

"It's Sunday," Hannah pointed out. "Don't you want to take a break?"

Rick made a face. "I thought I was supposed to put my bucket-of-bolts back together and get lost. Considering Maria follows me around and might be out there hiding in the bushes, I think it's a good idea."

It wasn't a good idea to Grace. She'd never say it out loud, but she didn't want Rick to leave.

"Rick?" she managed to force out of her mouth. "Eat lunch with us, will you? So we can talk? Hannah and the twins like Maria, and Kyle would marry her tomorrow if she'd have him, but I think it's wise to watch your step with her. If you agree, then maybe the three of us should put our heads together and try to figure out why."

The tension ebbed out of him, and he breathed a sigh of relief. "I'd win the jackpot if I knew the answer. Her hands have Super Glue on them, but it's not the first time she's said I've done something I didn't and it upsets me. Two weeks ago, she said I offered to take her shopping on the Avenue. I did no such thing. I hardly ever go there and probably wouldn't unless..." His cheeks darkened, and he looked away. "Unless I was in a serious relationship."

Los Gatos's Avenue sported businesses for the rich, including everything from the finest wedding apparel on the West Coast to staggeringly expensive diamonds.

He tossed the pizza on a paper plate, zapped it in the microwave, and set it on the table. He then took off for the garage.

"Good move, Evans," Hannah muttered, giving her friend a tacky grin.

"Knock it off, Fleming," Grace said, her cheeks blazing with embarrassment.

Rick was back in a minute from the garage fridge with three sodas. He handed them out, filled three glasses with ice, and slid them to the girls. The girls, in turn, made sandwiches and joined Rick at the table, but his tale of dates with Maria were few and straightforward.

"There has to be a way to unravel the mystery of Maria Del Rey," Grace muttered.

"Yeah. So you can get rid of me."

"What? No. In fact…" She gulped, shocked when she realized she almost admitted she resented the woman.

"In fact, what?"

"Never mind."

Rick paused mid-chew, amazement on his face. "You want me to stay," he ventured at last.

Hannah coughed. "Don't push it, Bro."

"No, I want to know what Grace is thinking."

"And I don't want to tell you."

"What, that you'd like my company?"

"As long as you're in the garage," Grace mumbled, staring hard at her half-eaten sandwich.

Rick barked laughter. "Yeah, I see how this works. You're interested when Maria's around, but one-on-one—"

"Hey! No aggravating the cook," Hannah protested. "We're having Tacos de Cerdo tonight. That's why Grace cooked the pork this morning. If you upset her, we might get canned pork and beans instead."

Rick snorted. "You do Mexican well, too?"

"Lugar Rosa should be jealous she doesn't work for them," Hannah said.

"Wow. My favorite Mexican restaurant in our hometown. So, only tacos? Or do you make a full dinner plate, like in a restaurant?"

Grace smirked at the challenge. "Tacos and all the trimmings, all from scratch. Spanish rice, refried beans, salsa, the works. And if I don't set anything on fire or get hit by an airplane, it should be pretty good."

Rick shrugged. "Fine. I'll put you to the test. I'll be back for dinner but not a moment sooner."

He gobbled the last of his lunch and left Grace with Hannah in the way-too-big, echoing kitchen.

"What happened to our babysitting job?" she asked.

Hannah laughed. "Ah, come on. Aunt Sharon didn't expect us to keep our eyes glued on three teenagers twenty-four-seven. She wants us to have fun, too, and I told you this could happen. Our job is to keep an eye on the monsters to make sure they don't take advantage of their parents being away and to be there in case of an emergency."

Grace shook her head and breathed easy. "I think a good book on the patio, with our sodas and chips, and maybe even a long nap, sounds great."

"It does, doesn't it? Although Damien might call. If he does, I'll disappear so we don't bug you."

Grace nodded, knowing in her heart Damien would call and Hannah would leave her completely alone. It didn't matter. She was tired and may not be able to stay awake anyway.

Sure enough, after they entrenched themselves on their chaise lounges, Grace got lost in her book and fell asleep.

Who knew how long later, Grace roused, aware of conversation in the background. She recognized Hannah's voice but sat up straight at the tone.

"No, no! That can't be."

Hannah was crying! Something was terribly wrong.

Grace jumped to her feet and dashed to the side of the house, where Hannah leaned against the wall, tears trailing her face. When she saw Grace, she nearly dropped her phone in her hurry to grab her hand.

"Hannah, what's wrong?" Grace hissed.

"Yeah, okay. I'll get there as soon as I can. Thank you, Janice. Thank you, thank you for calling."

The call ended and Hannah stared at Grace, her brown eyes swimming with tears and pain.

"That was Damien's mom," Hannah said, choked up. "They were having family and church friends over for lunch, and you know they live near that busy corner of Dry Creek and Sycamore in San Jose? Damien had to park across the street, and some kids in a pickup took the corner way too fast and couldn't stop in time. They hit him, Grace! They hit him. He's in critical condition at the hospital. I have to go. I have to…" She gasped for air and fell into Grace's arms.

"Shhh, shhh," Grace calmed her, patting her friend's back and hanging on for dear life, hardly able to make sense of it. Damien hit by a truck? How serious was it? Would he live? What would it do to Hannah to lose him? "It's okay. Let's get your clothes packed and I'll drive you—"

Wait? What was she thinking? She didn't have her license. Besides, the kids needed an adult here, and Rick wasn't the one hired to take care of them. He had a car to fix. He was a guy, and he'd probably let the kids eat top ramen and mac and cheese until they died of malnutrition.

Grace pried Hannah's arms loose and guided her into the house and to the stairs.

"Start packing," she told her. "I need to talk to Rick."

Grace put aside her concerns about how broken Hannah looked as she hurried into the garage.

"Rick?"

There was no sign of him.

"Rick!"

The sound of metal wheels rolling across concrete preceded him shooting out from under his car. He sat upright, more grease than ever on his face, and stared at her in surprise.

"Something wrong?"

"Yeah, big wrong. Damien's mom just called Hannah. You won't believe it, but Damien was hit by a pickup truck as he was crossing the street. He's in intensive care. Hannah's freaking out."

"You're joking. Oh, my gosh." He jumped off the creeper and stalked toward her, making her wonder if he would run her over to get to his sister.

They headed into the kitchen, Grace telling him, "I'll help her finish packing. Someone's got to be here for the kids."

"I don't know if Hannah should drive by herself," Rick said.

"Then you should go with her," she said, reminding him she didn't have her license. He should go, but Grace felt sad, needing him in a strange way, too.

They hurried upstairs.

"Let me grab a change of clothes, and I'll drive you," Rick told Hannah.

"No. Please. You need to finish your car and Grace needs your support with the kids. They might give her static. They're teenagers, and Cherise is turning into a bit of a pill."

"Yeah, I noticed. But you're upset. Driving isn't safe if you can't keep your mind on the road."

"I insist. I'm focused. I promise." Hannah turned to Grace. "Please be okay with this, Gracie. Aunt Sharon and Uncle Luke are counting on us, and if you and I can't be here, then you and Rick need to be."

"I'm on it. Be safe, Hannah. Call as soon as you arrive and again when you know what's going on."

"Of course."

Rick ran to the bathroom to wash the grease off his hands and face and grabbed Hannah's bags. The three of them hurried downstairs. Grace felt hollow inside as she stood on the drive, watching her best friend drive away.

It wasn't supposed to be like this. For as long as Hannah and Damien had dated, Grace had seen the future in all its happy yet sad glory: Hannah in love. Hannah so happy she was in heaven. Grace, seeing her best friend becoming permanently and forever someone else's best friend.

There were times she resented it, even if she knew it was right. But now? She wanted to curse Murphy. Instead, she bowed her head, tears streaming from her own eyes, and said a prayer. The doctors and nurses would do all they could do, and Hannah would be there to give Damien strength and courage, but the Father of Creation—not Murphy—would make the final decision about whether Damien lived or died.

<hr />

Rick's heart took a leap when he saw Grace praying. She was praying? He knew she went to church with Hannah, but he wasn't convinced she believed. Seeing her like this had him mesmerized. Was there anything be more wonderful than knowing the girl he cared for all these years had faith in God?

He tentatively stroked Grace's back to comfort her. Her eyes met his, glistening with tears, and his heart sank. She'd endured so much pain and unhappiness in her life. His choices shouldn't have been a part of it.

"We'll both pray for him," he murmured. "God answers prayers."

A quick, wry smile jerked the corners of Grace's mouth. "Always. But not always the way we want Him to."

His heart pinched again. She was enough of a believer to understand this was true. If the Father decided to take Damien home, there was nothing any of them could do about it—except carry on in his place.

"The power of prayer should never be underestimated," Rick insisted. He'd seen miracles in his own life. He hoped Grace would see one now.

Grace gave him a feeble smile, wiping her cheeks and giving a wet sniff. "Jesus healed the lepers and raised the dead, right?"

"Right."

"Then I suppose anything is possible."

Rick gave her a soft, tender smile. "It is, Grace. We're neither alone nor forgotten."

Grace nodded, standing quiet and thoughtful for a while. "We should call the kids and tell them what happened. They at least need to know Hannah's gone and why."

"I'll call Kyle. You tell the girls. I don't think they know Damien well, but it wouldn't be fair not to tell them. I'll also talk to my mom. I doubt Hannah thought to contact her."

Grace agreed, headed inside where she dropped into a chair to stop her legs from shaking, and called the twins. They'd only met Damien a couple times, but they knew how much Hannah loved him. Charlotte sounded sad; Cherise seemed quieter than usual. Grace wondered if this was one of those "wake-up call" moments for a teen showing signs of rebellion.

As upset in their own way as Grace, the girls asked to stay the night with their friends. Under the circumstances, Grace consented, provided they came home for breakfast. She needed to stay in touch with them. They agreed without argument. They also asked how their previous plans would change. With Hannah gone, there was a lot they might not be able to do. Grace wanted to pretend none of this happened, that Hannah would return and they could get back on track.

Instead, Grace had to face the prospect of being alone with Rick for the next couple days in a huge house, a meal to make for dinner meant to feed a dozen, and way too many hours to worry about Hannah and Damien.

———

"Hey," Rick said.

"Hey," Grace replied.

"It smells fabulous."

"Thanks."

Grace felt awkward as she sat down at the table. Yep, she was alone with Rick, and he was alone with her. They were alone together.

Her heart fluttering, she focused on the food rather than him, sitting across from her, looking as handsome as ever and ready to inhale what she made. She'd only cut the portions in half, in case the kids came home. They didn't, so it would give them leftovers during the week.

"Shall I say gr—uh, bless it?" he offered, bowing his head and giving a sincere prayer for nourishment and also begging the Lord to watch over and help Damien and Hannah and comfort Damien's family.

"Amen," she murmured with him, and they began filling their plates, although Grace had lost her appetite.

She also didn't know what to do with the silence hovering around them. She was too used to noise: family noise—her family, or the Fleming family's, or at her and Hannah's apartment—or the cafeteria lunches at school and the lunchroom at work.

Afraid to say the wrong thing, she said nothing. Rick was making quick work of his meal, but she gave herself permission to savor it, pleased by the results of her efforts.

"Mmm, this is great, Grace," Rick managed to say between bites. "I haven't eaten like this in... I can't remember when."

"When you went to the Lexington House?"

He paused, first thoughtful and then embarrassed. He shook his head. "There's no comparison. If everything you cook tastes this good, you might be better, but comparing well-done Mexican to upscale snob isn't fair."

"What?" Grace said, hand over her mouth to prevent laughing food all over the table.

"Okay, so, the snobs would take a teensy bite of this and a tiny bite of that and pronounce them 'exquisite' or 'delectable' or 'smooth

118

on the palate.' I enjoy what I can describe as delicious, and this is it. Thank you. You've helped salvage a tough day."

"You're welcome, I think." Had he given her a fair compliment? Should she be pleased or offended?

Rick grinned. "See, I think the snobs are so busy trying to arrange food to look like works of art on fancy plates and competing with each other on how to describe meals that would starve a rabbit, they've forgotten the majority of us merely enjoy eating food that's real. This is real, Grace. Honestly. Trust me. My mom can't cook, so my parents love to eat out. We got used to it as kids. I've lived alone for most of the last five years. I can cook simple stuff, but I prefer a good restaurant, dine-in or take-out, to my own cooking, and I know when something's good. This is good."

Rick tried to watch Grace without her realizing he was doing it. She had such difficulty taking compliments, and her tentative smile plucked at his heartstrings. She loved to cook, and she loved making people happy with her cooking.

He thought she was amazing. He could tell she was comfortable with her abilities—she just didn't feel comfortable with the attention.

Rick hadn't realized the depth of Grace's insecurities before. Not that it should surprise him. She didn't really have a mom. Trudy Evans' poor health forced Grace to take over maternal responsibilities very young. Most people would think it made someone grow up quickly—and it did—but it also prevented that person from growing up in a social sense. It was one thing to get younger siblings dressed, fed, and off to school each day, but she had to include cooking, cleaning, laundry, and running errands on her bike. She had to set doctor appointments or walk the kids to the dentist. It was altogether another thing learning how to fit in with her peers.

Rick mostly stopped making fun of Grace in grade school—unless Scott or Sean forced his hand. Seeing her take the razzing with her head held high, never saying a word back, dug at his conscience. Scoldings by his parents or their pastor made him feel even worse.

But when Hannah told him about the cruel mistreatment too many peers inflicted on Grace, he'd wanted to fight for her. He would have done so if not for his brothers. The pranks were the worst, like the boy who waited until she was went to sit down in class and jerked her chair out from under her. The mocking laughter from the class as she tumbled to the floor humiliated her. Or what about the jerks who squirted honey inside her locker—and all over her books and papers—at their middle school? One of the worst took place her junior year in high school. Three girls got together and devised a terrible plot to make fun of her.

Hannah said a boy named "Paul" called and asked Grace on a date. He snuck flowers onto her front porch the night before the date and secretly left a note for Grace on her desk at school the next morning. He asked her to wear Sunday best to go to dinner at a nice restaurant.

The Evans' budget had to stretch to buy a dress for the occasion, but her mom was thrilled for her. Hannah helped with her makeup and hair the night of the date. Then she gave Grace a hug, ordered her to have a good time, and headed home.

Paul was supposed to pick Grace up at seven o'clock. At seven-thirty, he still hadn't arrived. She was still waiting at eight-thirty, nine-thirty.

She called Hannah at ten o'clock, in tears. She'd been stood up. It was all a prank. There'd never been a date. Paul was just a jerk of a guy who had no intentions of taking her out.

Furious, Hannah did some digging. When she discovered the three girls behind it, one with a deep voice playing "Paul's" part, the others doing the rest, she made the decision not to tell Grace the truth. There was no Paul, only mean girls. It was worse than what Grace already believed.

There were some legitimate dates in Grace's senior year, but Hannah was tearful when she talked about all the things that went right at first, the hopes Grace developed, and how awful it was when it all went wrong. The only constant in Grace's dating experience was Rick, and she never consider their dates dates—until right before That Night.

Then Rick lost her *because* of that night. All these years, he longed to comfort Grace, to make life right for her. Winding up here at the cabin with her had been an amazing coincidence, although a smile tugged at the corners of his mouth. He wasn't sure he believed in coincidences. The powers of Heaven? That was a different matter.

He already felt a difference in their relationship. They'd been able to talk, and he at least made a stab at apologizing to her for what happened That Night. He'd been able to help around the house and with the kids, and she seemed to appreciate the care and support he offered after she hurt her shoulder.

Now, he faced a different quandary.

He felt obliged to stay here with the woman he'd once cared more about than anyone else in the world—maybe still did. He wanted to remain close and hoped to work his way into Grace's good graces— he grinned at the silly play on words. But he'd have to be careful with her.

Maria had changed the entire dynamic. His stomach tied itself in knots at the thought. He knew Grace sensed his attraction to Maria, which was true, at least physically. But he still harbored doubts about the woman, which he attributed at least in part to the feelings he still held for Grace. If she weren't around, he might have tried harder this week to get to know Maria better. But Grace was here.

And they were in the house together, alone. No Hannah. No kids. No Maria. And he knew his pastor wouldn't approve. Beyond Rick's youth standards about not dating until sixteen and only double dating until eighteen, youth and young adults were advised never to be alone with a date in anyone's home—especially in a bedroom.

Many of his friends outside his church brought their girlfriends home, played games in their rooms, watched movies on Netflix, or made out with the door shut. Rick had been taught to be an old-fashioned gentleman, and he stuck to his guns. Beyond the doctrinal part of it, he had no desire to end up a teen dad. When he finally became a father, he wanted to be ready in every way possible.

This meant he needed to find a way past Grace's defenses without giving her the wrong message. It was like tip-toeing through a minefield.

⁂

Rick pushed his plate away and groaned. "It tastes so good, I want to keep eating, but I'm about to pop."

"Compliment accepted," Grace said, allowing herself to smile.

He smiled back. "I know you learned to cook to help your mom, but when did you realize you had a knack for it?"

"I have no idea. Mom called me a natural. She and Dad even talked about sending me to chef school, but I wasn't interested. I've wanted to teach as long as Hannah has, and I have no desire to stand on my feet twelve hours a day, six days a week in a hot kitchen."

Rick nodded. "I can imagine. It takes a special personality to survive in the restaurant business. So, when you're not working, going to school, taking care of Hannah, or taking care of your mom, what else do you do?"

Grace chuckled. "I don't take care of Hannah. We take care of each other. Danny and Chloe help with Mom now that I'm in school and living in San Jose. I work at a pet shop not far from our apartment. A lot. I need the hours."

"Doesn't leave much time for R&R. You're not dancing anymore? I know Hannah quit in her junior year."

Grace stilled, her gaze dropping to her hands, which were fiddling with her napkin. "Uh, no. No dancing anymore."

"Why? You were so good. Did you lose interest in being a ballerina?"

Rick Fleming had thought she was good? Grace knew he'd been forced to attend his sister's recitals, but she had no idea he had an opinion one way or another about the quality of her performances.

Grace ruminated about telling the truth. She was so used to hiding herself from others, keeping her disappointments and embarrassments to herself, it was hard to allow herself to be open with anyone. Particularly someone who mocked her years ago. Even Hannah, who'd been the most loving person in the world, didn't know everything. Still, Hannah had told Grace dozens of times that she needed to take a risk once in a while. She'd find more friends if she would just be herself. But did Grace dare take that risk with Rick?

"I was good. Good enough our studio's owner had me on her short list to join her top team. I had a few bugs to work out, but if I'd succeeded, I'd have gone with them to New York City to compete."

"Wow. What happened?"

Grace sighed, thinking back to one of the most devastating of all the tricks Murphy ever played on her. It wasn't fair. But then, who'd ever said life, or Murphy, was fair?

"We only had five guys at the studio, but four of them were on the team. Unfortunately, three were assigned six of the seven serious ballerinas and couldn't take me on. The fourth one, Mike, had the remaining ballerina. He was a great guy, but he was shorter than I am, which is a scary mix. Diana, my teacher, encouraged us to work together on the basics, with the promise she'd have one of the taller guys step in for riskier stuff when we were closer to our next recital.

Our partnership worked so well, Mike got full of himself. He convinced me that we'd be fine." She paused, chewing on her lower lip.

"What happened?"

"He pushed it. Insisted we were 'gonna rock it.'"

"And?"

Grace met Rick's gaze, puzzled by the worry and compassion she saw in his eyes.

"I gave in, and he dropped me." As if on cue, her left knee twinged and she flinched. She had a habit of rubbing it, which she did now.

Grace massaging her knee reminded Rick of the scars on his hands.

"Messed up my medial meniscus," she added. "Surgery, physical therapy, the whole bit, but when all was said and done, I couldn't dance anymore."

Rick sat back, stunned. He didn't know Grace had surgery. "Are you kidding? That's terrible."

"I'm lucky I didn't break my neck or my back."

"Is it the reason Hannah quit?"

Grace shrugged. "She wasn't that excited about dancing in the first place. We just wanted to do something together. When I had to stop, she called it quits."

Rick stared at his laced fingers, his hands rested on the table, and shook his head. "I gotta say, you do seem to have had more than your fair share of trouble."

"You think?" she said, making a face before breaking into a wry smile. "I wish problems came with a merit system. I would have met my lifetime quota a few years ago."

Rick laughed. "I'll second that. Who do we talk to to work out the specifics?"

Grace's smile faded. "According to Hannah, it's God. So far, He only listens to me about half the time."

"He always listens, and if He gives you what you want at least half the time, you're doing a good job."

"I didn't say He gave me what I want. In fact, I'm pretty convinced when He does answer He's telling me a big, emphatic 'No.' The rest of the time, it doesn't feel like He heard a word I said."

"Maybe you're..." He paused.

"What?"

"Never mind."

"No, say it."

Rick shifted in discomfort when he said, "Maybe you're too much inside yourself. We all have crummy things happen to us. Perhaps not the way you seem to, but it's possible you just need to shake it off and go on. Not be so focused on it." The wariness on her face troubled him. "Or it could be the Lord's trying to fine-tune you. What if he sees such promise in you, he's giving you a few more challenges than the rest of us so you can be ready to face something in life we won't? Or can't?"

Grace felt the color leave her face. Was he serious? Did he think she was selfish or too self-absorbed? Did he really believe God would pick on her more than He did everyone else because He had some cockamamie mission for her to accomplish in life? This was why she rarely told anyone else what happened to her. It was hard enough when people didn't believe she faced real challenges every day, but having anybody suggest she was making more of it than it was...

She couldn't help the harsh tone in her voice when she responded.

"So, when I went to college, how was I supposed to interpret God's hand when I ran across a few of our high-school classmates and they found new ways to humiliate me?" she asked. "Like, locking me in the janitor's closet and posting it on social media. Or, the one time I was the butt of a joke for a guy's hazing into a fraternity? I was lucky. I made friends with a girl in my math class who whispered to me what they were up to. I managed to turn it against them without them knowing I did it. If she hadn't helped, you can't imagine what they had planned for me."

"Grace, I wasn't criticizing. I was—"

"And what about the real dates, or a few blind dates? What about the fantastical events that happened again and again: the power going out at the theater, or my date getting attacked by hornets?"

"You've never had a good, fun date in your life?"

She realized he didn't believe it, and in all honesty, she didn't blame him.

"I had several, and some of them even survived me. A couple wanted to take it a step further, but in all honesty, over time I discovered they weren't...."

She came to a halt as if she had run into a glass wall, stunned by having come so close to telling the truth. That none of them had been Rick Fleming.

"What? They weren't good enough? Decent guys? Respectful?"

"You wouldn't understand," Grace said, pushing away from the table. "I wasn't interested, Rick. That's all. Excuse me. I'd like to clean the kitchen and check my emails for more homework. I need to take my mind off Hannah and Damien."

Rick clammed up after that, insisting on cleaning the kitchen with her but doing so in silence. She managed to thank him before hurrying upstairs.

CHAPTER 11

Grace stared at the computer screen, which gave birth to no new homework, then turned to look out the window at the top of the staircase. The early evening sunshine shown brilliantly. She had no intention of sitting here, doing nothing. A nature trail bordered the homes around the lake, and a walk along it was in order.

Thankfully, Rick had gone back to the garage. She slipped out the front door, but having no idea where Hannah kept the key, left the house unlocked.

The shift from air-conditioned coolness to summertime heat actually soothed her. She loved summer, when the days were long and hot and lazy, when the trees and lawns were green and the summer flowers bobbed in the breeze. Her fondest memories were of eating cold watermelon while sitting on her backyard swing or running through the sprinklers to cool off.

It was a decent walk down the driveway to the trail. Overhung with trees, the trail followed the road's many twists and turns. The village had long ago planted hedges between the street and the trail, separating the bikers, joggers, and hikers from the traffic on the road. Grace had no idea who maintained it, but she appreciated it. When they were kids, she and Hannah used to ride their bikes here. It was a tough road, with hills both high and low and some dicey turns to negotiate.

Grace wanted to laugh when she remembered she never rode the trail without getting at least a skinned knee or elbow. Of course, Hannah got her fair share, too, which proved it wasn't only Grace's jinxy nemesis Murphy—or ineptness.

"Lord, I don't know what to do," she murmured, surprised at how good it felt to say it aloud. "It's probably best Rick and I stay away from each other. I mean, everyone near me winds up collateral damage. Mom's health. Dad's relationship with the family... Even my brother and sister, who've always been jealous of my being so close to Mom. If only they tried harder..."

She paused. That wasn't fair. The problem was, in many ways, Grace raised them and they looked to her for help and encouragement. Mom couldn't do much for them. These days, Mom was virtually housebound, and although she did what she could, when her heart had had enough for the day, she had to lay low.

"I can't figure out the clumsy curse, though. I really don't, Lord. You know it's not like I try to knock things over. Or forget everything. And it's not Alzheimer's. Even though I'm too young for it, the doctor ran the tests for the gene anyway, and that's not the problem. I'm the Bad-Luck Queen, and I get distracted and forget stuff. Like baking powder in pancakes. And my driver's license. Hannah forgot her bathing suit, Rick wasn't supposed to be here, Maria arrived, and now, Damien…"

She threw her hands out to her sides. "Would they all be better off if you did let an airplane fall on top of me? Not that I want anyone on the plane to die, I just mean…"

She turned a corner and passed an open section in the hedge—which allowed traffic to access the driveway heading up the hill to her left—and paused when she saw a group of youths playing volleyball in the front yard. The house on this property sat closer to the road than the Flemings' cabin and not so high, and there were adults on a decking fronting the lawn. They were having a great time.

The kids were laughing and teasing each other as the ball flashed back and forth. Grace stood still, watching in fascination. Other than PE, she'd had little opportunity to play the game and didn't care for it. She had small wrists and the ball always seemed too heavy. Serving left blisters on her arms, which she hated, and playing team sports was unpredictable with her. In most cases, someone got hurt or her team lost, and it was usually her fault.

At that moment, someone spiked the ball and it flew toward her. Mouth ajar and eyes wide, she put out her hands and by some incredible sense of luck, caught it.

"Good catch!" one kid hollered. She jogged over to give it to him. "Thanks, lady," he said, making Grace smile.

He was probably Kyle's age, pimply-faced and sweaty, nearly a man himself, yet calling her "lady," like she was old. The boy tossed the ball back to the other side, where a tall young man, most likely nearer twenty, prepared to serve.

"Game point!" his teammates hollered, and Grace stood at the edge of the "court" transfixed.

The young man set up the serve, pulled his arm behind him, and swung. The ball whistled through the air and—

"Grace? Grace? Please, wake up, Gracie," Rick urged, praying she was okay.

"Hmm?" She stirred, blinking at him.

"Are you all right?" he asked, panicked.

"What?" she lifted her head and looked around at the wide-eyed group of people bent over her, then dropped back into the dirt. "Wow. What happened?"

"Sorry, lady," the young man who served the ball apologized. "It was an accident."

"It was?" she asked, confusion beetling her brows.

"You and the ball had a head-on collision," Rick explained. He helped her sit upright, worried about her pale skin and the tennis-ball-sized bruise on her forehead.

She blinked several times, brows squeezed together. "Did the volleyball survive?"

The silence was quickly followed by snorts of laughter.

"Ah, man, you're a good sport," one of the boys said.

The three girls in the group knelt down to pat her on the leg, and the youth's parents murmured they're own encouragement.

"Yeah, she is," Rick said, his heart warm with the realization. Grace would rather make light of the situation than embarrass the kids or make them feel any guiltier than they already did. "Can you stand? I brought the Escalade to drive you to the ER."

"I can stand, but no ER. I'm fine." She offered her hand, wincing when he squeezed the blister on her thumb.

"Sorry. Sorry," he said, wondering where it was safe to touch her. Her shoulder, her thumb, her knee, her head—and who knew what parts of her had hit the ground when the ball cold-cocked her. She offered the other hand and gingerly came to her feet, wobbling a little bit. He dusted her off and put an arm around her, not caring if she protested. He didn't want her to fall again.

"So, what's the prognosis?" she asked. "Do I have a chance?"

He laughed. "Knock it off, Evans. You're too dang cute right this minute."

She looked away, but not before he saw the left side of her mouth hitch up in amusement. "If I'm cute, you won't call 911. I can't afford an ambulance ride, so I'll do whatever I can to stay cute."

Again, he laughed, but right this minute he wanted to take advantage of her weakened state and kiss the daylights out of her. Maybe he should let her faint and do CPR. Mouth-to-mouth would be a lifesaving measure for his heart.

"Take it easy, lady," the teen boy said, waving at her before they drove away.

Grace smiled and returned the wave, then closed her eyes and leaned into the headrest as Rick backed out of the kids' driveway and headed to the cabin.

"So, how did you find me?" she asked.

Long story, he thought, *although things happened quickly.* "I went upstairs to find another repair book I brought with me, and when I found you gone, I got worried. You weren't in the backyard, which left only two places you'd likely have gone: the lake or the trail. I didn't see you on the pier, which left two more possibilities to consider: you'd fallen in the lake and drowned, or you were on the trail. I found the front door unlocked, which is a big no-no in Fleming-land, but it gave me the clue.

"I jogged along the trail, supposing you were headed for the small park at the south bend. You and Hannah loved going there as kids. I was shocked when I found you on the ground and those kids and their parents running over to see if you were breathing. When I arrived and told them I knew you, they let me take over. Your color wasn't too scary—well, it was awful, but you were breathing fine, and I didn't think anything was broken—but you wouldn't wake up. So I ran back for the car to take you to the hospital."

"Not going to a hospital," she repeated.

"How's the headache?"

"Who says I have a headache?"

"You were demolished by a volleyball, your head hit the ground, and you were passed out for at least five full minutes. You probably have a concussion, and considering you have your eyes closed against the sunlight, I'm pretty darn sure you have a headache."

"Wow, aren't you Sherlock Holmes!" she said, but she said it without snark.

"I hope not. He was a drug addict."

"No, he wasn't. You need to get your literature straight."

"I need to come around and get you, miss literature expert. I don't want you walking inside alone."

He guided her through the front door and to the nearest easy chair, but he insisted she not fall asleep. He went for the bottle of ibuprofen and a glass of water.

"My favorite friends," she muttered before gulping the pills. "You shouldn't leave home without them."

"Yeah. Except I think you would have been better off not going out alone."

Grace snorted. "My best friend is off weeping over her boyfriend, in case you forgot, so I didn't exactly have someone to walk with."

"You could at least have told me you were leaving and where you were going. You're lucky you hadn't gotten far before this happened. What if it had been a rabid dog or a bear or a perv?"

"Oh, give me a break, Fleming," Grace moaned. "I have a headache."

He burst into laughter, and her eyes popped open, swimming with tears but also filled with amusement.

"You're something else, Grace Evans," he said, unable to stop the warmth flooding his voice. She blushed, red and furious, and he knew she hadn't missed his meaning. "I'd be happy to walk and talk with you whenever you want to go out," he added.

She blinked hard and a tear dampened her cheek. "Very chivalrous of you. Right now, I'd prefer to rest for a while. And then I might take a shower. I think I have seven different kinds of dirt and gravel in my hair."

"And an eighth ground into your clothes."

"Great. No wonder you think I'm 'something else.' I probably look like road kill."

"But as my mom says, you're also wash-n-wear, so I wouldn't freak out about it."

Grace dared to chuckle but put a hand to her head with a soft gasp. "No jokes. No laughing. It hurts."

"Let me grab my laptop so I can do some work while I sit nearby. I won't bug you, but you can't fall asleep, and I want to help if you start feeling worse."

"I'm feeling better," she insisted. "But... I'd rather not be alone."

"You got it," he said, and he went for his computer.

When the ibuprofen kicked in and her headache backed off, Grace appreciated Rick's help upstairs to the bathroom door. The shower felt so fabulous she wanted to stay there all night.

She carefully washed her blistered shoulder and the handful of bruises on her forehead, but the back of her head, and her backside? Not so fun, particularly since the fall from the volleyball aggravated the pain in her back caused by Kooky Kathy. Add a blistered hand, and she grimaced at the thought of tackling buttons, snaps, and zippers. Her nightclothes came out instead, a pair of capri leggings and a sloppy T-shirt. Not particularly fashionable, but she didn't care.

Forget makeup. It was too close to bedtime anyway, and she figured Rick had already seen her at her worst. Her hair went into a wet ponytail, which was a mess because of her hand and shoulder. Leaning into the mirror, she groaned when she saw the bruise the volleyball imprinted on her forehead. The crisscross hatching of the seams looked like someone had stretched chicken wire over her head.

Lovely.

Rick winced at seeing how much the volleyball bruise had darkened. By tomorrow it would turn all the colors of the rainbow. He doubted Grace would be happy with that.

"You look better," he said, which anyone would—despite the bruising—after washing away the dirt and sand. He helped her sit gingerly on the closest couch.

"I could still pass for a zombie," she grumbled.

Rick cleared his throat against laughter. "Ah, come on. Give yourself a break. You've had a heck of a time since Friday."

"You think? It's been such a fabulous vacation so far, I can hardly wait to do it again next year." She stared at him for a minute and then broke into laughter herself. It jarred the headache and had her pushing her good hand against her temple again. "I should be grateful I haven't broken anything yet."

"Let's not go for 'yet.' Let's try for optimism. You're not going to break anything."

"Yeah, I think I'll stay safe here, in the loft, and let you wait on me for the rest of the week. Hopefully, the kids will drop by once in a while so I can report to Hannah and Aunt Sharon that they're still alive."

Rick looked at her aghast, a hand on his chest. "Can you stay away from a kitchen that long?"

Fighting a grin, she made a face—still a little pale but much improved. "Please don't tell anyone I'm an addict."

"I think it's why my aunt hired you."

"Oh, yeah. I guess you're right. I haven't gone longer than a day without cooking something since I was about five."

"Chocolate chip cookies?"

"Tollhouse, of course."

"You're killing me, Gracie. They're my favorite."

"I know. I used to make them for you and leave them at your house. I didn't care if you thought your mom or Hannah had made them. I just wanted to make you happy."

He sat next to her, careful not to touch her, his cheeks warming when she perused his face. Those gorgeous cornflower blue eyes seemed full of questions—then she glanced away, toward his laptop, sitting open but dark on the coffee table.

"What kind of work did you bring with you?"

"The totally boring kind. To most people anyway. I'm a computer geek for Uncle Luke. His company designs software, especially for big businesses, hospitals, that sort of thing. I'm only working on the business management end of my accounts this week."

"Really?" Her surprise came across as genuine—maybe even impressed. "Didn't you go to Berkley to become an architect?"

"Wow, you remembered. Scott and Sean didn't want to join Dad's firm, but I did. Over time, I found myself more and more drawn to the technology and less and less interested in architecture. Dad finally encouraged me to talk with Uncle Luke, and I decided to follow in his footsteps."

"Your poor dad. He must be disappointed."

"Nah. He's proud of us all. Scott surprised us and became a pilot. He works for Delta. And believe it or not, Sean's a physician's assistant."

Grace sat stunned, not able to imagine either of his two rowdy brothers doing something productive. He couldn't hold back more laughter.

"Yeah, I know you're thinking, but boys do grow up. At least most of us do. Scott's married, with a beautiful three-year-old daughter. My mom's suspicious Julia is pregnant again, and she's hoping for a grandson this time. Sean's engaged. Lisa is a nurse-midwife at Hazel Hawkins in San Jose."

"Wow," Grace said. "Your brothers are normal people."

"Actually, I think they're aliens in disguise, and the world should beware. What about me? Am I normal people?"

"Maybe, but you need help with your grammar. Do you work in San Jose?"

Rick grinned. "No. I work from my house. Uncle Luke has employees like me all over the country. Less overhead, a more relaxed environment, more flexibility. Makes for greater creativity."

Grace's smile faded into a solemn look. "Time goes so fast," she murmured. "I wish I'd realized the horrors of the school years wouldn't last forever." She snuggled back into the couch.

"Horrors? I loved school," he murmured, wishing he could snuggle up next to her.

"Yeah, you were a jock, class president, and voted one of the most popular guys in school in your senior year. You had a different take on things."

"You knew I was voted… Gee, I'm flattered."

Grace's cheeks reddened again. It made him want to kiss her. He always thought she kept an eye on him, but Hannah would never admit it.

"Is school better now?" he asked. He hoped so. He hated the idea Grace might still be struggling.

"In a way," she replied. "I'm doing an online class this summer, which is a reprieve. During the regular year, with my classes getting more and more difficult, the students are older, more responsible, and less likely to tease. Although I'm not too popular when Murphy messes with group assignments that affect other people's grades."

"I can imagine. You're not dating?"

She barked laughter. "You're kidding, right? *If* I had the time—a big if, considering my schedule—most of my peer group is married or living with someone. At this point, the drunken bum freshmen have been replaced by men either old enough to be my father or dead-set post-grads who consider everyone else in school an enemy on the bell curve for the A's. I do my best to keep my nose clean and to the grindstone."

Rick didn't know what possessed him, but he leaned close and examined the tip of her pert little nose.

"Mmm," he grumbled. "I'm not sure I see the grindstone callouses. Maybe this is one right there?" Then, with a fingertip, he stroked the side of her nose, amused when her breath left her and she stared at him in shock. With two fingers, he traced her delicate cheekbones, the skin soft and smooth. Of their own volition, three fingers laid against her cheek slid down to her jaw and lifted her chin. Her lips were moist and pink and far too inviting. She shivered as he leaned closer, his mouth brushing lightly against hers.

The front door flew open and banged shut, and they jumped apart, Grace wide-eyed like a scared rabbit, Rick breathing hard with stifled anticipation.

"Anybody here?" Kyle called. "Rick? Grace? There's no one in the garage, so I wondered..." His footsteps thundered up the stairs, but he wasn't alone. Two more sets of feet followed.

"Yeah, we're here," Rick responded, rising and distancing himself from Grace. He wanted to scream when he saw the betrayal on her face. She thought he didn't want to be seen with her. He shook his head slightly and murmured, "Sorry, Grace. It's best I set an example for Kyle, which means I really shouldn't be here alone with you. Church dating standards, you know?"

She didn't seem entirely convinced, but Rick felt fairly certain she did look relieved.

"Hey, what's up?" Rick asked Kyle when he, Jeff, and Ethan reached the top of the stairs.

Grace managed to twist around on the couch to see the boys. A part of her resented Rick for pulling away, but seeing the suspicion on Kyle's face changed her mind. Especially since it wasn't the expression of a young man wondering what his cousin and his sister's best friend were doing; it was the gleam of a young man who was dying to tease them about it.

The knowing smile disappeared when he got a good look at her. "Uh, what happened to you?"

The bruise on Grace's forehead suddenly felt like a giant, ugly postage stamp.

"Grace had an accident," Rick interjected. "She went for a walk, and the neighbors down the street spiked a volleyball right in her face and knocked her out. She might have a mild concussion."

"Are you kidding? That sucks," Kyle said. He glanced at Rick. "I guess Rick's taking care of you, huh?"

"He is," Grace said, hoping her cheeks hadn't lit on fire again. "Ice packs, glasses of water, keeping me awake so I don't slip into a coma, that sort of thing. Are you guys running off, or do you want to play here for a while?" She hoped not.

"No, no, we're leaving," Kyle said, to her relief. "We've been on Xbox at Ethan's place, but I forgot to bring my *Rocket League* game with me."

Rick's brows twisted with skepticism. "It took all three of you to come after it?"

"Oh, no, man. Ethan's dad gave us his car and some money to pick out some ice cream in town. Any word on Damien?"

"No," Grace and Rick said at the same time.

"Hope he's okay." Kyle glanced at Grace again, making her blush in discomfort. "You, too," he said to Grace, before heading off to collect his game.

"Grace, do you know Ethan and Jeff?" Rick asked.

"I've met them a few times at your folks' place when Kyle and the twins were visiting. Hi, boys. How are you?"

Jeff was tall and blond, Matt short and dark, but both were lean, like Kyle. Seeing her struggling to get off the way-too-cushy couch, Rick reached a hand out to help her, taking care to avoid her blisters and bruises. She extended her hand and the boys gave awkward handshakes.

"Do you need anything from town?" Kyle asked when he returned.

Grace was charmed by his gracious offer. "No, I'm fine. Thank you for asking. You boys have fun."

"We will," all three said, and then in a rumble of descending footsteps and another slam of the door, they were gone.

Rick stood far enough away to not "accidentally" bump into Grace. He searched her face, and she wondered what he was thinking.

"So, was that a close call, or Murphy's accidental rescue plan?" he asked, one corner of his mouth twitching in amusement.

Grace tipped her head in confusion. Rick took a tiny step closer, close enough she could feel the heat from his arms. She didn't realize a lock of hair had worked its way loose from her ponytail until he gently slipped it behind her ear, leaving her tingling.

"We almost got caught. Close call? Or did you wish them here to rescue you from me?" The amusement in the green depths of his eyes glittered.

"I... I didn't know I needed rescuing," she murmured, hardly able to speak for lack of breath.

"The last time it happened, Sean ruined everything," he said, now so close she had to look up at him. "I wish I'd..." He left the rest hanging, abandoning Grace to her imagination—which became reality when he cradled her face between the palms of his hands and bent down to press his lips to hers. Sweet and tender, it felt better than she'd ever imagined, so wonderful it nearly took her knees out from under her.

Rick drew her against his rock-hard chest, Grace's heart thundering inside her own. Her headache was nearly gone, but maybe the accident had addled her brain. What else would make her feel faint like this?

Or maybe it came from what she could only describe as pure pleasure? From having Rick thread his fingers into the hair at the nape of her neck and lift her face to his. From having him kiss her again, long and slow and frightfully delicious. The power of it overwhelmed her to the point she could barely open her eyes to catch his adoring gaze. It overwhelmed her with the need to return the kiss.

She wove her own fingers into his hair and leaned into him, tingling from head to toe at his soft gasp of pleasure.

"You're so beautiful, Grace," he whispered in her ear. "I've wanted to do this for a long, long time."

His lips captured hers again, the kiss deepening, the power of it taking Grace to places she'd only read about in books. Tingling heat spun through her, burning her cheeks, racing down her spine to her toes and rushing back, only to settle somewhere deep in her core. She wanted him more than she'd wanted anything in her entire life.

She slipped her hands under his shirt and against the warm skin and firm muscles of his back—then gasped when Rick pushed back from her and grabbed her wrists. She flinched at his grasp on the blistered hand.

"Sorry," he said, letting go while shaking his head. His chestnut mane had somehow gotten even more mussed than usual, and he ran his fingers through it, trying to tame it. His breaths were ragged, but the pleasure was gone from his face.

"Yeah, me, too," she said, taking another step back. "Don't want to make a big deal out if it, right?" It was tons easier on him and less embarrassing for her to give him an easy way out.

"No, Grace, that's not it, not at all. Please." He drew her into his arms and kissed the top of her head. The affection felt different, tempered, gentle. She had no idea what it meant. She only knew her heart was well on its way to its demise. It couldn't survive Rick Fleming one more time.

"Surely Hannah explained our church dating guidelines, right?" His voice rumbled in his chest. "She dated a lot in high school."

Grace shrugged. "Sort of. I mean, mostly she said her dates were none of my business. Until she met Damien. She was never head-over-heels with anybody until him, and she's still pretty private about their relationship, because...." She paused, finding two plus two did make four. "Oh. Okay, I get it."

"What?"

She leaned back to meet his gaze. "They belong to a 'wait-'til-you-get-married' group. That's what you mean, right?"

Rick gave her a lopsided smile. "Yeah, something like that. Only it isn't only about waiting for marriage—it's about avoiding the edge of the cliff. Temptation can trounce the best of us. And I want better for you. I mean it. You deserve it."

Grace wasn't sure how to feel about what he said. She'd grown so used to disappointment, she feared it was just an excuse.

Rick seemed reluctant when he let her go. "How are you feeling?"

"Better."

"It's still too soon for you to go to sleep." He gave her a sheepish grin. "And I refuse to leave you alone. If we're going to hang out together, we need a distraction. Like a movie or a game?"

"No games with you, Fleming. A movie will have to do." In fact, it felt amazing as they settled on the couch and Rick held her good hand in his, and she allowed herself to lean into him. Over the years, she'd had very few dates that progressed to this point and none like this. None like Richard Fleming.

She prayed it would do nothing but get better from here.

CHAPTER 12

Hannah called near the end of the movie. She'd arrived at the hospital and gathered as much information as she could but hadn't seen Damien yet. His parents were there, hugging Hannah and desperately anxious to get news from the doctors. She promised to call back and keep Grace updated, day or night.

Afterward, Grace was no longer into the movie and neither was Rick.

"How would you feel about praying together for Damien and Hannah before we settle down for the night?" Rick asked, searching her face.

Grace agreed but asked him to offer the prayer. She didn't feel competent enough yet. She enjoyed kneeling beside him in front of the couch and hearing the love in his voice as he begged the Lord to strengthen Hannah and everyone taking care of Damien and who loved him, and if it was His will, to heal him.

Rick offered a hand to pull Grace to her feet, his other hand cupping her cheek. He stroked it with a thumb, then bent to give her a kiss that tumbled her heart several times without setting off too many sparks.

"If you need me, don't hesitate to call," he said. "And I want to know about Damien the minute you hear anything."

Grace nodded good night, padded off to her room, closed the door behind her and crawled into bed. Lights off, she lay there for what seemed forever, reliving Rick's kisses and wondering when she would wake up from the dream and find it never happened.

At some point, the exhaustion closed in on her and she drifted off to sleep.

The night grew end-of-June hot, and Grace's worries about Hannah and Damien and everything happening with Rick made her sleep restless. Her phone hollering, *"Grace, pick up the phone! Grace, pick up the phone!"* all but threw her out of bed.

"Hello?" she mumbled, not sure which body part ached the worst.

"It's me," Hannah said. She sounded tearful.

"Hannah," Grace said, throwing her legs over the side of the bed and sitting up. "How is he?"

"It's bad," Hannah admitted. "He's got several broken bones, but he also has head injuries, and they've put him into a medically induced coma to allow his brain to heal. I'm so scared."

"But what do the doctors say about his prognosis?"

Sniffling and nose-blowing were followed by Hannah catching her breath. "We have to wait and see, but the neurologist said he's seen worse accidents and full recoveries, so there's hope. I thought I'd die when they let me visit for a few minutes. He's in traction and bandaged like a mummy. I didn't even recognize him. His face is so bruised and swollen…" Hannah broke into tears.

"It's okay, Hannah. It's going to be okay." Grace needed to believe it like Hannah did. But what if it wasn't? What if he died? Or worse? What if he lived through it and remained in a vegetative state for the rest of his life? Damien was smart as a whip. Nothing would be worse for him or his family, for anyone, than ending up brain-damaged and in a wheelchair.

"Pray for him, will you?" Hannah begged. She always encouraged Grace to pray, and for once, Grace was glad.

"I already have. More than once. Last night, Rick and I prayed for him together."

"You did?" The astonishment in Hannah's voice made Grace smile. "Oh, Grace, how wonderful. You guys are getting along?"

How much should Grace tell her? It felt wrong to share her precious moments with her best friend right now. "We're okay," she admitted, forcing herself not to make a big deal out of it. "Missing you, you know, and worried about Damien. We did let the kids stay overnight with their friends. It was just too, well, depressing to make them hang around."

"Oh. So, you and Rick are there alone."

Grace wanted to laugh, despite the circumstances. "Yes, Mother Hannah. And we're fine. Rick and I aren't dating, you know."

"Uh, yeah, right, of course," Hannah replied, but there was hesitation—maybe even worry—in her voice.

"What time is it?" Grace asked, wanting to know, but also wanting to change the subject.

"Five o'clock."

"Monday morning?" She didn't realize she'd slept that long.

"Yeah. I just reached my folks' place. I desperately need to sleep, clean up, and head back to the hospital."

They talked for a few more minutes, and after their goodbyes, Grace pried herself out of bed. She agreed to let Rick know about Damien as soon as she heard, but she wasn't going near him without getting dressed and doing something with her hair. After that, she needed breakfast and a coffee.

She tapped lightly on Rick's door as soon as she could face him, hideous bruises and all. He was already dressed when he pulled the door open, his face tight with worry. She relayed the information, seeing his relief when he understood Damien had at least survived the night.

They went downstairs together, and when Grace set about making herself some cereal and toast, Rick did the same.

"The kids will come home this morning," he commented, stirring creamer into his coffee. "But bad news gets in the way of their fun."

Grace sighed in understanding. "Yeah, I remember those feelings when I was a kid. Mom's heart problems terrified me, but when I got used to the idea it wasn't going to go away and she also wasn't going to die in the near future, it was… inconvenient. I also felt guilty for it, but…"

"Like I said, kids can't handle things maturely."

She smiled, loving the way he encouraged her to forgive herself. "So, what do we do with them if—when—they do come back?"

Rick shrugged. "You guys had plans, right? Weren't you taking the boat out for the day?"

"Uh, yeah. No," Grace said, shaking her head. "We were, but Hannah drives the boat, not me. I wouldn't even consider it."

Rick laughed. "It's not hard to drive. In a lot of ways, it's simpler than driving a car."

"Yeah, but in a lot of ways, it's not. Other boats on the lake going every which way, people in the lake, no lines on the road, and I tried and failed to park it a few times."

"Park it? You don't park a boat, you dock it."

"Yeah, well, I tried to run the boat over and through the dock. Not doing it again."

He laughed again. "Point taken. Okay, for now, I have a car to work on, but if the brats come back and want to go out, I'm available. Just remember, the less time I spend with the car, the longer I'm hanging around this place."

Grace rolled her eyes, not yet willing to concede she didn't want him to leave but frantic at the idea he would.

Kyle and his friends showed up first, bounding with enthusiasm. Kyle asked how Damien was doing, but then the boys rushed around filling the cooler with ice and sodas, inflating flotation devices, collecting fishing equipment, and getting it all to the boat. The girls came soon after, also concerned about Damien but insisting on helping Grace pack their lunches in the chest. Kyle begged to drive, insisting they didn't need Rick, but Grace gave him an it's-not-happening look before reminding them all to put on their lifejackets. Once everyone was ready, she summoned Rick.

"Ah, darn," Rick said to Grace when he arrived, his eyes glittering with mirth. "I was finally making some progress. You're sure you don't want to drive? I could stay here and work on my car."

"The boat remains tied to the dock until you put on your life jacket and take over the wheel," she replied with a smirk. "No Rick, no boat."

The lake was serene, the water as still and shiny as glass. Overhead, a lone eagle watched their progress as they navigated from one fishing spot to another, having no luck. Grace actually loved to fish, as long as she didn't skewer herself with the hooks. She didn't even care about catching anything. The hours of serenity and an excuse to read a book made the morning beyond pleasant.

She had a few nibbles later in the morning, more than anyone else did, but nothing more. She didn't mind. Today, she was doing all of this with Rick nearby. He was even there to help her when the wake from a passing speedboat almost tossed her into the lake.

Near lunchtime, Rick drove them to a shallow inlet where ski boats and serious fishermen normally didn't go. Basically a huge swimming hole, the inlet had a wide beach on the south side perfect for sunbathing. Smaller boats had already dropped anchor, with several families on shore enjoying the serenity. Surrounding wooded areas provided picnic tables, and the pleasant smell of food cooking on barbecues permeated the air.

Kyle helped Rick anchor the boat close to shore, and the three teen boys stripped to their swim trunks. They insisted on muscling the ice chest to the beach and claimed a picnic table in the shade where the group enjoyed their lunch and rested for a while. Starting to feel the aftermath of the last few days, Grace took another dose of medication.

Kyle was first to head into the water, the girls on his heels, and Ethan and Jeff hooted and raced after them, their splashes sending water sky high.

Rick rose to join them, leaving Grace weak-kneed at the sight of his six-pack and well-tanned torso. "Come on, Grace," he encouraged her. "It's too dang hot to sit here and watch the water go by."

She grinned her agreement then gasped at how cold the water felt as she walked in. At least it was a break from the heat. Once she got used to it, she closed her eyes, lay back, and floated on the surface, acting as if she was really on vacation.

"Kyle's back on the boat for the flotation gear," Rick said a little later, dog-paddling toward her. "I think one of the chaise lounges has my name on it. What about you?"

She nodded, and Rick asked Kyle to toss two of them over. Before Grace knew it, she and Rick were basking side by side on the lounges. Not sure if Rick cared about the kids discovering their newfound relationship—whatever it was—Grace smiled when Rick threaded his fingers through hers to keep them from drifting apart. So many feelings rampaged inside her, she struggled to get them in order. She felt sick for Hannah and Damien, but there was nothing she could do for them. It was a beautiful day, a beautiful place. And it was a beautiful moment with a beautiful hunk-of-a-man holding her hand. It was simple and quiet and good.

Before she knew it, the intoxicating warmth, the lapping water, the distant sound of people having fun, a stomach full of food, and ibuprofen-induced pain relief—on top of the early morning wake-up call from Hannah—lulled her into dreamland.

Grace's eyes popped open. The sun, a scorching ball of fire, hovered above her. She lifted her head and looked around, seeing the kids climbing onto the boat and jumping off again, cannonball-style. They were having way too much fun.

And Rick was as sound asleep as she'd been.

"Uhm, Rick?" Grace said, prying her hand loose from his. Her fingers had gone to sleep, and she had to work to get the feeling back into them. "Rick?"

"Yeah, yeah, what? What the heck?" He dropped his legs to either side of his lounge and sat up. Sleep still clung to his gorgeous eyes, and his hair stood straight up on the left side.

It made Grace laugh.

"What's so funny?"

She laughed again. "Love your new hairdo."

His hand found the outer-space creation, and before he could blush, he rolled off the lounge. The ice-cold splash sprayed Grace and made her gasp. Oops. She was sunburned. Oh, great, add that to the list of injuries. She never did believe sunscreen worked, and this proved it. She put on enough sunscreen to butter toast, but it hadn't done her a bit of good.

Abruptly, the lounge pulled out from under her, and gasping, Grace managed to suck half the lake into her lungs as she went under the water. She surfaced fighting for breath, arms pell-mell as she thrashed about like a two-year-old in a bathtub. Coughing and retching, she wished being embarrassed by vomiting in the lake was all she had to worry about.

Next thing Grace knew, Rick grabbed her from behind and squished her enough she was sure he'd ruptured her spleen. A mouthful of water gushed from her lungs and, thank you, Lord, precious oxygen took its place.

"Sorry, Grace. I didn't mean to drown you," Rick said, turning her around and letting her float face-to-face with him as she coughed and coughed. "I was just goofing off," he admitted, panic on his face.

"Yeah, I know you Flemings." *Cough, cough.* "You love to live dangerously and…" *Cough, cough.* "…assume the rest of the world…" *Cough.* "…can keep up with you.*" Cough, cough.*

He chuckled and then pressed a kiss to her brow. "Probably truer than I want to admit. Are you okay?"

She coughed again. "Yeah, I think so."

"Can you climb back on your lounge? I'll tow us back to the boat."

Grace's face blazed when she saw the kids all whispering and elbowing each other as Rick grabbed the cords connected to the front of both lounges and dragged them toward the pontoon. Grace's nearly drowning and Rick kissing her on the forehead hadn't escaped their attention.

Cherise and Charlotte helped pull the lounges in, and Grace managed to haul herself up the ladder and into the boat. It wasn't easy. The blisters and sunburn plagued her every inch of the way.

"Oh, man, Gracie," Charlotte said, her face scrunched with concern. "You're burnt to a crisp."

Grace replied between more coughs, "Yeah, I noticed. Where's the aloe burn gel?"

Cherise retrieved it from the back of the boat and helped Grace apply it, although Grace wouldn't let her even close to the snap-back blisters from the broken bowstring. Touching it felt miserable even when she applied it herself.

Rick said. "Kids, we've all had enough sun for the day, and we need to take Grace home. She's had a rough few days and the sunburn isn't good."

They understood but still took their time going to shore for the ice chest and their other belongings. Grace sighed then turned around and ran right into Rick. He grabbed her arms then leaned down and kissed her sweetly.

Gasping for breath, she coughed again. "What was that for?" Not that she didn't like it, she just hadn't expected it.

He grinned wide. "I missed the opportunity to use mouth-to-mouth on you during both the volleyball fiasco and the near-drowning incident here. Thought maybe you could use it now. Come sit in the shade. I'll bring you something to drink."

Grace settled on a seat under the boat's Bimini top, and when the boys delivered the ice chest, Rick snagged her an ice-cold Dr Pepper, her favorite. She savored the fizzy sweetness and the pleasure of feeling safe.

Rick fished out his own drink and pressed its coolness to one cheek. The other hand dangled at his side, and Grace got a good look at the ugly scars that stretched across the palm of it, evidence of a night gone awry, of a conflict between two brothers... because of her, and her heart sank.

"Oh, my gosh," she murmured, taking that hand in hers and then asking to see the other one. "I didn't really look at these scars before. I'm so sorry, Rick. This is my fault. I wish I'd handled things differently that night."

He gave her a weak smile. "We all do. Especially Sean. He really muffed it."

Grace paused, tipping her head to the side. He was going to blame Sean again? Sean was wrong, of course, but Rick still didn't seem to recognize his part in it. Too many times over the last few days he blamed the disaster between him and Grace on his brother. Didn't he think he needed to make his own amends?

"He wasn't alone in the process," she pointed out. "I jumped to conclusions, and Sean did goad us, but you were mostly avoiding him. Don't you think you should have been more, well, proactive?"

Rick's eyes narrowed. He clearly didn't like what she suggested. "Sure, but none of it would have been necessary if he hadn't started everything, or better yet, not forgotten his hat."

Grace felt a chill trail its way down her spine, and not the romantic variety. "But what about the next day or the next week, or whenever there was another confrontation? When would it have ended? Would you ever have been willing to stand up for me?"

Rick's expression darkened. "It didn't cross my mind at the time. All-out war put me in the emergency room and gave Sean a major attitude adjustment. By then, I'd blown it with you, and I've had a hard time forgiving him for it."

Grace turned to watch the kids bring the last of their things to the boat. "Funny. Sean made me furious, but all these years, it's you I've had the hardest time forgiving."

The silence between them drew her gaze back to Rick's. The hurt on his face was unmistakable. He didn't know what to say. Despite his having apologized a few days ago, Grace didn't think it was completely sincere.

"Wow, Gracie, you look like a lobster," Kyle said as he came aboard.

"One that's been tossed on the barbie," she quipped, although her heart wasn't in it. She wondered if sunburned welts could turn into cancer. With Grace? Probably sooner than later.

"Man, you need to get home and out of the sun. Can I drive?" Kyle asked Rick.

"Uhm, no, I'll drive," Rick replied. "You do great in the open, but you're still a bit rough at docking."

"I can't get better without practice," Kyle insisted, irritated.

"It's not a good time, Kyle. How about the next time we go out?"

Kyle blew out a breath of exasperation and joined his friends at the rear of the boat. They dried themselves off while Kyle shot Rick resentful looks. It appeared he wanted to show off in front of his friends. Worse yet, he'd been told no in front of them.

The twins sat on either side of Grace, Charlotte daring to pat one of Grace's hands. "I'm so sorry. Bad things happen to you all the time, don't they? I don't get it."

Grace grinned and pointed at Charlotte's reddened shoulders. "I'm not alone, dear heart. You're burned, too."

Charlotte and Cherise immediately jumped into comparing notes on their own burns. Instead of sounding upset about it, they extolled the virtues of turning burns into tans. Grace wondered if youth was just born blind and dumb, or whether it just happened during the teen years. Maybe neither girl would be cursed with skin cancer, but why were they excited about taking the chance?

Grace was more than glad to return to the cabin. By the time they put everything away and showered, they were hungry enough Rick offered to throw an early dinner together.

"We've got tons of leftovers, Grace," he said in a neutral tone. "And the kids can help me. You need a break." He cast a suggestive look at teens, who nodded their willingness, worried about Grace and excited about the tacos they'd missed the night before.

Grace wouldn't argue. She was worn out and downright miserable. This time she downed two extra-strength acetaminophens, thinking she must be one step away from becoming a drug addict. The burn gel after her shower and the softest clothes she owned helped her settle onto one of the chaise lounges on the patio to await their meal.

The girls begged to have their friends spend the night with them, but Rick politely refused. It would be too hard on Grace. He did, however, give them permission to go to either Rachel or Skylar's house. Kyle and Jeff already planned to go to Ethan's for the night.

They'd only just cleaned up after dinner when Grace's *"Pick up the Phone"* ringtone for Hannah started squawking again. Grace grabbed it and stepped back outside to take the call in private.

"He's still the same," Hannah reported, her tone filled with fatigue and fear. "The nurses don't seem worried. They said it's all part of the healing process, but he looks dead. It's destroying me, Grace."

"I'm so sorry. Rick said he'd watch the kids. I'll take the SUV and be with you in just a few hours," Grace said, hoping that with all the stress Hannah would forget she didn't have her driver's license.

"No," Hannah insisted. "You can't do anything here, and my brother would let the kids get away with too much. Mom called Aunt Sharon, so she knows what's going on, and Sharon said she's tremendously grateful you're staying and keeping everything together. She told Mom she'll pay you twice what she planned to pay."

"That's not necessary, Hannah. I..." She knew Hannah wanted Grace to hang around Rick and hopefully work things out, but Grace didn't even want to think about that right now. "I can't help wondering what happens if the situation with Damien…. I mean, the kids and I should go home if…."

Hannah struggled with tears as she said, "If the worst happens, like… I have to go to Damien's funeral, Aunt Sharon and Uncle Luke will come home. If not for you being there, they already would have."

Another sigh, another link chaining Grace to the cabin and Rick. "Okay. Give everyone my love and call again soon."

Grace, returning to the kitchen, discovered the kids determined to tackle another game of Monopoly before heading their different ways. Exasperated and sore, she excused herself and went to bed early.

Rick wanted to stop Grace and talk to her. Her earlier comments upset him, and he wanted to set her straight. If it weren't for the exhaustion on her face and the pain he knew she was in, he'd have confronted her.

When he had time to think, however, he knew it was better to let it go. Her criticism had cut him to the quick, and he wanted to argue with her about it, but words from his youth pastor from years ago stopped him.

"If you need to argue your point, you've already lost your battle," he told the teens. "The Devil loves an argument, and arguing leads to more and more serious conflict, maybe even permanent injury to a relationship or worse. The truth wins the day every time. Let it be your guide."

But Grace couldn't have been the bearer of truth. How could she? She wasn't there during the fight. She had no idea how hard he'd fought for her. She had no right to judge him.

He huffed and headed into the house. The kids would have more fun playing their game without him hanging around. He needed his rest, too, if he wanted to have a clear mind when he faced Grace in the morning. He only wondered what he would say to her that could make any difference.

CHAPTER 13

Morning came and Grace, needing more than ever to work out the aches and pains, determined to take another walk. The possibility of getting hit by a volleyball on the path today seemed highly unlikely. She slathered on more sunscreen, grabbed a water bottle and her cell phone, left a note on the kitchen counter for Rick, and popped her earbuds in before heading out the door.

She wasn't on the road two minutes before her mother called.

"Gracie!" Mom cried, chipper this morning. "How's the vacation going?"

Grace paused, a lump gathering in her throat. She wasn't ready to tell her mom the details, but she needed a listening ear. She did her best not to cry as she talked about Damien, but her mother's own grief and tenderness made the tears flow.

"Oh, sweetie, you should have called me. I could at least be a listening ear. I wish I could do more. If I could, I'd be happy to take over a handful of teenagers so you could go be with Hannah."

"I know, Mom," Grace replied, wiping her face. Her mother had never really handled teenagers. That had been Grace's job, to the point she hadn't been a real teenager in her own right.

She passed the house where the volleyball attacked her, noticing there was no sign of the spheroid monster anywhere. The house was quiet, as if no one was awake yet.

"It's okay, Mom. No one can help Damien right now except his doctors and nurses. And maybe God. The best I can do is pray for him, you know."

"Yeah. I'll do that, too, honey. I'm glad Hannah encouraged you to lean on God. I should have prayed more when you were younger."

Grace didn't comment. She knew her mother had a bitter place in her heart for being dealt such a difficult hand. Her dad was even worse, but he softened as he grew older and got to know Hannah better. Hannah had that effect on people.

"It's fine, Mom. I know how you feel. I have moments when I want to yell at God." She described what she'd gone through the last two days, worried about her mom's reaction. "I'm okay. Really. I feel good today." Or at least her breakfast of toast, juice and acetaminophen had made her feel better. "Please don't get upset. It's hard on you. I just wanted to forewarn you before I came home with a few bruises."

Grace's mom paused and then laughed. "I don't know what I'd do if you came home without bruises. You always have bruises."

They changed the subject to Chloe and Danny and how they were doing. Things were going well for them. They were always busy and had both found "friends" who seemed to be more serious than friends.

After Grace ended the call, she allowed herself to enjoy her hike. With the Fleming teens gone, she didn't need to rush back. They might want to carry on with their plans today, but she wouldn't mind if they didn't. More time at the lake held no appeal.

Tomorrow was different. They were supposed to head into town and spend the afternoon and evening there, maybe even have dinner out. She needed a break from the cabin.

And she didn't want to be alone with Rick.

She found more homework assignments waiting for her when she returned, did some housework, and Rick stayed scarce. The clanging in the garage sounded serious.

Teens being teens, they took advantage of the situation to announce they were staying with their friends again. Grace reminded them that asking for permission was appropriate, and the requests came with a bit of annoyance. At least all three of the kids asked about Damien.

Hannah's phone calls throughout the day and into the night gave no new hope.

Wednesday promised to be hotter still. Grace took a long walk just after dawn and found it good to stretch her legs. When she returned to the cabin, all four girls had arrived. They hung out in the twins' room and listened to music and painted fingernails and toenails and gossiped about everyone they knew. That left Grace to tackle more homework and nod at Kyle as he and his friends bounced through the kitchen, laughing and roughhousing, on their way to the racquetball court downstairs.

Rick came inside to wash up and rummage through the fridge. She watched him as he guzzled a bottle of iced tea.

"So, are we going into town this afternoon?" he finally asked, seeming a little hesitant.

Grace felt her belly tighten. "That was the original plan. The girls' friends are here, and Kyle's downstairs with his."

Rick shrugged. "So let's do it after lunch, enjoy a little sightseeing on Main Street, go bowling. I'll take you all to dinner tonight."

"Are you sure? That's two nights in a row I won't be cooking. Isn't it a violation of my contract? Besides, even if I were in shape to do it, I don't bowl. I'd probably break something with the ball. And I'm not able to afford to eat out a lot. Nice idea, though."

Rick fought with a wry smile. "It was an invitation. Perhaps you've forgotten what one sounds like? You are not paying for dinner. I am."

"Oh." Grace tried not to laugh while also struggling with surprise. Would it be appropriate under the circumstances for her to accept?

Rick went to the living room and shouted upstairs. "Girls!!!" Cherise sauntered to the edge of the loft to glower down at him. "You guys still want to go into town? Bowling? Dinner?"

The girl's face brightened. "Sure. Can Rachel and Skylar come?"

Rick made a face only Grace could see. No doubt he wondered if these girls were capable of functioning without each other. "Check with their folks," he told her. He grabbed his phone and called Kyle, who had the audacity to refuse to join them. He and the boys were helping Ethan's dad work on his 1978 Jaguar.

"Man, I'm jealous," Rick grumbled, after telling Kyle he was on his own for dinner.

"Me, too," Grace said, itching to tease Richard Fleming for a change.

"What?"

"It would be lots more fun to take apart a Jaguar transmission than go to town," she said, which broke Rick's stiff expression and made him smile.

"You don't like to bowl, huh?"

"Uh, no. I'm along for the ride."

"Why don't you like it?"

Her eyes widened with her best you've-got-to-be-kidding look. "Me? I'm growing a new crop of sunburn blisters, I'm stiff as a board, and my bruises have bruises. Besides, I rarely set foot in a bowling alley." After all, the cost was bad enough, but who in their right mind would suggest letting Grace Without Grace throw around a ten-pound bowling ball?

"I'm not worried," Rick said. "You have to help me tonight. I can't handle four teenage girls by myself."

"Keep score for them while they play," she suggested, hoping he'd drop it.

"Nope. I won't survive it without you," he muttered, his cheeks darkening when she gave him a double take. He cleared his throat. "Come on, Evans, be a good sport. Your right hand still works and bowling won't hurt a sunburn."

Grace was terrified of humiliating herself in a bowling alley, but how did she refuse a guy who sounded a bit desperate? Was he really afraid of dealing with the girls? Or was he trying to hint he wanted to be with her?

She didn't have the heart to say no, but she dreaded the entire affair.

Making the brief trek to town, they did their sightseeing and revisited the village's small museum and historical sites. It seemed the Flemings never tired of them. At the small-scale six-lane bowling alley, Grace allowed herself to be put through the torture of checking out shoes and choosing the bowling ball that would probably kill someone.

"This is a terrible idea," she muttered when it was her turn to bowl.

"I'll help if you need it," Rick promised. "You can't enjoy life by avoiding life, you know."

Famous last words. Grace could tell he regretted them when she kept forgetting to let go of the ball and threw it into the air like a softball—not once, not twice, but enough times the alley manager finally asked her to either stop doing it or leave. Then she dropped the ball on Rick's foot and had him yelping and hopping around, moaning in agony—while the girls howled with laughter. Amazingly enough, she finally managed to knock down a few pins on several frames, which gave her some impossible spares, and she even got applause when she threw the last ball so hard it bounced into the alley next to theirs and knocked over half the pins on the other side.

"I'm so glad that's over," she said, handing in her rental shoes and dusting off her hands.

"Yeah, me, too," Rick muttered, making her laugh.

"See? I told you. I suck."

He squeezed his eyes shut and shook his head. "You don't suck. You're just… kind of crazy. You need to slow down, take your time. And practice. Practice makes perfect."

"Yeah, well, I don't have the money or the time," she snapped, wincing at how harsh she sounded. "Sorry. I mean, I'm drowning in student loans, you know, and living in expensive San Jose. It's hard enough to budget what I can't live without. I'm sure as heck not spending money on something I don't even like. Besides, the next alley manager might have me arrested for reckless endangerment."

Rick laughed. "You may have a point. I'm sure this one is posting your picture near the door as a warning to others." This time, Grace laughed, able to enjoy the teasing since she was in on it.

"Okay, girls, are we ready for dinner?" Rick asked the twins and their friends. Rachel hung up her phone.

"My dad's picking me and Skylar up," she said. "We're going back to our house to swim before dinner. Can Charlotte and Cherise come with us? Please?"

"Please?" the twins asked in unison, bubbling with excitement.

Grace watched with dismay as Rick weighed his answer. Finally acquiescing, he gave the house key to Charlotte. "Grab your bathing suits, towels, and sunscreen, lock the door when you leave, and hide the key in the usual place. We'll talk later about tonight's plans, okay? No leaving Rachel's place without permission."

"You're such a cool cousin," Cherise said, giving him a punch on the shoulder.

"We have to wait for Dad in front of the sheriff station," Rachel said to Cherise as they ran off with the other girls.

"You don't mind, do you?" Rick asked.

Grace sighed. "No, but maybe we should go back to the cabin. You can work on your car and I can cook."

"Nope. I invited you to dinner." He paused, pointing out the small, one-screen theater on the other side of Main Street. "And later we could catch the movie. I haven't gone to a theater in the middle of the week in years and I'd rather not go stag."

Grace had gone with hardly anyone but Hannah in years. The idea made her stomach flutter, and not in a totally good way.

"You don't mind it's an older flick, do you?" he asked. "The village isn't exactly on the current-movie track. At least they have hit movies when they do get them."

"I guess that's okay."

They did some more window shopping on their way to The Hungry Bass, where Rick planned to go to dinner. Grace admired a few of the adorable glass figurines in one shop, but she refused to buy any of them and wouldn't let Rick do it, either.

"I don't own things like this for a reason," she insisted. "They won't survive me."

Ahead, under the sign beckoning people to BJ's Grill, Grace saw a familiar figure turn right into its entryway. She paused, wondering if Rick saw her. One look at his face and she knew he had. He gave Grace a double-take, his eyes wide.

"I don't know why Maria would hang around here all alone."

"Me, neither," Grace said, feeling sorry for the woman. And still jealous. She kept her eyes averted as they approached The Hungry Bass, not wanting Rick to know how she felt.

The owner of the restaurant had done a recent remodel, and Grace enjoyed seeing the atmosphere transformed from a cheap diner to a nice restaurant.

The change in air flow from the air-conditioning slammed the door tight behind Grace when they entered, the cool air feeling wonderful on her sunburn. The hostess, an older but thin, swarthy woman, grabbed menus and headed toward a table at the back of the restaurant. Grace went to follow, but after only two steps, her shirt jerked her to a halt. She heard and felt it tear. It was her second favorite top, next to the peach one she soaked in the faucet at church on Sunday, and its long, flaring hem had been begging to get caught in the door. Grace felt stupid at finding herself held so tight she couldn't reach the door to open it without tearing the top worse than it already was. She was stuck there, like a dog on a short leash.

"Oops," Rick said, coming to help. He set her free, but she leaned away from him to inspect what turned out to be a vertical rip near the bottom edge of the hem on the right side, thankfully near the seam.

"You okay?" he asked.

"Absolutely fantastic," she said with exasperation.

Rick cringed when she showed him the damage.

"I'm so sorry," the hostess said, coming to assess the problem.

"I have a sewing kit in my purse," Grace said. "I'll pin it for now."

She held the top together on the way to their spot, amazed to sit at a table actually sporting a tablecloth and cloth napkins. She made quick work of pinning the seam, mumbling to herself: "Tacky, Murphy, tacky."

The menu made up for it, and Grace picked a thick, juicy steak, telling Rick she insisted on paying for it so she wouldn't feel guilty. He grumbled something about his dead body, but she ignored him.

"Rare. Like the cow's still kicking," she instructed the server. "I'll send it back if it isn't." Grace gave her a wrinkled-nose smile to soften her insistence, but the woman got Grace's drift. She meant it. She wasn't paying double-digit bucks for a dry hockey puck.

"A lady after my own heart," Rick said, ordering the same. Along with baked potatoes, fresh veggies, and salads with ranch dressing, it promised to be a meal fit for a ravenous queen and king.

Grace felt something shift in their connection. Rick relaxed and seemed more himself, and they both smiled when talking about mundane things like the kids and the weather. Their salads came quickly and the meal was fabulous, Grace even more impressed she didn't knock over their water glasses, although she did drop two forks on the floor. She had to sit, red-faced and sheepish, waiting for the waitress to bring one willing to stay between her fingers. She also managed to choke on her potato. It was so blasted hot! Rick looked ready to jump up and slap Grace on the back, but she gave him the evil eye for even thinking about touching her blistered, sunburned skin.

Gulping the cold water, she put out the fire, calmed her racing heart, and then addressed the rest of her meal, savoring every bite. It had been forever since she'd eaten in a restaurant that served something pricier than chicken nuggets.

"Your mascara's running," Rick said, hesitant to point it out.

Great. The hot potato had made Grace's eyes water. She probably looked like a crummy rendition of Kiss.

"I'll run to the ladies' room and fix it," she said, slipping off her chair and heading toward the restroom.

A tug on her blouse turned into a solid yank, which felt like she'd come to the end of a tugboat line. People cried out, followed by a terrible crash, and she turned around to see their entire table's dishes, flatware, seasonings, and condiments on the floor. Some of it was shattered on the tile, the rest was on the tablecloth, which was pinned to her shirt. The people around them stared at her, one older woman trying hard not to laugh.

Grace slapped her hands over her face and wailed. Could it get any worse than this?

"Grace! Grace," Rick said, grasping her arms. "It's okay, honey. Come on. Let's get you to the bathroom, and then you can tell me how I can help."

The server came to see what happened, and Rick explained everything while Grace unfastened the pins from the tablecloth. She bowed her head as she all but ran into the single-seater bathroom, slamming the door in Rick's face and locking it. She leaned against it and sobbed, wanting to disappear. She'd never be able to face another human being again, and her shirt was beyond repair. How would she even get out of the restaurant? Besides ruining expensive dishes and a tablecloth she couldn't afford to pay for, they wouldn't be able to go to the movie.

A polite knock at the door preceded the hostess calling for her. Rick must have told her Grace's name. Grace opened the door a crack.

"Miss Evans, I'm so sorry. Believe it or not, you're not the first person to have problems with our tablecloths. They're too big for our tables. Mrs. Chester, the owner, has ordered new ones, but they won't come until Friday. Please accept our apologies. Your entire dinner's on us, and you're both welcome to dessert, as well."

"I don't know what to say," Grace replied, filled with relief, "except thank you. But I have another problem." She showed the woman the damage. "If I give you money, could you have my..." What was Rick? He wasn't her boyfriend. "Could you have my date find me a shirt somewhere?"

"Oh, that might not be necessary, miss," the hostess said. "We have a never-ending lost-and-found supply, and I think I have a couple of blouses your size. I'll be right back." She returned in a few minutes with three tops—all nice enough Grace had no idea how people had lost them. Who took a shirt off in a restaurant and left it there? Still, she knew from high school and college friends who became servers, it happened more often than people realized.

A lovely flowered blouse fit even better than the ruined one. Amazing. She pocketed her pins and tossed the old shirt in the trash, fixed her face and her hair, and slipped back to the table, her head bowed in embarrassment.

Rick placed his hand on hers, sending her heart bouncing at his touch. "Are you okay? I'm so sorry that happened. Do you want to stay since they're footing the bill?"

"No. I just want out of here."

"I don't blame you," he said, tossing a twenty-dollar bill on the table for the tip. He walked close, protecting her from the curious glances of the other diners as he escorted her from the restaurant.

"Can we still see the movie?" he asked, peeking at his watch. "It's *The Fault in Our Stars.*"

"You'd be crazy to take the risk. We'd be taunting fate."

He sighed with patience. "I don't believe in fate. And it's worth the risk."

The movie was worth it? Or she was? Her heart tumbled at his kind smile. It reminded her that she still cared about him, even if he hadn't apologized exactly the way she wanted him to. "So maybe avoid the popcorn, candy, or soda that I'd probably spill on you and we'll be okay."

Rick returned her smile with one she couldn't resist. "Don't worry about it. Maybe the theater will have an extra pair of pants lying around."

Grace laughed and ended up with a big bucket of popcorn in her lap, a large soda in her cup holder, and Peanut M&M's in her hand. Amazingly, no one was drowned or damaged during the movie. When the flick grew sad enough Grace needed a tissue, Rick handed her a napkin and let her cry on his shoulder. Although he hesitated for a moment, he put an arm around her and pulled her closer. Grace couldn't resist snuggling into him and allowing his comfort to slow her tears.

It was late when they returned to the cabin. While they were still sitting in the Escalade, Rick contacted Kyle to see if he was coming home. He wasn't. Charlotte and Cherise begged to stay another night with Rachel at Skylar's place, and neither he nor Grace objected.

House key retrieved from its hiding place in the front planter, Rick let Grace inside. She mounted the stairs and headed for her room, far too aware Rick was on her heels. She faced him not far from her bedroom door, knowing she'd be ungrateful not to thank him for a wonderful night—even if it hadn't started out a date.

"Thank you," he told her, surprising her.

"For what?"

"For letting me be a part of your day. I had a great time."

"Despite my trying to break your foot with a bowling ball and making a fool out of myself in a restaurant full of people?"

He shrugged, although the humor danced in his eyes. "Incidental. And it was a terrific movie. It, uh, gave me an excuse to hold you."

Her smile faded when he stepped closer. She should step away. They hadn't worked out enough of their differences. He leaned toward her. She should stop him, she told herself, but when his lips touched hers, it felt as amazing as before and her feet wouldn't move. His arms slipped around her and pulled her against him, his kiss delicious, their breaths mingling together. She needed to stop it, but it was the last thing she wanted to do.

When he let go, his smile seemed troubled, and she wondered if he felt as confused as she did.

"Good night, Grace," he said. "Get some rest. You deserve it."

Then he slipped into his own room, leaving her standing there, thinking how it didn't happen this way in books or movies. It didn't happen like this in the movie they saw tonight.

But, strangely enough, it felt right enough when all else seemed to have pushed her life off its axis.

***

Another early morning phone call came from Hannah. She was at her parents' house again, quiet and resigned. She hadn't lost hope, she said, but Grace felt she had. The sadness in her voice was as powerful as last night's movie. The longer they kept Damien in a coma, the greater the chances he would ever regain consciousness.

Grace felt selfish for wishing she could talk to her best friend about Rick. She wouldn't burden Hannah with her own woes, but she needed a sounding board, and Mom wasn't the right person, either.

Tossing and turning, sleep evading her, she finally did what Hannah always suggested. She slid out of bed to her knees and talked to the Lord. She prayed for Damien and for Hannah and for Rick. And she prayed for answers. She had no idea how to fix any of this, but maybe Someone Upstairs did.

The kids were home bright and early the next morning. The original plan on the day's agenda had been to consider camping overnight on Haylee's Peak, a campground near the top of Mt.

Haylee, the tallest mountain near Secret Lake. Grace didn't feel comfortable camping without Hannah, and Rick didn't want to, either. Thus, the kids begged for the second item on the day's list. They wanted to head with their friends and their families to the Peak anyway, where a company had three zip lines. In Grace's opinion, it was the craziest sport next to bungee jumping. Or possibly spelunking. Or rock climbing, especially free climbing. She shuddered at the thought.

She kicked back on one of the semi-circle of shaded flat-rock benches when they arrived, content to enjoy the beauty of the place while people-watching. It annoyed her to see the twins, and even Rachel's parents, teasing a reluctant Rachel into taking the line. Grace wanted to lock the girl in the Escalade. No one should goad someone into doing something that frightened them, especially a parent.

In the end, Rachel went, and when she returned, she was roaring with laughter and begging to do it again.

Well, Grace, you are now part of an even smaller minority. Her heart froze when Rick approached her, the same expression on his face he had yesterday when he was determined to make her throw a bowling ball. She raised a finger, the look she put on her face enough to curdle milk.

"Don't ask, don't tease, don't argue," she said. "I am not leaving this mountain hanging from a rope."

Rick laughed and ran his fingers through his hair. "Charlotte was giving me grief. She thought we were abandoning you. I came to keep you company."

"Nope." Grace raised her cell phone. "I have a reading assignment for school. I even have reception right now, believe it or not, so I'm good."

Rick shook his head and walked away, but deep in her heart, Grace wondered if this was a glimpse into the future if they got together. Would her clumsiness and her affinity for accidents keep her always sitting on the sidelines? Would Rick grow tired of going off to do things she wasn't willing to do?

It didn't sound like a very good formula for a successful relationship. Maybe she was wrong to entertain it.

Rick felt like he was choosing his family and their fun over Grace. He wanted to go back and sit with her, but he had an obligation to keep an eye on the kids. Aunt Sharon and Uncle Luke had brought them here many times over the years, but they were all daredevils, and even in the best of circumstances, there were risks.

So, for now, he would let Grace at least pretend to do her homework. Besides, it put some distance between them, which he needed right now. His feelings were as chaotic as the sea in a storm. He cared, he worried, he needed her—but he didn't know what to do with her yet, and he was still irked at her insistence he needed to take more responsibility for what happened five years ago. What he did need was more time to sort it out.

He only knew he couldn't take another five years.

Grace downloaded her assignment and began reading. It reminded her of how deeply she loved literature, the beautiful prose that people didn't seem to appreciate enough these days. It swept her into a world that reminded her that life itself, even in its darkest times, was still beautiful.

Later, feeling a touch nostalgic, Grace called her mother's number, but it went to voicemail. Mom was either busy or resting. Feeling a little stiff, Grace dared Murphy as much as she dared, walking to the edge of one of the cliffs to admire the lake and the spectacular view around it. More people needed to take time to appreciate things like this: the clear blue sky above, the bright blue lake below, the amazing contrast of the green forest and rich, brown earth. Grace loved Hannah for introducing her to this place. She wished Mom was here to see it, and it made her sad that it would never happen.

Flashes of old memories, sepia-shaded moments that formed Grace's childhood, popped into her mind: having to do most of the housework after Danny was born. Changing his diapers and bathing him when she was barely strong enough to lift a growing baby. Making Chloe's lunch because Mom couldn't stand long enough to do it. Sitting with her dad, when she'd grown older, as the doctors explained what was wrong with Mom, a moment blazed into her mind forever.

Trudy Evans apparently suffered an infection when she was young that had gone undiagnosed. Left untreated, it damaged her heart. By the time they found the right doctors, it was too late. It left her weak and tired most of the time. She had to limit her activities and

160

subsist on a host of pharmaceuticals. She refused to lug an oxygen tank around with her during the day, but she needed one at night. She might live a long time, but not a particularly exciting life.

Grace fought back tears at remembering the doctor's strange sense of humor. He told Mom that if she wore out her present "model," she'd have the fun of joining the lottery for a new one—a transplant. He looked shocked when Trudy Evans told him she'd never agree to a transplant. Later, Grace tearfully asked her mother why.

Mom laughed and then wept a few tears, hugging Grace and trying to comfort her daughter about what appeared to be her own death sentence. "I can't hope someone else will die so I can live, Gracie. Let them have their lives. I don't have a right to it."

Grace took a deep breath. The idea rubbed off on her. It was an odd concept in today's world, where permanent-press shirts, self-mending zippers, and replacement body parts almost seemed synonymous. Faced with the same possibility, Grace realized she might not want a transplant, either.

"Oh, my goodness, guess who's here!" a familiar voice said, hurtling Grace back to reality.

"Maria?"

"Are you okay, honey? You look kind of sad." Maria stood beside her, her lovely face seamed with concern.

Grace huffed laughter. "My face isn't sad, it's abused. I had a run-in with a volleyball. Still have a bit of a headache."

Maria mewed sympathy and offered more pain medication.

"Nah, I'm fine. What brings you here?" Why did she suddenly have the feeling Maria's arrival wasn't a coincidence? Rick's complaints that she followed him around were seeming too well-founded.

"My hotel has a lobby brochure rack, and I found this place's pamphlet. I love zip lines. Rick is here, too?"

Grace glanced over her shoulder. "And the rest of the gang. I'm here in case someone needs a Band-Aid."

Maria gave a wry smile and stepped a little closer to Grace, leaning into her as she peered over the cliff. "Heights are frightening, aren't they?" she said.

The tone in Maria's voice struck Grace with a moment of vertigo. What did she mean by that?

"Not a fan," Grace admitted.

Maria grinned at her. "It's a long way down, for sure."

As she leaned into Grace even more, Grace couldn't help imagining the horrors of being pushed off the cliff. She huffed a deep breath and stepped away.

"Excuse me. I've got homework to do." She went back to her wonderfully safe bench, and when she glanced up, Maria was nowhere in sight. How did she do that? Come and go without warning? Especially in those bright colors she always wore. Grace dared pray Rick would stay away from Maria. She was convinced the girl was warped. Maybe not Kooky Kathy warped, but still… odd.

The prayer went unanswered. When their group had its fill of zip lining, Maria was hanging on Rick as they headed toward Grace. Even worse, Rick appeared to be having fun. A lead bar settled in Grace's stomach when Kyle admitted he'd invited Maria to lunch back at the cabin. Grace had to be nice. Wanting to maim Kyle didn't seem terribly Christian.

Having the kids at the table helped mitigate the situation. As soon as the teens took off with their friends again, Grace bit her lip against a smile when Rick also bid Maria farewell. Maria spared Grace a dark look when Rick wasn't paying attention, and once more, right before he closed the door on her. Again came the chill that twisted Grace's spine. Jealousy she understood. This felt different.

"I need to get back to my car," Rick said, his gaze searching her face. "Too much goofing off has put my car repairs back another day. Maybe more."

Grace nodded, glad he couldn't read her mind. She longed to have him put his arms around her and kiss her, but she didn't think it was a good idea right now.

The mudroom door closed, and she curled up on the couch to rest. She did feel better today, but she was still tired. Their time apart would give her a little more time to think—and pray.

CHAPTER 14

It was dark when Grace roused, absolutely starving, and realized she'd fallen asleep. Again.

She sighed to herself. At least she got a little rest while Rick puttered around in the garage, although she felt bad she'd missed dinnertime. At least she'd put some chicken and vegetables in the Instant Pot on slow-cooker mode after breakfast and before they left for the mountain. By the way it smelled, it was done.

"Grace? Are you awake yet?"

Grace jumped, then sat up too quickly, grunting as stiffness stabbed her neck and shoulders. Her heart hammered at having Rick surprise her. Well, that, and seeing him wiping his hands on a dishtowel. At first, she feared he'd gotten grease all over the towel, but then she realized he was drying them after a thorough washing.

"No," she murmured. "I'm still asleep. You're talking to my voicemail."

Rick chuckled. "Thought so. I put dinner together. You ready to eat?"

Did she understand him right? He got dinner ready?

He helped her to her feet and walked her to the island bar, where he'd set out two simple place settings and the food—and pulled out her chair for her. It felt strange to be pampered this way. After all, she wasn't an invalid.

"I'm glad you planned ahead," he said. "Made it quick and easy for me."

Grace gave him a pained smile. "I don't dare face life without planning. I never know when Murphy's going to feed me to the lions."

He chuckled. "No lions so far. Heartless bows and arrows and ferocious volleyballs have taken the cake."

Grace snickered. "Vanilla or chocolate?"

Rick shook his head. "You have a crazy sense of humor, Grace. Dry, but long-suffering. Is this your way of coping with life's hurdles?"

"You finally figured me out. If I can't change the accidents, laughing about them when I can helps take the edge off."

The food took the edge off the hunger and fatigue she felt, too. When they finished, Rick pointed toward the pitch-dark outdoors.

"I bet it's a great night to see the stars."

Grace loved being away from big-city lights, and when Rick turned off the kitchen lights and led her outside, she was awed at the Milky Way's celestial grandeur.

"Beautiful," he murmured, although his voice raised goosebumps on Grace's arms when he said it looking at her, not the sky.

"I love it here," she replied, her voice unsteady. "It's quiet and peaceful. No freeway. No cars or planes or trains."

"Just nature at its best," he agreed. His fingers intertwined with hers, capsizing her heart. "Grace—"

"Grace, pick up the phone! Grace, pick up the phone!"

Peace fled.

"My phone! I left it in the living room. It's Hannah!" Grace started for the house, but Rick stopped her, insisting he could move faster. Afraid of the dark but anxious to talk to her best friend, she persisted in following him at a hurried walk.

Rick threw open the door, and Grace followed him into the pitch-black kitchen, stumbling when her shoe caught the edge of the threshold. She went down so fast, she didn't have time think about it, landing face first on the tile. She lay there, hardly able to believe it. Clumsiness was one thing, but this vacation triumphed all others. Hopefully she hadn't broken anything.

She rolled over and stared at the ceiling. "Thanks, Murph," she said. "What? A little dig, to get even with me for not chancing the zip line? I figured you preferred a more dramatic ending to my puny existence."

Murphy didn't answer, but Grace wouldn't be surprised if he was just around a corner snickering. Then she heard footsteps nearby and worried Rick would step on her.

"Hold on! Let me stand up!" she said. The footsteps stopped.

"Grace?"

"Uh, yeah. I need to move out of your way."

"Where are you? Did you fall down?" The flashlight on his phone blazed to life and scorched her eyeballs.

"No, the floor had something it wanted to tell me," she muttered, shielding her face with her hand.

He gave a belly laugh. "Well, I guess a good conversation with Aunt Sharon's tile is better than falling down."

She groaned. "Why is that the first thing you assumed happened to me?"

"Because you said you needed to stand up, and I didn't think you'd lie down in the doorway to admire the stars. Of course, I didn't consider the possibility you wanted to chew the fat with Mother Earth."

Grace heard him trying hard not to burst into laughter.

"Alexa, turn on the lights," he commanded, making Grace feel even more stupid. She could have done that. The room came to life, and Rick's humor faded when he saw her struggling to get to her feet. It faded even more when he helped her to feet and handed her the phone.

"Is he better?" she whispered, not sure she wanted to hear about Damien.

He shook his head.

Grace took a deep breath to calm her nerves before saying hello to Hannah. She needed to be strong for her best friend. "Hannah?"

Tears and sniffles were all Grace heard for far too long, then Hannah got enough air to reply. "He's worse. He had a bleed in his brain. They had to go in and relieve the pressure."

Grace thought she might fall again. He wasn't better. He was dying. Anguish filled her face, and she turned to Rick, needing his strength, his kindness. He was there without her saying a word, holding her against him and stroking her hair. Giving her the strength Grace wished to give Hannah.

"I'm so sorry, Hannah," Grace said, her own voice thick with tears.

Hannah broke down and sobbed, and a short while later, Hannah's—and Rick's—mom, Marilyn Fleming, came to the phone and spoke briefly with Grace. They could do nothing for Damien but wait and pray, and she asked Grace and Rick to also pray for Hannah. She needed all the help heaven had to give.

Rick took the phone from Grace and set it on the table next to him. Grace found herself once again wrapped in his arms and weeping into his chest. Never had she felt this sort of pain, but she'd also never been offered such tenderness from a man, not even from her own father. She cried not only for Hannah and Damien, but for the sorrow lurking inside her, the heartbreak which far too often made her feel so small and vulnerable. When she shed every tear she owned, Rick offered her some tissues. This time she didn't try to clean his shirt with them.

"I can't believe this," she said after mopping the tears from her cheeks and blowing her nose. "Why does this happen to everyone around me? It's upsetting enough I get hurt. Why is it everyone I care about suffers, too?"

Rick's brows furrowed deep. "Don't you dare, Grace. This isn't your fault. Bad things happen to good people—and bad people—all the time. You're not responsible for the world's ills."

Grace shook her head. "I swear I'm just a walking jinx. Hannah has a perfect world when I'm not around, but as soon as we're together, something happens to one or both of us. I'm so tired of it."

Rick raised her chin and gave her a stern gaze, reminding her of her late grandmother when Grace whined too much.

"Hannah's world is no more perfect than anyone else's. She gets hurt, she gets ill, she makes mistakes. So do I. Murphy doesn't exist, Grace. Like I said before, I think maybe you're trying too hard."

"Okay, so I need to relax. But I can't change the fact I'm clumsy." She felt a touch annoyed.

Rick shrugged. "My grandmother's clumsy, too. I've seen it with my own eyes, but it doesn't have anything to do with bad luck or Murphy. Grace, you can't take the world on alone. God is there to guide you, to forgive your weaknesses—"

"He doesn't even know who I am," she snapped, feeling the anger stirring around, deep inside her. "He couldn't care less what happens to me."

"So not true," Rick said with determination. "Look, I'm going to go out on a limb here and quote one of my favorite scriptures. I recite it any time I'm feeling down, so don't think I'm berating you. It's from Romans, Chapter Eight. 'The Spirit itself bears witness with our spirit, that we are the children of God: And if children, then heirs; heirs of God, and joint-heirs with Christ...' There's more to it than that, but this part says a lot.

"We are children of God, Grace. I am His son. You are His daughter. How can a man not love and care about his daughter? And

He's not just a man, He's king of all creation. He loved us so much He gave us a savior, the Son of Man, and because of the Savior's suffering—far greater than everything you or I have ever suffered put together—we can become joint heirs with Him. Heaven is our real home, not this place. Here we have to fall so that we can learn to get back up again. We make mistakes to learn to become better people. It's not a curse, sweetheart, it's an opportunity. I know it's not fun sometimes, but I think Christ would say the same thing about dying on the cross."

Grace felt gut-punched. No image felt clearer to her than the idea of an innocent man being crucified for her. Jesus would understand. How could He not?

Hannah was always begging Grace to read the Bible. Grace had tried hard over the last couple years but still didn't understand a good part of it. Hearing these verses spoken this way, with feeling, from someone who felt such love for a being Grace didn't fully understand, gave it a whole new meaning.

"Heirs of an eternal kingdom?" he said, stroking her arms gently. "Immortality? God's plan for us is amazing. We just need to exercise faith. Nothing is a waste—not one experience, not even if we're wrong—if we trust in Him. All that's required is to do our best to follow in Christ's footsteps. It's not easy, but it isn't impossible."

Grace loved the warmth she saw in Rick's eyes; the passion for what he believed. She wanted to melt into him, to hold him tight, to let him hold her up. They came naturally into each other's arms, his head dipping down as he kissed her like she'd never been kissed before.

Pleasure turned into burning desire, and she drew in a fervent breath, opening her mouth to his, welcoming the kiss. It fed her need as well as it stoked it, sending heat flowing through her. His fingers tangled themselves in her hair while he kissed her cheek and her nose and nuzzled her ear. Her toes curled, and she hung onto his shirt front, afraid if she let go, she'd melt onto the floor. She kissed him back, loving the taste of him, the scent of sandalwood and citrus which had become so dear.

Rick's arms stiffened, curbing Grace's eagerness and making her pull away. Seeing the worried look on his face made her realize she was asking for something that wasn't true to Rick Fleming's principles, and if she'd learned nothing else on this trip, she knew those principles meant everything to him. Out of breath, she leaned her brow against his chest, heard his heart thundering behind his ribs, and knew it was as difficult for him as it was for her to contain the fire they ignited.

"Grace," he murmured, lifting her chin, "we have to be careful. You know we not only can't step over the line, we'd best stay a good way back from it."

She snorted laughter. "Easy for you to say. It's not my line. It's yours." Rick look dismayed, and she realized she'd disappointed him. "I'm sorry. I didn't mean it the way it sounded. I understand your moral code. but I've never had to worry about having one. I had no idea this felt so... *good.*"

Rick groaned and leaned over to touch his forehead to hers. "I've wanted you for as long as I can remember. I was too young to understand it when I first decided you were the cutest girl in the world. I only knew what my mother called puppy love was a pretty powerful creature."

"Are you serious?" Grace leaned back to better see his face. He was serious. "Your mom thought you had a crush on me?"

Now Rick laughed. "She didn't think it, she knew it, and she was on my case all the time about how a gentleman treats a lady. I was a boy, and I wasn't supposed to like girls because they were gross, and it was even grosser having my mother know I lost my brains whenever you were in the same room. That's why I did what boys do when they can't deal with their feelings. I made an idiot out of myself, and I made fun of everyone: you, myself, my brothers. I'm so sorry, Grace. And I'm so sorry my brothers made your life miserable."

Grace scanned his face, stroking his cheek, tormented by what he'd said.

"Rick, your brothers made their own mistakes. Those weren't your fault. Being big enough or strong enough to stop them wasn't the issue."

"What do you mean?"

"Your brothers annoyed me, along with a lot of rude kids in the world. You knew they hurt me, and I could see it bothered you, but you didn't stop it."

"Like I told you, I had to lay low with my brothers. If I ignored them, they went away and left me alone. If I fought them, I got pounded—and sometimes my friends did, too."

Grace shook her head and stepped back. Rick's arms dropped to his sides.

"You were twenty years old That Night, Rick. You can't blame your mistakes on your brothers forever. You need to take responsibility for what you didn't do. You didn't stand up for me. I needed you to declare your feelings for me by setting your limits on how they treated me."

"Okay," he said, hooking his thumbs into his pants pocket. "It didn't work out that way, just like you wouldn't let me come and apologize."

"Would you have apologized for your part? Or said you were sorry that That Night happened? It's not the same. I know what I did was wrong. I was mean, and I threw you out of my life. I've apologized for that, too, but I'm not blaming a bit of it on Hannah or anyone else. It was my fault alone. I think I understand what your church preaches about the importance of forgiveness even when it's hard. Isn't there a connection between forgiveness and repentance? You can't really repent if you don't take full responsibility for what *you* did wrong. How can I fully forgive you if you don't offer a sincere apology?"

<hr>

The color drained out of Rick's face. She held a grudge against him all these years because he hadn't apologized the right way? He didn't know why it annoyed him, but it did. He shook his head and took his own step back.

"I never needed you to apologize for what you did," he told her. "You were right, and I knew it. But I did stand up for you. I got into a fist fight with my brother and was permanently scarred because of it. I'd do it again in a heartbeat, but it was Sean who caused it. I'm sorry about all of it, and I'm hurt that you still hold it against me."

<hr>

The air deserted Grace's lungs, what was left of her heart in agony because of what he said. "You believe in your Savior and your God, but you don't know how to take responsibility for your mistakes, Richard Fleming. You have no idea how to offer a sincere apology. When you do, let me know."

She turned on her heel and managed to make a quick exit, hollering at Alexa to light her way to her room. She didn't intend to slam her door, but it felt good when she did. She locked it for good measure and fell on her bed, wincing at the pain not on her body but in her heart. She beat her pillow several times then lay there, unable to move, breathing hard in anger and frustration.

"I know a few scriptures, too, Ricky the Rude," she muttered. "From the book of Proverbs, Chapter Sixteen: 'Pride goeth before destruction, and a haughty spirit before a fall.' I have a feeling God would consider your refusal to see the truth as prideful. Pride has made you blind. You don't even see the mistake you made."

A grim smile crept across her mouth. "And if I understand how this works, if you make a mistake, you can learn to become a better person—but only if you acknowledge your mistake, confess it, and ask for forgiveness." She buried her face in her pillow. "The only question is whether your pride is stronger than your feelings for me. It's not my call, but it's the wedge you drove between us five years ago, and the wounds can't heal until you take it out."

<hr>

The teens remained scarce on Thursday, as did Rick. Sequestered in the garage, he only came in to make his own breakfast and lunch.

Grace ignored him, sitting out in the fresh air on the patio and concentrating on her homework, until the day grew too hot. The solitude became both boring and stifling. She went upstairs to finally make her bed, then sat on it and stared around the room. It was beautiful, but it felt sterile and empty. She'd rather be back in her apartment. It was small, but it felt like home, proof money couldn't buy everything.

Hannah's bed was a little rumpled. She'd sat here while collecting her things to race off to Damien's side. The drawer to the nightstand stood slightly ajar, too, and Grace saw a dark object inside it. She opened the drawer and took a deep breath when she saw Hannah's Bible lying there. She didn't even know Hannah brought it. She usually read scripture on her iPad.

Lifting it, Grace returned to her bed and sat back, flipping through pages in a book as foreign to her as France. The admission didn't feel good.

For some crazy reason, she found herself compelled to drop to her knees and pray. She prayed for Damien and Hannah, for herself, for her mother, and especially for Rick. But she also prayed for help finding answers to her life. She couldn't go on this way.

Feeling drawn to the topical guide, she sat back on the bed and browsed through the seemingly never-ending pages until her eyes fell on the topic of forgiveness. Some of the verses bothered her, some weren't as clear as she'd like, but some hit the mark—enough she was willing to pursue it.

Feeling more positive, she returned downstairs to make dinner. She ended up eating it alone and retired to her room with her Kindle because she had nothing else to do.

On Friday, the kids descended on the cabin at nearly the same time as the day before, their friends in tow, hoping to go to the lake again. Not before raiding the kitchen for food, of course. Grace, who felt as if her main purpose for coming to the cabin had been hijacked, gladly took on the role of KP commander, giving orders and directing her helpers and their helpers.

The boys cheered when she pulled out the waffle maker and pans for hash browns and Denver omelets. The twins made juices—orange for most of them, grape for Grace. It was her favorite.

Kyle extricated Rick from the garage and insisted he join them when the doorbell rang. The surprise on their faces meant no one expected company. Rick headed for the front door. Curiosity had the kids following, and Grace wasn't about to be left out.

Shock hit her when she saw two deputies standing on the porch, and she was grateful Kyle reached out to steady her. She had no idea how deep the Fleming connections ran with Secret Lake Village law enforcement, but she feared they'd come to bring word Damien had died.

A moment later, her head spun in the opposite direction when she saw Maria step out from behind the officer on the right, a large handbag over her shoulder and a combination of embarrassment and worry on her face. What in the world was going on?

"Hey, Rick," the cop on the left said.

"What can I do for you, Deputy Marcos?" Rick asked, his brow creased.

Yep, he knew the deputies.

"We got a call from dispatch. A complaint from your neighbor to the north—" He pointed in the direction of the garage. "They said someone was prowling around the house. We found this young lady in the bushes near your backyard fence. She says she knows you. Is that true?"

"Maria? What the heck?" Rick scowled.

"I'm so sorry, Ricky. I wanted to surprise you."

"Uh, yeah, you did such a great job you're one step away from getting arrested. Where's your car?"

She winced, her eyes filling with tears. "I left it in the turnabout at the bottom of the driveway. I didn't want you to catch me. When I saw you in the garage, I knew I'd have to hide somewhere until I could sneak up to the front door. And then…" She waved her hand at Marcos and his partner.

"I assume you don't intend to press charges," Marcos said, his own annoyance surpassing Rick's.

"We're acquainted. No, I won't press charges. Thank you, deputies. I appreciate your diligence. If she'd been a thief, this would have been a different story."

The deputies said their farewells and, after giving Maria a stern warning, left her standing there, her face pale and her shoulders stooped.

Grace felt sorry for her, even if she didn't like her. She was firmly convinced the girl was stalking Rick, but she couldn't possibly believe this was a smart way to win a man's heart, could she?

Kyle, of course, had different feelings. Still infatuated, he and his friends jumped in to invite her to breakfast. Grace wanted to scream in exasperation, and she could see Rick felt the same way, but neither wanted to make a scene. Charlotte set another place at the big table in the formal dining area, while young hands transported the food from the kitchen.

"Good grief," Maria said, eyeing the spread with amazement. "Are you expecting the entire village for breakfast?"

"No, we were waiting for you," Kyle replied, his hazel eyes twinkling. "I guess Gracie decided to make enough for an army, so here we are."

Maria laughed, setting her bag under her chair and taking her seat. "Yes, here we are." Her dark, almond-shaped eyes turned to Rick, filled with hope. Rick sighed and asked Kyle to say thanks for the food this time.

Conversation remained general, covering their stay, their fun, their plans. Rick ate quietly, his gaze flicking to Grace occasionally, reminding her of their disagreement on Wednesday night. Then Maria sought his attention, and he gave it to her, undivided and with far too much warmth. Grace stabbed a bit of sausage, stuck it in her mouth, and ground it to bits between angry teeth.

"So, Grace," Maria said at last. "I haven't learned much about you. Do you work? Have a boyfriend?"

Grace paused, her last forkful of food on its way to her mouth. Was that a hint that Rick was hers, not Grace's? She cleared her throat to avoid uttering a nasty reply. After a brief explanation about her college work, her future employment goals, and her job at the pet store, she added, "The boyfriend thing is in limbo."

"Your life sounds wonderful! Boyfriend things are the hardest, of course, but you'll find someone. I'd love to go to college, but my family doesn't have the money and needs my help. I work at Pablo's, my parents' restaurant in Los Gatos."

Rick leaned toward her in surprise. "Pablo's? I love the place. It's small, but I don't think I've ever had better enchiladas."

"Thank you for saying so. My father has terrific business sense, and Mama's a great cook, so it was a match made in heaven when they opened their restaurant. It's just not what I want to do with my life."

"What would you like to do?" Grace asked. She tried hard not to be catty, but she hoped Maria wanted to become an astronaut and head for Mars.

"I'm good with numbers. I'd love to manage a bank, which means I need a degree in business or finance."

"And experience in banking," Grace pointed out. "Why don't you look for a job as a bank teller? Most banks love to help their employees improve their education."

Maria's face darkened. "My parents won't let me. They need me in the restaurant. Sometimes I wish I could win the lotto or some sweepstakes so I could help them out and then be free to do what I want to do."

Grace had to admit Maria had a sad situation. In some ways, they had something in common: difficulty reaching their goals because of money and family needs.

"Can we take the boat out now?" Kyle leaned over to Rick and asked in a hushed voice. Turning to Maria, he asked if she brought her bathing suit.

She smiled and pointed toward her large bag. "I pack a change of clothes and my swimsuit every day. It's a little far to the hotel if I need them."

"Super. You have to come along," Kyle said without permission, jumping up to start clearing the table.

Rick seemed glum, but when Maria turned her million-dollar smile on him, he glanced at Grace and then returned Maria's smile. "Let's get this done. The lake looks great today, even better than yesterday. I don't plan to go out tomorrow. With all the people coming in for the celebration, the lake will be worse than standstill traffic on the freeway, so we should take advantage of it now."

The kids laughed and hurried to clean the kitchen.

"You coming, Gracie?" Charlotte asked.

Grace was touched to see the sincere hope in the girl's eyes. She hated to dash them. "I've got tons of homework, honey, and my sunburn needs to stay indoors. I really want to enjoy the celebration tomorrow, and getting too much sun today might ruin it for me."

And being around Maria for too long might lead to somebody's murder—not necessarily Grace's. A shiver ran through her at remembering Haylee's Peak.

She thought she saw Rick's eyes dim with disappointment, but it was brief and she wasn't sure. Afterward, he and Maria headed out the door shoulder to shoulder.

Grace had trouble focusing on her homework, imagining instead a variety of ways to send Maria into Dante's Inferno. If only doing it wouldn't make Grace one of Maria's neighbors in Dante's Circles of Hell.

Later, she tried to call Hannah. It went to voicemail. She called Mom, finding Trudy Evans armed with the compassion of a saint. Her mom had called Marilyn Fleming to offer her sympathies regarding Damien.

"The doctors are still hopeful, Grace. You know how much I've gone through in my life. Besides my own problems, I've lost both my parents and my grandparents, a few friends, and your father's oldest uncle. When a situation is hopeless, doctors rarely mince words. They also don't give hope when there isn't any. Marilyn said their church has held a group fast, and their prayer circle is offering prayers night and day. I may not be able to attend church, but I do believe in prayer."

"Which means you believe in God, right?" Grace said. "Mom, why didn't you share this with us when we were kids?"

Her mom was quiet for a moment. "I made the same mistake you're making, Sweet Cheeks. I blamed my ills on God and had no idea why he was picking on me. By the time I remembered my own religious upbringing and began to make peace with it, I felt I'd be a hypocrite to try changing things with you and your siblings. Dad and I decided we'd do our best to live by example and leave ourselves open to answering questions when you were ready. I've hoped all these years you'd see I'm not afraid of dying. This is why, Grace. I love the Lord, and I know he'll take care of me."

The lump in Grace's throat returned, so big she was sure it would strangle her with grief and anger. She doubted most children would choose religion if they weren't exposed to it. She said so, and Mom agreed and said she regretted it but couldn't do anything about it.

"Learn from my mistakes and yours, honey," she said. "We can't change the past, but the future is full of promise."

Before she knew it, Grace was teary-eyed and sharing her troubles about Rick and admitting how hard it was to love a man who seemed dedicated to his beliefs but couldn't apologize like he should.

"Gracie, Jesus never said someone has to ask for forgiveness to be forgiven. In fact, he said the opposite. He's divine. He will forgive those that he feels deserves it—and won't forgive those who don't. But of us? We aren't perfect, so we have no right to judge. He expects us to forgive everyone, no matter how reprehensible the offense."

Grace found it hard to swallow the idea, but as they ended their call and she returned to her homework, she had to admit there was merit to it, even if she wasn't sure she could do it.

The day felt flat without Grace, but Rick had to admit he enjoyed Maria more than he'd expected. Except for her constant questions. What was with that? Was she writing a book?

He paused at the thought. His parents and his aunt and uncle dealt with all kinds of people in their jobs. Reporters were notorious for pushing their way into their lives. Was Maria looking for information to toss to a hungry magazine or newspaper editor? Worried, the idea had him pulling the kids aside one at a time to remind them to keep personal information about their family to themselves.

CHAPTER 15

Lunchtime heralded the return of the Fleming/Maria crowd. The kids took their food outside, while Rick, Maria, and Grace ate in the kitchen. Nothing felt better, even with Maria hanging around, than air conditioning on a day which had already climbed well above a hundred degrees.

Later, the twins brought Maria and Grace the projects they planned to enter into the contest tomorrow. Aunt Sharon didn't know how to cook, but she could crochet, and she'd been teaching her girls for a while. They each finished a pair of potholders right before coming to the lake.

"These are the best potholders I've ever seen," Maria declared, admiring them with enthusiasm.

"You think so?" Charlotte said, excited.

"I know so. My grandmother is award-winning and would love them."

"I think Char's is better," Cherise said, her nose wrinkled. "I'm not so good at the artsy stuff. Char likes to paint and is learning to knit and sew, and she's really good at crocheting. I prefer riding horses. Gracie, you should come to my next horse show. Gala is turning into the best jumper in the world."

"I'll be there in a heartbeat," Grace promised, adding to herself that she'd go even if Hannah disowned her and Rick turned his back on her. Cherise entertained aspirations about the Olympics, and Aunt Sharon and Uncle Luke had the money and the connections to make it possible. "You're a fantastic horsewoman, Cherise, and horses are gorgeous creatures. They're also a lot more loyal than boys."

Cherise laughed, making a face at Rick. "Yeah, but boys are pretty fun, too."

The girls pushed their potholders back into their backpacks and then stood back while Kyle showed off his entry for the woodworking part of the judging. Everyone gasped when he brought out an intricately carved 1960 cherry-red Corvette. He'd equipped it with everything from the gills near the rear wheel wells, to the bumpers painted to look like chrome.

"Great job," Rick remarked.

"It's magnificent," Maria said, breathless, making the boy blush the same color as the car.

"It is, Kyle," Grace agreed. "You've worked on this for a long time. Didn't you start it when your grandpa was still alive?"

The boy shifted at the reminder. "Yeah, I've dabbled with it off and on for a couple of years, but I was almost done when I heard about the contest."

"It motivated you," Grace said, her eyes twinkling. He grinned and nodded.

"What about you, Grace?" Maria asked. "Are you entering anything?"

"Possibly some candy. My grandmother gave me her recipe for divinity many years ago. It's something many people don't even eat anymore—mostly because it's like fruit cake. If you don't make it right, it's disgusting."

The others laughed, but Grace realized this held true about many things in life. Powerful lessons from the past could change or improve lives, but only if they were used right. If not, younger generations didn't value them.

She glanced at Rick, wondering what he was thinking. She was coming to respect the words of wisdom Mom gave her. No one was perfect, and Rick was truly an awesome guy. It was wrong not to appreciate that.

Maria hung around, even when dinnertime came and visitors should go home. Grace knew it was small-minded to let it bother her, but she wished the girl would give them some space. No doubt, Grace had no right to resent Maria's interest in Rick—or his in Maria—if he'd decided to give up on Grace. Grace just knew she wasn't ready to give up on Rick.

Maria watched as Grace prepared Mu Shu Pork, the Fleming kids' favorite of her meals. Rick was the only one who hadn't known her hands had prepared it over the years. According to Hannah, he and his brothers swooped in after she left and chowed down what they thought were restaurant leftovers.

Rick's eyes grew wide when he took note of the night's fare. Grace could almost gloat at the thought his mouth was watering and that this might be a talent Maria didn't possess.

"This dish is Grace's signature favorite, Maria. You'll love it," Charlotte said, handing her a bowl of the best sticky-rice in the world to take to the table.

The others grabbed the rest of the offerings: deep-fried, breaded shrimp; plump, crispy egg rolls; made-from-scratch Chinese pancakes; and yummy sweet and sour sauce. The hot Chinese mustard and plumb sauce Grace had brought from home to cut down on the preparation time. Rick delivered the pork filling for the pancakes, the others laughing and jeering when he declared this was his serving. Where was everyone else's?

"Would you like to bless the meal, Grace?" Rick asked.

The request came so unexpectedly, Grace almost declined. Then she bolstered her courage and did so, and everyone began passing the food. She didn't miss the soft look on Rick's face. He liked hearing her pray.

"I have to have these recipes," Maria insisted after taking a bite of each dish. "Do you share them?" she asked Grace.

"Actually…."

"Even if she would, I don't want her to," Rick said. "Hannah once told me Grace wants to publish her own cookbook someday, and giving away the recipes would be counter-productive. Don't you agree, Maria?"

Both Maria and Grace stared at him, Grace wondering where he'd gotten that idea. She'd shared it with Hannah years ago, but Hannah wasn't supposed to talk to Rick about Grace. Besides, why would he care? Grace was about to ask, but the strange look he gave her warned her to silence.

After dinner, the girls insisted on baking cookies, and Grace decided to make a double batch of her divinity now, so they could taste some of it tonight and have less hassle getting to the park tomorrow, too.

"This is divine," Rick said later, taking his time munching on the small mound of candy.

"Duh. That's why it's called divinity," Cherise said, laughing.

Rick laughed, too. "Yeah, I guess you're right. I can't imagine this not taking the blue ribbon tomorrow, Grace. It's fabulous."

Aunt Sharon's sainted offspring stayed home that night—without their friends. Grace was more than grateful Maria didn't ask to sleep on the couch. The girl lavished Rick with affection, but he didn't let her kiss him goodbye, which made Grace want to smile. If he'd been smitten with Maria Del Rey, he would have welcomed her with open arms.

Still, he buried himself in the garage again while the three Fleming teens went out back to set up the badminton net. Grace loved badminton, but she didn't care to challenge Murphy and she had more thinking to do.

Tired of voicemails, she texted Hannah, sad when a returned text informed her that Damien had not improved.

Grace sighed with sadness. In a way, she empathized with Damien. She felt like her heart was on life support. Maria's advances and Rick spending the day with her had made it impossible for Grace to talk to him, and even if she did, she had the awful feeling it was too late.

Resentment was the cause of it. Grace had harbored it way too long. Holding grudges wasn't what anyone with half a brain should do, even if it was a common human failing. Mom was right. She should forgive Rick no matter what. It might not matter to Rick, but it would be good for Grace.

Needing a diversion, Grace found herself drawn to one of her favorite pastimes: making homemade bread. She had plenty of time to get it raised and out of the oven before everyone went to bed, and there was nothing to equal a slice of hot, fresh bread, slathered with butter or honey or even a spoonful of jam.

She sat at the table reading her book while the two loaves raised and again while they baked. She'd nearly finished the romance, and she got so locked in, she didn't notice the time passing.

With the bread done, the tops lightly greased, and both covered with a clean dish towel to cool, Grace went to finish the last chapter, tearful at the close call in the struggling romance, and smiling when the couple finally declared how they felt about each other.

She jumped when the mudroom door swung shut and Rick walked into the kitchen, sniffing like a drug dog.

"I smelled something incredible all the way out in the garage. You're killing me. Did you make bread or something?"

She smiled and rose to slice off two pieces, buttering hers and leaving Rick to take care of his own. He closed his eyes and savored it, offering soft moans of pure ecstasy.

"This is the best thing of this entire day," he murmured. His eyes popped open. "No, my week. I know you made a lot of bread at our house when we were kids, and my brothers and I had to make ourselves scarce so you wouldn't hide it. You and Hannah were afraid we'd eat it all before dinner."

"Because you sometimes did," Grace pointed out.

"Nah, maybe just half a loaf."

"Yeah, and the rest of it at the dinner table if your mom didn't put a muzzle on you guys."

He took another relished bite. "I'd wind up big as a house if I ate like this every day, but I wouldn't mind getting used to it."

Rick hadn't shaved that morning, and his evening stubble was thicker and darker than usual. His hair was a bit tamer, but it was still amazing. He didn't look like a wannabe-mechanic-slash-computer-geek; he could pass for a magazine model. How was it possible? And at the end of a very busy day?

The kids were embroiled in another game outside, and Grace knew from the score Cherise hollered they still had a way to go. She took a deep breath and faced Rick, hoping he'd listen.

"Can we talk?"

His chewing slowed, but he swallowed and shrugged, dusting the crumbs off his hands over the sink. "Sure."

He seemed all business now, his friendliness tucked into some corner of his soul where he kept it safe from Grace.

"I need to apologize. Again. I was wrong on Wednesday night, and I'm sorry. I hope you'll forgive me. I've been doing some soul-searching and some reading... in the Bible... and I've begun to realize I either expect way too much or way too little from other people. A part of me makes excuses for everyone else because I'm so broken I don't feel I have the right to expect anything from others. That's why I don't stand up for myself the way I should. The other part of me feels so broken, I need everyone else to be perfect to help me out, and it's not fair that I'm disappointed when they're not."

Rick's brows pulled together. Perhaps he didn't know what to make of her confession.

"You know I was hurt when you didn't protect me from Sean, but if I'd let you and Sean talk to me the next day, we probably would have resolved it. If I understand it right, the Lord expects us to forgive, whether we receive an apology or not. If I don't, then I'm the sinner."

Rick stared at her for a moment before responding. "That's the way the gospel works. It's more for our own good than for the person we should forgive, especially if someone doesn't feel like he or she should apologize."

Grace pushed away her disappointment. It would do him some good, too. Apologizing was the same as repenting, and repenting healed the soul. Maybe he didn't think his soul needed healing.

She nodded, glad to have done her best to "clear the air" between them. It hadn't brought any great exclamations of joy or rediscovered love, but it felt right.

She touched the bread loaves and found them cool enough to slice and bag. She turned her back on Rick as she did it, watching the knife slice its way, back and forth, through the yeasty-sweet-smelling loaf.

The rustle of clothing, the soft step of shoes on the tile, made Grace freeze in place. Rick stood close enough behind her she felt the warmth radiating off his body. He leaned toward her, his breath ruffling the hairs at the nape of her neck. It elicited a cascade of tingles which caused her shoulders to curl forward, as if to guard her heart.

He bent down and pressed his lips to the right side of her neck. The shiver it triggered bunched her stomach into knots and sent her heart galloping. Leaning into her, his chest against her back, he kissed her again. Sliding his hands down her arms to her wrists, he helped her set aside the knife and threaded his fingers between hers. Hands locked together, he wrapped their arms around her and hugged her tight.

Her breath stuttered, her heart racing from being enveloped against him while he rocked her gently from side to side. His teeth nibbled her ear lobe, and she shuddered with pleasure, completely helpless when he turned her to face him. Careful to avoid her injuries, he laced his fingers together at the base of her neck, his thumbs caressing the curve of her jaw. His forehead pressed against hers, he closed his eyes and held still.

"You're quite a woman, Grace," he said. "I wanted to talk to you, but Maria was hanging around and I was still smarting from our last discussion. I had a long talk with my Father in Heaven last night and had my eyes opened more than I liked. The truth is that Sean and I deserved what you said to us, and I understand why you would wash your hands of me. I deserved that, too. You know I would have apologized had you let me, but you're right. You wouldn't have gotten the apology you deserved if I'd given it back then. I was trying to pile blame for my own sins on my brothers. I'd kowtowed to them for so long, I'd forgotten I was a man and needed to shut Sean up, whatever it took. I assumed you'd understand, but we'd played too many gags on you over the years. You had no way of knowing I was serious. I needed to face all of it, and I needed to make my intentions toward you known. Now, this many years later, I realize I've harbored my own grudge against you. You made me see myself as I was, and it wasn't pretty. You also wounded my pride, which needed to be deflated, but it hurt."

Grace felt stunned to see his eyes redden.

"I'm sorry, Grace. For everything. For every time I hurt you and every time I didn't stop my brothers or the kids down the street or the kids at school from hurting you. How could I have done that when I've been crazy about you most of my life? Please. Will *you* forgive *me*?"

Grace felt a happiness she'd never known before blossoming in her heart. This was the most perfect apology she'd ever had, the one she'd always wanted, but more than that, one interwoven with snippets of love.

"Without question," she replied, joy lightening her heart.

He smiled back, bending over to kiss her brow and her eyelids, his lips searing her cheek and down the length of her neck in a dance as old as time itself. When his lips captured hers, the ecstasy of it had her gasping for air. She'd had no idea until now what it was to care for someone so completely it would almost hurt.

Rick embraced her, kissing her deeply and building the passion burning between them. Grace caressed his back and his arms, the powerful muscles of his chest. The scruff of his beard tickled the palms of her hands; her thumbs stroked the softness of his lips. She wanted more than anything to make love to him.

She forced herself to laugh and pushed him back a little. When he seemed confused, she took his hand and kissed his fingers.

"The kids may be outside, but you know we're not alone. Lucifer would love to ruin what we have. We can't give him the satisfaction."

Rick laughed, too, taking a deep breath and trying to relax. "Good call, Evans. Let's keep it light."

"For four more days alone together in this house, Fleming. It makes it harder to behave but not impossible. No wonder your church has its standards."

"Yep," Rick agreed, wiping a tear from one eye and blinking hard. "But after we get home, we can start courting, right?"

She laughed. "Courting? That sounds delightfully old-fashioned. I vote for courting."

"And kissing, at least a little bit," he said, giving her a quick peck on the lips.

"Maybe a little more than a little bit—but not right now," she insisted, raising a hand to stop him. "I'm barely able to keep my act together. Don't push me."

Rick chuckled. "Likewise. In fact, I'd best snag the drink of water I came in for and then lock myself in the garage. Or maybe you should lock me in the garage so I can't get back in."

One more quick kiss and they separated, Grace feeling as if she'd just stepped out of a dream—or had she stepped into one?—as Rick abandoned the kitchen.

July 4th. Grace couldn't believe it was here.

The meteorologists predicted a clear, sunny, triple-digit day, which would fill the small community pool with people and the lake with boats.

Grace had chosen to make bacon and fried eggs for her breakfast, along with toasted slices of her fresh bread, and the longing looks on the kids' faces had her chuckling. She offered them a deal.

"You guys make our picnic lunch—sandwiches, chips, whatever you want—and I'll make your breakfast."

She didn't need to say any more.

Rick joined them a little later than usual, freshly showered. Everyone else had eaten, so when Grace offered his plate to him, he snagged a piece of bacon and popped it into his mouth while still standing.

She raised a brow at him. "Really? It's a good thing Cherise blessed the food this morning or you'd be considered a heathen."

He chuckled then paused to watch her as he licked the grease off his bottom lip, slowly, almost seductively. Grace wanted more than anything to kiss those gorgeous, full lips.

"Uhm, are you two okay?" Charlotte asked, her brows pulled into knots.

Grace turned away quickly, feigning ignorance. "Does something seem wrong?"

Cherise snorted. "Not wrong, maybe, but completely different. When you first got here, Gracie, you were about to bite my cousin's face off. Now?" She turned her glittering eyes on Rick. "You look like you'd like to eat him."

"Cherise!" Grace snapped, her face burning with embarrassment. "That isn't nice."

Charlotte stepped back, her eyes wide as saucers. "Wow. Smack me. I totally missed that one. Good call, Sis," she said, slapping hands with Cherise. "Hey, Cuz, you aren't supposed to be sharing the same house alone with your girlfriend." She flashed them a tawdry grin.

Rick laughed, raising his shoulders. "I'm not copping to anything. I see you guys got our picnic together. Kyle, did you put the chairs into the Escalade for the fireworks tonight?"

Kyle gave Rick a knowing grin. "Chairs, blankets, and the small ice chest with sodas in them."

"Good man," Rick said. "Make sure you guys don't forget anything. I'm not coming back for cell phones, hair brushes, purses, bathing suits—"

"We've got it all, Dork."

"Cherise," Grace corrected her again.

"Oh, sorry, dearest most wonderful cousin, we've got it all. Can we have part of the allowance money my folks left for us?"

Rick snorted, but Grace couldn't help chuckling. Thankfully, Hannah had left the funds in her room for Grace. She gave each of the kids enough to keep them happy for at least a little while.

"Grace, pick up the phone! Grace, pick up the phone!"

Hannah! Grace wrenched the phone out of her hip pocket, all other thoughts fleeing.

"How is he?" she asked when she answered the call.

"He's awake! Gracie, he's awake!" Hannah shouted, laughing and crying all at once, and making Grace pull the phone away from her ear. She put it on speaker phone to save her ear drums and let the others hear.

"He recognizes everybody, and he remembers everything except when the truck hit him, and it's okay because he doesn't need to remember that."

"Oh, Hannah, that's fantastic."

The twins jumped up and down, clapping their own and each other's hands in excitement, and Kyle and Rick pumped their fists.

"What now? How long will he be in the hospital?"

"They don't know yet, but he's out of the woods. It's okay if he stays here for a month as far as I'm concerned, as long as he's okay."

"What about the boys who hit him? What's going to happen to them?"

There was a long pause. "They were drinking, Grace. They're in a heap of trouble. But Damien's such a great guy. He won't press charges. The cops can't ignore it, of course. They broke the law, and someone could have died, including them. But Damien talked to them on the phone and he forgave them, and one of the boys… the driver… he broke down and cried."

Grace's throat tightened. She had compassion for the boy. He'd done something terrible and must feel wretched, but such complete forgiveness would do something special to a person. It would touch the soul.

Forgiveness. It was a powerful reprieve. An incredible mercy.

Tears burned Grace's eyes.

The astounding news made Rick want to fall to his knees right then and there and give thanks. Grace's face glowed, and he suddenly didn't care the kids were watching when he gathered her into his arms and held her tight, the tears in his eyes matching the ones of hope in hers.

Grace sniffed, smiling her gratitude.

"Must have been the prayers," he murmured. Then he bent and pressed a soft kiss to her lips. Charlotte gave a quiet gasp and Cherise snorted, but he ignored them.

"Yeah," Grace agreed, her gaze locked with his. She appeared thoroughly amazed. "I guess prayers really do work."

The trip to town took longer than usual with way too many cars coming into the village off the freeway and way too few places to park. At least Marty had decided to allow the community to use his store parking lot—for a price.

"Three dollars?" Rick frowned. "Come on, Marty. If we have to pay for it, make it hurt. Most fair lots charge five or six bucks."

"You want to pay more?" Grace asked in bewilderment.

"Nope. Just think Marty's too nice a guy." They both laughed.

The kids' friends were waiting for them, the four girls running off to the recreation hall with the twins' potholders. Kyle's buddies accompanied Kyle to the woodworking area with his Corvette, and Rick and Grace submitted Grace's divinity. There were dozens of entries, and despite Rick's belief in her candy, Grace knew she had plenty of competition.

"Hey, Rick," Kyle said, running toward them full of excitement. "They set up a shooting gallery at the far end of the park. Can you believe it? They're only pellet guns, but the prizes are cool. Ethan and Jeff's parents are on their way with the guys. I need you to sign a permission slip."

"I'll walk over with him," Rick told Grace. "Find the girls and have fun. I'll call you when I'm ready to get back together."

Grace agreed and located the four girls hovering outside the recreation hall doors.

"Let's go see what Search and Rescue has going on," Cherise said, dragging Grace toward the west side of the park. The team had brought a few horses for children to pet while the officers explained their role in a rescue operation. A short distance away stood a fenced area, set up for the Search and Rescue dogs to demonstrate their skills to the audience.

"Cherise! Charlotte!" a voice stopped them, and Grace's heart nose-dived when she turned to see Maria jogging toward them. Today she was more casually dressed and seemed more serious, but she still managed to look like a movie star.

"Maria!" the girls cried in unison.

"Hey, girls. Grace," Maria said.

"Maria," Grace replied, thinking something felt off about the woman. "So, you decided to stay for the celebration."

"I wouldn't miss it," Maria said, her expression almost a challenge. Was she as uncomfortable around Grace as Grace was around her?

"Come on, Gracie," Charlotte said, tugging on Grace's hand. "Skylar's and Rachel's parents are holding a place for us."

Their group joined the girls' parents and siblings with the horses and dogs, but afterward, the girls wanted to take off on their own. Watching them having so much fun made Grace sigh. She used to love running around with Hannah and the twins when they were younger. It looked like those days were nearly gone. Peer groups and cell phones had taken their place.

Most of the vendors were under canopies, a few in tents with fans. Grace was sure it was already pushing one hundred degrees at ten o'clock in the morning. The sweat rolled down her face, and she wanted to kick herself for having forgotten her hat in her bedroom. Even if Rick agreed to go back for it, she didn't want to lose their parking place.

Grace wondered why Maria stayed with her as she walked, but then the interloper asked, "So, where's Ricky?"

Stalker. I wish you'd leave Rick alone.

"With Kyle at the shooting gallery. He's under eighteen and needed adult permission."

Maria's lips pulled into a sardonic smile. "Perfect. I need to talk to you, Grace. Alone."

Alone? As in, without witnesses alone? A sense of alarm raised goosebumps on Grace's arms.

"Uh, I guess, but Rick will be right back," she replied. Hopefully sooner rather than later.

"Which means we have little time," Maria said. "I've kept too much to myself about the Flemings, but it's unfair of me to not warn you."

CHAPTER 16

The goosebumps turned into alarms inside Grace's head. Grace knew more about the Flemings than Maria ever would. As a whole, they were a highly respected family, so what kind of scam did Maria hope to pull off?

Steeling herself, Grace fell into step with Maria, back toward Main Street and away from the crowd. Maria seemed so sure of herself. The casual flip of her hair, her runway-model saunter. She intimidated Grace.

"Ricky's hiding the truth from you, Grace," Maria began. "I could have embarrassed him a dozen times over this week. He's lied to you and hurt me. We've been dating for a while, but something happened and he's avoiding me. I have religious roots like he does, but I guess you might say I'm a modern woman. I wanted to move in with him, and it offended him. We had a fight. He wouldn't even give me a chance to apologize. He just stopped taking my calls."

Grace felt the world reeling and thought she'd fall off it. This was so bizarre she couldn't quite grasp it.

"Maybe he hasn't told his family about us, but he not only sent me flowers..." She paused before presenting her left hand to Grace. "He gave me a promise ring. A month ago."

There it was. Not a big ring but definitely expensive, the round-cut diamond sparkling in the late-morning sun. How had she missed it? Stunned, Grace didn't know what to say or think, and the tears blossoming in Maria's eyes baffled her.

"You don't want to get involved with a guy whose heart belongs to someone else or who would lie to you. He and I need to settle our differences."

Grace felt the ire churning in her gut. How could Maria suggest Rick was tainted goods and then say they had to work things out? It sounded ridiculous.

"We have a history. It may be short, but it's… powerful. You've seen him with me. You know he cares for me."

Grace knew Rick was attracted to Maria. What man wouldn't be? It didn't matter. Maria wasn't the one Rick kissed this morning. Straightening, Grace turned back toward the carnival.

"Thanks, Maria. I've heard enough. Rick's a big boy. He can make his own decisions."

"Wait. Please." Maria's pleading felt real. "You haven't heard it all. Like, how I got to know the Flemings. I graduated from high school when Ricky did, and I know his brothers, too. In fact, I dated Scott first for a while, but we broke up because he tried to force himself on me. Sean was the one who pulled him off me. Scott married a few years ago, but I fear Julia will have a rough marriage."

"Maria—"

"Sean felt bad about what happened and took me under his wing. We started dating. He was more fun and less physical, but he wasn't faithful. More than once. He's with Lisa now, and I hope she knows she can't trust him."

Julia. Lisa. Where had Maria learned all this without knowing the Flemings? Grace couldn't make the pieces fit together.

Maria continued. "Mac Larson is one of Ricky's best friends. He introduced us because he thought we'd make the perfect couple, and we would. Ricky needs a carefree woman, one who's in it for the long haul, and someone who doesn't… well… drop or break everything. He's patient, but you know he'll get fed up with it. I wouldn't want to be a pity date, and that's all you are to him, you know."

Grace's eyes widened and her jaw tightened with each of Maria's comments. Pity date? Her blood boiled. Pity dates didn't include kisses that left two people breathless, or looks of affection that could last forever.

"I don't know what's going on here, Maria, but I don't believe you. Stay away from me, and stay away from Rick."

She turned and fled toward the carnival. The east side of the park lawn was filled with people and canopies, and she had to dodge women with small children, boys with toys they bought from vendors, old people hobbling on walkers—

"Woah—"

She crashed into someone and gasped when she saw it was Rick. She held her breath, wondering if she saw something different on his face, something that came even close to what Maria said.

"Grace! What the heck? You look like you've seen a ghost. What's wrong?"

It came sputtering out of her, so disjointed Rick asked her to repeat it. She growled the story, and Rick took a step back, brows beetled and mouth hanging open.

"Are you serious? She said that? She's a lying snake. Where is she?"

They scanned the crowd, but neither saw any sign of her.

"This isn't funny," Rick said, shaking his head. "I'm beginning to think she has a box of screws loose."

"None of it's true, right? Do you think she might be dangerous?" Remembering the way Maria acted at the edge of Haylee's Peak came back to haunt her. Had she really been tempted to push Grace off?

"What? You think she'd kidnap me and make a kept man out of me?" He almost sounded amused.

"Or maybe she'd take you to a cabin in the mountains and use a sledgehammer on your legs to keep you a prisoner?"

Rick huffed. "Way too creepy. No, I think she's getting desperate and trying to scare you, Grace. Or she's after something else. Like, what if she's a reporter, digging for a story?"

Grace shook her head. "I guess it's possible, but something in my heart tells me it's not that simple."

"Yeah, me too. Pray about it, Grace. We need the Lord on our side."

Grace nodded. The Lord and maybe half the Mendocino County Police force. "You're sure Scott and Sean never dated her?"

Rick's face scrunched in disbelief. "Are you kidding? I think the bigger question is where she got all the information about my family. I mean, she has to either be a conniving journalist or a crazy stalker to have dug so deeply into my past."

And in different ways, both sounded dangerous. "Well, she's gone now. Let's hope she figures she blew it and will get lost."

Rick put his arm around her. "Yeah. Let's hope so. Forget her. Relax. Let's do some tent-style window shopping."

Grace chuckled. Even if she wasn't into trinkets and such, she wanted to go everywhere and do everything with Rick today.

They passed hawkers and food carts, artisans, musicians, and insurance salesmen. Rick insisted on buying her a caramel apple, a shave-ice, and a broad-brimmed sunhat.

"Thank you," she said with honest appreciation. "My freckles and my sunburn thank you, too."

"You're welcome, and it looks great on you."

Grace grinned, loving the quick kiss he gave her as they continued through the rows of tents and tables.

The loudspeaker announced the judging for the arts and crafts competition was finished, drawing a crowd to the recreation hall. Grace and Rick found the kids already there, wound tight with excitement.

"Wow!" everyone said when Grace's divinity took first place, and Rick gave her a hug. "Wow," she said, blinking in surprise. "I don't know what to say." She wanted to laugh, thinking it was a miracle she'd gotten the divinity to the contest without dropping it in the first place, but she'd also beaten more than twenty other entries.

The girls were excited their potholders tied for second place, behind an amazing crocheted afghan, and the Fleming crowd clapped and cheered when Kyle took Best of Show in the wood-carving department with his Corvette.

"Terrific job, everyone," Rick said, high-fiving the kids and hugging Grace again.

The rec hall needed to be prepared for the annual fundraising dinner that night, so the participants collected their entries and locked them in their cars. The kids' friends ate with their families, while the Flemings and Grace took their picnic lunch and blankets to a shady spot away from the crowd. They talked about all the fun they had while enjoying their sandwiches—and Grace's divinity.

Headed for the pool after lunch, Rick and the kids changed in the locker rooms while Grace found an umbrella table on the pool decking. She wanted to join them but not as much as she needed to coddle her injuries.

The day's pleasantries crept into Grace's bones. Knowing Damien was out of danger, that Hannah would survive the disaster, and that Rick deeply cared for her made her more relaxed than she'd felt in a long time.

Then the chair to her left shifted and she looked up, blinking in surprise as Maria sat down beside her. The woman set her elbows on the table, clasped her hands, and leaned toward Grace with her head turned away from the pool.

"You told Ricky what I said." It wasn't an accusation, just a statement.

"Of course. He denies it."

"Of course, he did. He doesn't want you to know the truth. I know I probably sound pathetic, but I love him and he loves me. He'll get over being mad at me, and he'll dump you. Protect your heart, Grace. He's playing you. Unfortunately, the Fleming men are good at the game."

Grace felt as if her heart had been pulled from her chest and smashed on the concrete. The Fleming boys had been good at playing people—particularly her—when they were younger. What if Maria was telling the truth now? What if Rick really was only making a fool out of her?

"Would you stay with a guy who cheated on you?" Maria asked, her gaze intent.

"No," Grace replied, "but Rick isn't cheating. For one thing, he can't. We're not... exclusive." In her mind, she was, but she didn't have the right to speak for Rick and they hadn't gotten that far yet.

"Ricky's the only one I would forgive," Maria insisted, "because he's everything I've ever wanted in a guy. He's handsome, fun, and rich. Remember?"

She showed off her ring again, making Grace want to drag Rick out of the pool. He needed to explain this. He needed to confront Maria himself. She stood, the chair screeching across the concrete behind her.

"I said I don't believe you, Maria, and you need to leave us alone."

Grace marched off to find Rick. The pool was crazy-busy, with all the splashing and laughter and screeching making it impossible to hear. When she finally found Rick and got his attention, she pointed toward Maria—but once again, found her gone.

⌒ ⁂ ⌒

"You don't believe one word of it do you?" Rick said when he climbed out of the pool to discuss the new confrontation.

"I'm sorry. I'm an idiot, but I need you to reassure me," she insisted. "You can't imagine how convincing she is. You should see her ring."

He shouldn't let her comment offend him, but it did. His scowl deepened. "Anyone can buy—or even borrow or steal—a ring, and I can't believe you'd even think about taking her word over mine. My phone's in my pool locker. Let me borrow yours and I'll call Scott. You can talk to him yourself."

He dialed his brother on speaker phone so Grace could hear Scott's comments. Unfortunately, it went to voicemail. Rick left a message and hung up, his irritation palpable. He tried again with Sean but had the same result.

"Forget it," Grace said, obviously not happy with the situation but trying to placate him. "I can't let her get to me." Phone in hand, she returned to the table and kicked back.

Rick sighed. He knew Grace would require tons of patience. She'd been through a lot in her life, but it bugged him that she would give one ounce of credence to Maria's insane accusations.

An hour later, Rick dried off and joined Grace at the table, content to sit back and watch the fun. He'd never seen so many people in the village's public pool, and there were still scores of people patronizing the vendors while the lake remained full of boats of all kinds.

Rick lost track of time, but a while later, Cherise came to them, wrapped in her towel and shivering. "Hey, have you guys seen Charlotte?"

Grace shook her head.

"Only in the pool with you and your friends," Rick said. "Why?"

"She went to the bathroom a while ago, but she didn't come back. I went to check on her, but she isn't there, and we can't find her in the pool area."

"What about Skylar?"

Cherise's face went blank. "I don't know. I wasn't looking for Skylar, but I haven't seen her either."

Rick mashed his hand against his face. This was all they needed. A couple of maverick teenagers.

"I'll go check the bathroom myself," Grace volunteered. "Maybe she stepped outside for a minute and Cherise missed her."

"Thanks." Rick was grateful. After all, he couldn't go into the girls' bathroom to check it out.

Replaying Grace's conversation with Maria had him on edge. The minute he saw Maria again, he was going to put an end to this.

When Grace didn't return, he paced outside the bathroom door for what seemed forever. He finally sent Cherise back inside to find her. She returned far too quickly.

"Ricky, Grace isn't there, either. Where did they all go?"

"I don't know. Find your brother and meet me out front. Something's off. If we don't find them soon, I'm heading for the sheriffs' station."

When Grace marched into the women's bathroom, she called for Charlotte. The only answer was the echo of her own voice. She checked each stall and then dared open the curtains to the two showers. The bathroom was empty.

Frustrated, she headed through the locker room into the hallway which led to the ticket desk at the front door. No one was there right now, and the door was locked to incoming traffic. The pool must be filled to capacity. No one else would be admitted until a significant number of people left. Grace wondered if, for some reason, Charlotte had come out this way and discovered she couldn't get back in. If so, she might be wandering around the park, trying to find a way to get in touch with them. Like all the rest of their group, her cell phone was in her locker.

Grace combed Main Street before heading across the lawn toward the vendors. Late afternoon was hot and still. She stood in a spot where she felt she had a good vantage point, searching the crowd for any sign of a girl with red hair with purple ends.

"You won't find her there," a voice said in Grace's ear, making her jump. She whipped around to find Maria standing behind her, a knowing look on her face.

"Find who?" she asked with suspicion.

Maria laughed. "You know who I mean. Let's go for another walk."

"I don't want to take a walk. I'm trying to find Charlotte."

"And I know where she is, so humor me, okay?"

Grace felt her cheeks pale. Yep, something was seriously wrong with this girl. Grace had no choice, but her skin crawled when Maria looped her arm through Grace's as if they were best buds.

Dread grew into abject fear when they approached Maria's car. Grace recognized it, but a closer examination of the beat-up gray Cavalier jarred an idea inside her.

"If you know where Charlotte is, what are we doing here?" she asked.

Maria twitched a sly grin. "I'll take you to her. Get in."

"I'm not getting in your car. Tell me where Charlotte is!"

Maria leaned into Grace, nearly nose to nose, then muttered, "Look in my bag, Snoopy."

Maria opened the handbag hugging her waist and displayed the only object inside it besides her wallet—a small, black pistol. A soft gasp from Grace painted a nasty grin on Maria's face.

"It's about time you finally got it," Maria said. "I'm not willing to share, girlfriend. I want Ricky, and that's all there is to it. Get in the car, or I'll shoot you. If you cooperate, we'll make this quick."

Grace searched and prayed and searched some more for a way to ease the situation. Finally, she cleared her throat, fighting tears. "Your relationship with Ricky is between the two of you. I just want Charlotte." Had Maria hurt the girl? Had she done it because of Grace? Was she going to take Grace somewhere and kill her?

"She'll be fine if you do what I tell you to," Maria insisted, nodding toward the passenger door. "Now get in."

Grace did as she was told, her heart about to hammer its way out of her chest. She was on the edge of a panic attack.

Maria opened the door and slid into the driver's seat but didn't close the door. Handing Grace a sheet of paper and a pen, she said, "Here. Write the note I'll dictate to you. If you don't, your little friend will die."

"Where is she?" Grace insisted.

Maria laughed. "Locked in the trunk, *honey*, and I promise you, at one hundred and ten degrees, it's a dangerous place for a drugged-out fourteen-year-old girl to be."

Grace nearly panicked. "No! You can't! Maria, please let her out. You don't want to go to jail for murder."

"She won't die, but if she did, I'd make sure the cops think you're responsible. Now, here's a piece of paper and a pen. Write Rick a farewell letter. Tell him you found out what sort of a selfish player he is and don't ever want to see him again. That you never, ever want to hear from him or any of the Flemings again, including Hannah. Then sign it. I'm taking you to a bus stop in Ukiah and giving you a one-way ticket home. If you climb on the bus and promise you'll never repeat our enlightening conversation, I'll make sure sweet Charlotte is back at the cabin by Monday morning. If you tell anyone, none of you will ever see her again. If you say anything in the future, believe me, I'll know and I'll hunt you down and make you pay for it."

Maria meant it. Grace could see it clearly written on her face. The woman wouldn't hesitate to kill her or Charlotte, now or six months from now.

Her hand shook as she wrote the note, words which made her sick to her stomach. When she was done, Maria took the note and pen and demanded Grace's cell phone. She took it, turned it off, and pocketed it. "You won't be getting this back."

The beat-up car managed to race up the street, out of town, and onto the freeway toward Ukiah. Grace was stunned when they reached a bus stop on one of Ukiah's main streets, where Maria handed her a one-way bus ticket she bought… *yesterday*. The woman was truly deranged.

Maria checked her watch. "The bus will be here in ten minutes. I'll park at the back of the lot in the shade. If you're good, we'll stay here and keep Charlotte as comfortable as we can."

"No," Grace insisted, "the shade isn't enough. She can't breathe. Let her out of there. I'll behave. I promise. I won't tell a soul."

Maria grinned. "I know you won't, because Charlotte stays where she is."

"Charlotte!" Grace cried out. She needed to know the girl was still alive.

"Shut up," Maria commanded, grabbing Grace's wrist with a bone-breaking grip. There were a few people sitting on the sheltered bench at the bus stop who turned to glance at them.

"Charlotte, are you okay?" Grace cried once again, but this time, Maria whipped the gun from her purse and pointed it at Grace's stomach.

Grace thought she might wet her pants. This was far worse than a highway patrol officer in a convenience store defending himself from a flying burrito. She yelped, seeing stars when Maria backhanded her with the pistol. Everything went gray until the sounds around her faded to near nothing before returning to normal.

"Don't make another sound," Maria warned her through gritted teeth. "I'll drive to the nearest patch of woods and make you wish you were never born."

Grace blinked, cringing when she saw blood pouring out of her nose onto her shirt. She touched her nose and gasped from the pain. No doubt it was broken.

"Here." Maria opened her glove compartment and grabbed a small box of tissues for Grace. "There's a bottle of water on the floor by your feet. The bus is here. Wash your face and get going."

Grace did as Maria said, pinching her nose to stop the persistent bleeding, then opened the door and said, "Rick won't marry you, you know."

"Of course, he will. He's in love with me. I told you." She turned the ring toward Grace. "Just remember, Grace, if I can't have him, no one can. He needs me, and he knows I need him. Have you seen his house? It's beautiful. I belong there. Don't you get it?"

Grace suddenly did get it, and she stepped out, knowing there was no way she could talk Maria out of her delusion.

CHAPTER 17

"You still haven't seen Grace, Charlotte or Skylar?" Rick asked Cherise and Kyle when he found them. He'd taken a complete tour of Main Street and through the carnival and hadn't located them. Afterward, he collected his phone and spoke with Deputy Hadley at the station. On his phone, he found a picture he'd taken of Grace and Hannah on the boat. It was the only one he had to help the department identify her.

When Cherise and Kyle said they hadn't seen them, Rick asked them not to involve their friends or their friends' families in the situation yet, not even Skylar's. They needed to avoid upsetting people until they were sure they had a problem. The thought led him to the next logical question.

"What about Maria?"

They hadn't seen her, either.

Rick blew air out between pursed lips, baffled.

"Hey, can we have some help here?" a young voice called from up the street near Marty's.

All of them froze, shocked by what they heard.

"Charlotte!" Cherise cried, bounding down the sidewalk like she'd been blown out of a circus cannon.

Rick's mouth dropped open when he saw Charlotte and Skylar, both wearing their bathing suit cover-ups and flip-flops, toting carry-boxes filled with double-scoop ice cream cones.

"What the heck?" he asked, glaring at his cousin when she arrived. "We've been looking all over for you."

"Maria gave us money and sent us on a scavenger hunt. We've had so much fun! She said if we found everything, we could buy everyone's favorite ice cream."

"And you didn't think to ask for Grace's or my permission first?"

Charlotte scrunched her face into a what's-the-big-deal look. "Maria said she would tell you," she replied.

"Oh, look! You girls did such a great job!" Maria called out, stepping up behind Rick out of thin air. "Wasn't scavenger hunt fun?"

"Yes!" the two girls cried, laughing.

"You had no right," Rick snapped.

Maria had the courtesy to act sheepish. "I heard what you said. I'm sorry, Ricky. I couldn't find you to tell you what was going on, but I'm sure the ice cream will make up for it. Charlotte and Skylar, let Kyle hold the cones so you two can pull the others out of the pool. We need to distribute this stuff before it all melts."

Rick felt as if he'd been stuffed into an old *Twilight Zone* episode as the girls ran toward the pool to do as she asked. He'd awakened from one nightmare into another, from losing Charlotte and Grace, to finding Maria was the instigator of a different kind of trouble.

"Where's Grace?" he asked, barely civil.

Maria's eyes widened. "She's missing?" she replied. "Where was she the last time you saw her?"

Rick glared at her, ignoring Maria when she offered his favorite rocky road ice cream to him.

"She has to be here somewhere," Maria said. "Unless she doesn't want to be, but it would be rude of her to leave since she's supposed to be watching your cousins, right? Although it sounds like they've been with their friends a lot, and you're fine with it. Maybe she decided she wanted to go home." She paused, chewed her pecan praline ice cream, then swallowed. "Perhaps Grace's mom got sick or needed help. Have you tried calling Grace? Or maybe texting her?"

"Yeah, both, several times, and the calls go to voicemail," Rick said between gritted teeth. He didn't know who to be upset with now, Maria or Grace.

What felt terribly wrong before now had him scared.

"That's not very nice of her," Maria grumbled.

"We shouldn't be eating ice cream. It's dinnertime," Rick said, glancing at his watch. The foot traffic had dwindled to almost nothing. Although plenty of people were headed off to either BJ's or The Hungry Bass, the vast majority were lining up outside the recreation hall for dinner. "If Grace is upset about something, she'll probably join us when she gets over it."

As soon as he said it, Rick felt as if he'd betrayed Grace. He was the one upset, not Grace. She'd asked for simple reassurance Maria was telling a pile of lies. He wished he'd been more understanding. He grabbed his ice cream from Maria and tossed it in the trashcan. Her eyes widened in disapproval.

"I'm going to let the sheriff know we've found Charlotte and Skylar," he grumbled, leaving Maria to follow the girls.

"They're safe and sound," he told Hadley in the station's front office, "but I'm still worried about Grace. Will you keep an eye out for her?"

"As best we can, but she's an adult. Unless you have some proof of foul play, we can't use valuable manpower to find someone who doesn't want to be found."

"Understood," Rick said. "But I have a feeling she's not safe."

Prickles kept racing up and down Rick's spine. The way Maria was chumming up to his cousins bothered him, and when he joined them in line, the way she stroked his arm and leaned into him as if they were a couple sickened him. The kids seemed confused, especially the twins, but Rick signaled them to stay quiet.

It was then a thought dawned on Rick, one he believed came from a place greater than himself. If Maria knew why Grace vanished, he needed to take advantage of her friendliness rather than alienating her. Maybe she'd slip up and give it away. After all, Grace didn't have a car, and if Rick understood Grace's circumstances, she certainly didn't have the funds to take a cab home. A bus, perhaps, but the closest one was in Ukiah and was also expensive, and how would she buy it? She didn't have her I.D. with her.

What he still couldn't fathom was why she'd do that in the first place. Grace might have reservations about Rick because of Maria, but he didn't think she was rash or rude. She'd gone in search of Charlotte, not to run off and throw a temper tantrum.

The line had shortened notably when Deputy Hadley approached Rick, a piece of paper fluttering in his hand.

"One of the Ukiah deputies found this about half an hour ago. Just got around to bringing it to me. You need to take a look at it."

Rick felt the ground tip beneath him when he read the words which didn't make sense. "Where did you find this?"

"It was stuffed into our mail slot," the deputy said, pointing toward the station. "What do you think? Is it Miss Evan's handwriting?"

Maria peeked over Rick's arm and gave a soft gasp. "Ricky, this is awful. I feel so bad."

Rick wished Hannah was here right now. She'd be able to tell him if Grace had written this. "I haven't seen Grace's handwriting since she was in high school. But why would she break up with me by leaving a note at the station? I know her well enough to believe she'd say it to my face if she wanted me out of her life."

"So, there's no bad blood between the two of you?"

"None. Just the opposite. As I said, Charlotte disappeared and Grace went to see if my cousin was in the pool bathroom. Charlotte just returned with her friend, but Grace hasn't."

"Would she have any reason to go home unannounced?"

"Not that I know about."

"Are you sure?" Maria asked, leaning into Rick, her lovely face filled with sympathy. "Maybe something happened. Like, to her mother. And you know Grace has financial difficulties, don't you? Maybe that's the problem."

"Yeah, but—" Rick bit off the rest. Grace's family had always had financial headaches, which was why he didn't believe she would leave a paying job like this. He also couldn't believe Grace would be inconsiderate about saying goodbye—unless there was an emergency. Even then, she would have called or texted him.

Besides, how did Maria know anything about Grace's finances?

"Sorry about all of this," Hadley said, "but I think this note is your answer. Probably not the one you wanted, but it means we won't be looking for her anymore."

Rick nodded his understanding. He made a mental note to call Hannah later, when Maria wasn't listening, to get Trudy Evans' phone number. Grace's mom might have the answers to some questions.

"So, you've gotten to know Grace while you're here," Rick said to Maria. "You probably know more about her than I do. I'm… a little worried about what's going on with her. You want to share?"

"Oh, I doubt I know a lot," Maria said, her coquettish grin sending his heart spinning. She wanted to flirt with him? Now? This girl was clearly disturbed.

"But the financial stuff?"

"Just girl talk. You should forget about her. She's obviously not into you."

Rick sighed. Maria didn't know Grace or him. In his heart, he knew Grace wrote that note, but that didn't mean it made any sense.

Determined to slip past Maria's defenses, he changed tactics, unloading a pile of non-existent suspicions about Grace on her, and before he knew it, Maria was echoing him, even creating a few accusations of her own.

"I still can't figure where she'd go without a car, though," Rick murmured, watching Maria out of the corner of his eye. She tensed, tipping him off that she didn't want him to go in that direction.

Maria flipped her dark hair behind her shoulder and said, "There are shuttle buses helping with the tourists. She could certainly take one to a bus stop in Ukiah."

It bothered Rick that Maria knew this. She'd never been here before. She didn't know Ukiah or Secret Lake Village. Normal people didn't look up information like this for the fun of it, did they? No, Rick was convinced Maria knew more than she let on.

Grace leaned back in her seat, her head protesting as the bus bounced its way southbound on the 101 freeway. Her bloodied nose wouldn't cooperate, and from time to time she had to grab another tissue to staunch the bleeding. Her box was almost empty. The sun was nearing the distant horizon, its red-gold haze all but blinding her swollen right eye. It was past dinnertime, and her stomach growled in protest. The occasional glances from other riders made her uncomfortable, too.

"Honey, are you okay?" an older woman finally asked, leaning across the aisle to touch her arm.

Grace jerked away, not expecting either the contact or the concern. What should she say? If she told anyone the truth, Maria would hurt Charlotte.

She struggled with another round of tears, imagining Charlotte in the trunk of Maria's car, dying from heat prostration, with Rick, beside himself that his cousin was missing and convinced that Grace had run out on him. Or worse. That he believed she was responsible for Charlotte's disappearance. Maria might hurt him if Grace told on her, but she wasn't convinced the deranged woman wouldn't hurt Rick anyway.

"Oh, my, you're in a pickle, aren't you?" the woman asked, her gentle touch sparking something in Grace's heart. "Here, move over and let me sit beside you."

Grace slid into the empty seat to her right to let the woman take hers. The woman's husband leaned forward to watch them, the concern on his face as authentic as his wife's.

"Your nose is broken, sweetie. Did someone hit you?"

Grace couldn't speak for fear she'd break down and sob, but she did nod.

<hr />

Rick found a table in the recreation hall with enough chairs for their entire group, and they took turns getting food from the serving tables. Old friends came by to say hello, and Rick tried to pretend nothing was wrong as he visited briefly with them.

When he chatted with Maria, he did his best to act like a high-school jock as he told story after story about girls who hurt his feelings in the past, even girls who never existed. Maria cooed over him, offering to help make his life better.

"I'd do anything for you, you know," she said. "I really care about you."

"Wow." Rick turned to face her. After three dates, and the last one basically a disaster? How could anyone fall in love like that? "That's amazing, Maria. You're a special girl. One of a kind."

She glowed, and Rick began the journey he dreaded, making her think he'd fallen for her while finding a way to determine if she had anything to do with Grace's disappearance.

<hr />

"That's right, Deputy," the bus driver said on his radio, confirming the entire conversation. "Miss Evans is on my bus. She looks like someone took a sledgehammer to her face, and she says a woman, a Maria Del Rey, hit her with a gun." He reviewed the conversation, reassuring Grace he'd gotten the crux of the situation straight. She wasn't the one in danger. It was Charlotte.

"This Miss Evans is Grace Evans, correct?"

"Yep, that's her."

"Can she hear me?"

"She's right next to me. She can hear you fine."

"Grace, this is Deputy Hadley. Do you know Rick Fleming?"

Grace nearly burst into tears again. "Yes. He's my... my boyfriend." She hoped he was. Unless the note Maria made her write ruined everything.

The deputy went on to explain the situation in Secret Lake Village. Grace sat, lips parted and eyes rounded, as the deputy told the entire story, from Charlotte and Skylar having been sent for ice cream to the note that had mysteriously appeared on the sheriff station door.

"Charlotte's safe?" Grace rasped, relief a tidal wave flooding through her.

"She's fine, but you don't sound too great. The accused, on the other hand, is clinging to Mr. Fleming like a barnacle on a ship. If she has a gun, we don't want to confront her. She could panic and hurt someone. We'll keep an eye on her until we can find a safe time to catch her. In the meantime, we need to get you back here as soon as we can so you can press formal charges."

"But how?"

"You hang tight. A CHP officer has already been dispatched to bring you back. We'll have EMT's waiting for you when you arrive."

"No!" Grace insisted. "If Maria sees the ambulance, she'll know something's up. I'll go to the hospital when this is over." When Hadley reluctantly agreed, she thanked him profusely. It was enough to make her want to cry again, only she didn't dare because it would make a worse mess of her bloody, swollen nasal passages, and she was sure it would be her undoing.

"You sit back, dear," the older woman said. "Here, my sweet Jake got some ice out of our little ice chest and wrapped it in one of his clean hankies. It'll feel good on your nose."

It did feel as good as a hard, cold chunk of ice could feel pressed against a broken bone. Grace sat back as suggested and began counting the minutes to climbing into a patrol car and speeding back to the village. She only prayed Rick didn't consider her the enemy.

Nothing Rick said got Maria tricked into giving away anything she might know. She seemed sincere, well versed in what she should know, oblivious to what she shouldn't, and far too conniving with the way she worded whatever she said.

The meal tasted like sawdust, and he pushed it aside, pretty convinced he wouldn't find food appealing again until Grace was safe and sound.

Part way through dinner, a country trio took to a small stage at the front of the room and played for a while. He hated it when Maria insisted he dance with her, but he did so to carry on his scheme. He also wanted to slap Maria's hands, which were too familiar by far, but he tolerated her behavior to avoid upsetting her.

After all, Godfather Michael Corleone's advice still rocked: to keep your friends close and your enemies closer.

It was nearly dark outside now, and it wouldn't be long before the fireworks started. They'd been set up during the day on a floating barge in the lake, and it would be a spectacular event for such a small town. The kids were getting excited about collecting the blankets, and Maria said she had a couple of lawn chairs for her and Rick in her car.

Rick wanted to scream. The last thing he wanted to do was watch fireworks with Maria Del Rey. Her advances had him concerned she really did want to throw him in her car and take off with him. Where? To the justice of the peace?

It chilled him to think of it.

"I've got to check in with Hannah about Damien, Maria," he said at last. The excuse appeared to appease the woman a bit—although she watched every move he made as he sauntered to the side of the room where it was quieter. He dialed Hannah's number, relieved when she answered on the third ring.

"Rick! Happy July 4th! Damien's doing so much better they're letting him eat. How's the crew?"

"Fantastic news. Give him our best. We're okay, but I need a favor. I also need you to trust me and not ask any questions."

Hannah was quiet on the other side of the line, letting him know she was listening.

"I need to call Grace's mom, but I don't have her number."

Another pause followed Hannah's giving it to him. "Rick, is something wrong?"

"No, Sis. It's cool. Go back to Damien. I want to ask Mrs. Evans something about Grace. You know, a little secret something."

He pictured Hannah's smile when she replied with an emphatic, "Oh, you bet. But you have to tell me every juicy detail later."

"You've got it," he agreed, praying it would be a good story.

His heart sank when Trudy Evans' phone went to voicemail. Hadn't Grace said if she didn't answer her phone, she'd gone to bed? And if she went to bed early, she was having a bad day?

"Mrs. Evans, this is Rick Fleming. Uhm, we have a situation here, and I need to ask you a couple of questions about Grace. It's important, so it would be wonderful if you could call me back soon. Thanks."

Disappointed, Rick pushed his phone into his pants pocket and headed back to the table.

⁂

Grace hung on for dear life as the patrol car roared up the freeway. The siren blared, and every car on the road slowed and moved over to let them through. The officer had pulled the bus over the same way and taken Grace off as quickly as her feet would move—with a bit of help from the old woman's husband and the bus driver, who didn't want her to fall.

Grace couldn't help sneaking a look at the officer. Surely, he remembered her. Surely, he had to wonder what sort of person she was, beyond being a thorn in his side twice over. Officer Tran stared straight ahead, his eyes hidden by his sunglasses and his concentration tight. At least the goose-egg on his forehead from a frozen burrito was gone.

Tran turned off the siren and slowed to normal city street speeds as they headed into Secret Lake Village.

"Can't go into town like something's wrong," he said to Grace. "Might tip off the suspect. I'm headed to the far end of Main Street."

He parked and pulled off his sunglasses to stare at Grace. "For now, you will stay in the car. The windows are dark, so unless someone comes right up to the car, they won't see you. I'll leave the doors unlocked so if it gets too hot you can get out, but remember, you're safe here. If you leave, not only could your life be at risk, but so might innocent bystanders."

Grace agreed but her head swam, probably from a concussion from being pistol-whipped. That's what the cop had called it—pistol-whipping. Leave it to Grace to manage not one but two concussions—and a broken nose—on a vacation in the quiet woods of Northern California.

Tran parked his car and left her there, strolling toward the sheriff station as if he didn't have a care in the world. Grace supposed he wanted to avoid getting Maria's attention.

Grace wanted to obey the officer, but sitting there, doing nothing, had her skin crawling. Where was everyone? Had Maria somehow persuaded Rick to trust her? If Maria got him in her car, what would she do to him?

At least she had hope Charlotte was safe. It was worth all Grace had gone through today. Now, if they could manage to corral the crazy woman.

Looking out the back window, Grace's heart seized when Rick, hand-in-hand with Maria, crossed the street and headed toward Maria's car. Seeing the two of them together and smiling seemed so wrong Grace was sure she'd fallen into a coma and was having a nightmare.

From the trunk, the pair removed a couple of low-sitting lawn chairs, while the Fleming cousins, arms wrapped around blankets, waited for them on the sidewalk. Fireworks. They wouldn't start until after dark, but people were already saving their spots.

Jealousy tore at Grace. It wasn't fair. This was supposed to be one of the best nights of her life. She should be the one watching the fireworks wrapped in Rick's arms, not Maria. The woman had ruined everything. Grace would *not* sit there and let it happen.

She climbed out of the car, glad her legs felt stronger, and bustled toward the sheriff station. She should go in. She should introduce herself and insist on being part of the arresting party that would put Maria behind bars for assault and battery.

The door to BJ's opened, and a woman gasped when she saw Grace. Grace cringed. Maybe this hadn't been such a great idea. No doubt, she looked like a train wreck, with her black eye and broken nose, twice its normal size and bent sideways. Blood stained her shirt—another ruined shirt to add to the others from this trip—and had dried under her fingernails. She dreaded what her mascara looked like, mixed with her tears and blood and smeared all over her face.

"Miss, are you okay?" a man asked, reaching toward her.

"Yeah, I'm headed to the sheriff's station," she said, avoiding him and hurrying on. She needed to do something before Maria saw her. The woman might bolt if she saw Grace, but Maria had a gun in her purse, and who knew what she would do if she got desperate?

Maria and the others disappeared from view and Grace relaxed. Then the station door opened and two men, one in a deputy's uniform and the other Officer Tran, walked ahead of Grace and toward the park and the recreation hall. From further away, two more deputies, among those who'd come to safeguard the festivities, approached. All four followed Rick and Maria, soon passing from Grace's view, as well.

Keeping her face turned downward, Grace shadowed them. If nothing else, she wanted to witness what was about to happen.

Unfortunately, Maria turned around and saw Grace before she noticed the cops. Maria went white but her cheeks flamed red. Immediately her hand went into her purse and Grace panicked. No! Maria was crazy enough to shoot anyone, and it suddenly dawned on Grace "anyone" included Rick. She warned Grace if she couldn't have Rick, no one could, and Grace may have just signed his death warrant.

Grace lost all sense of reason. A bullet shot at point-blank range would travel lightyears faster than she could run, but she ran anyway. Passing the cops, she elbowed a young boy out of the way and plowed into Maria.

"I'll kill you! I'll kill you!" Maria howled as they hit the ground, the woman trying to reach her bag while beating on Grace's blistered shoulder. Grace gritted her teeth and screeched, with pain, turning her face away to protect it while doing her best to grab Maria's wrists. She failed. The woman finally gave a mighty heave and threw Grace to the side, coming to her feet like she was on steroids. Maybe she was.

Grace lurched to one knee and grabbed for Maria's left ankle, amazing herself at having the wits to sink her teeth into Maria's calf. Maria screamed and fell, turning around to slap Grace in the face with the flat of her hand. Grace howled when the pain nearly blinded her.

Maria lurched back to her feet, and gasps and screeches all around told Grace the woman had drawn her gun. She looked up, head spinning when she saw the weapon pointed at her face.

"Maria, stop," Rick said, hands raised. He leaned over and offered Grace help up. She took it, trembling, and somehow managed to stand. "Grace may be clumsy sometimes but she doesn't need to be shot for it. Let's talk, okay? This isn't like you."

"It's her fault. She's trying to get between us."

"No. She's just worried about Charlotte, and we both know Charlotte's fine. Give me the gun, okay?"

"No. Grace has to go."

Grace's mouth dropped when Rick stepped in front of her and his entire demeanor changed. "That's not happening, Maria. You'll have to shoot me to get to her."

Maria screamed with rage, and Grace sobbed, terrified Rick would die to protect her from the woman. In the next instant, Rick's fist flashed out and knocked the gun out of Maria's hand and then he grabbed her wrist. The deputies and Officer Tran jumped in, and despite Maria's hissing, spitting, kicking, and trying to bite, they managed to handcuff her.

"You can't do this, Ricky!" Maria begged. "She isn't good enough for you."

Rick, pulling Grace against him, leaned into Maria and replied, "Grace Evans is ten times the woman you'll ever be, and I wouldn't have chosen you if we were stranded together on a deserted island."

Maria's jaw dropped in horror, and Grace's ears turned red as the woman called Grace a slew of choice names. Tran told her to shut her mouth and she did. The onlookers started shouting questions, but Hadley raised a hand. "We've got this, folks. Go on about your business." To Maria, he said, "Maria Del Rey, you are under arrest for kidnapping, assault and battery, and carrying a concealed weapon." He added her Miranda rights.

"You can't do this," Maria wailed, her tear-filled gaze attached to Rick's. "I need you, Ricky. I need to marry you. I love you."

Rick shook his head. "No, you don't. You don't know me well enough to be in love with me. And I love Grace with all of my heart, which I could never say about you."

Grace's head swam with everything she was hearing. Rick had protected her from Maria, he'd said she was ten times the woman Maria was, and he'd declared his love for her in front of his family and half of Secret Lake Village.

"But I *need* you," Maria insisted.

"You need his *money*," Grace taunted. That had been Maria's goal all along.

"You're my last hope, Ricky," she persisted, ignoring Grace. Tears drenched her face.

"Which is why you bought a ring and went on a vacation you can't afford," Rick said.

"I can't stand working at the restaurant. I want to go to school. I'm smart; I'm a hard worker. I'd make you a good wife and give you beautiful children."

"That's enough," Hadley said, grabbing one of Maria's elbows, while Tran took the other. To Rick and Grace, he said, "Sorry to ruin your night any worse than it already is, but you two need to come to the station and fill out some paperwork. After that, you, young lady, need to go to the hospital in Ukiah and get your nose put back in place."

Grace groaned at the reminder, grateful to lean into Rick and let him hold her up.

Rick turned to her and, really seeing her for the first time, gasped in shock. "Grace! Oh, my gosh, what happened? What did she do to you?"

She tried to talk but wound up crying some more, grateful to have him to hang onto her. She managed to tell the story, but all she wanted was for Rick Fleming to kiss her into delirium.

Then he did kiss her and she winced, thinking it might be better to fix her nose before she let him do that again.

The report seemed to take forever, but when it was done and Grace's phone was retrieved from Maria's car, Grace was free to go.

"Man, you look gross," Kyle said when they returned to the kids and explained the entire escapade to Skylar and Rachel's frightened parents.

"Doesn't feel too great, either," Grace admitted, still embarrassed.

"Yeah, I need to take her to a doctor," Rick told them, his arm still around Grace.

Everyone knowing Grace would again need space to get over this latest escapade when she got back to the cabin, Rachel's and Skylar's parents agreed to keep the twins again, and Kyle wanted to stay at Jeff's place.

"I'm sorry I had one moment of doubt about you," Grace said, on the edge of tears again as Rick headed her toward the Escalade.

"Maria played us both, Grace. Let's agree to let it go. You're quite a woman, you know, confronting someone like her."

"No," Grace said, grabbing Rick's shirt. "You risked your life for me. You put yourself between me and a gun. You're *my* hero, Rick."

He grinned, leaning toward her for another kiss when his phone interrupted them. Checking it, he realized it was Grace's mother. He stared at Grace, not sure what to say. He gave an abbreviated explanation and handed her the phone. She might as well tell her mother what happened now.

"I was in the washroom when Rick called," Trudy explained. "He sounded worried. What's going on?"

"Uhm, Mom, something kind of weird happened today. Well, it's been going on all week, but today was the icing on the cake. Don't freak out, but my nose is broken, I'm on my way to the hospital, and I just put someone in jail."

"What?!" Grace pulled the phone away at her mother's shriek. Putting it on speaker phone, like she had with Hannah, Grace spent the remainder of the ride into Ukiah explaining the entire week.

When silence met the end of her story, Grace wondered what Mom was thinking. It might not be good. After all, she had her prejudices against the Fleming boys, too.

"That's the craziest story I've ever heard, but I'm so glad you're safe, Sweetie. Uhm, so, have you worked things out? Are you and Rick *together*?"

He pulled into the hospital parking lot and found a space in the emergency parking area. He turned to face Grace, his eyes twinkling with delight.

"Grace? Are you together?"

"Uh, what do I tell her?" Grace said, not having the right to assume anything.

"How many of your prayers were answered today?" Rick asked, his grin broadening.

She laughed. "More than I can count. And yours?"

"The same."

"Did you see any miracles?"

"More than I could ever have dreamed possible."

"Me too. How many of them put us together?"

"All of them."

Now he laughed.

"Grace?" Trudy said. "Are you there?"

"Yeah, Mom, I'm here."

"I love you, Grace," Rick said.

"I love you, too."

Rick leaned over and pressed a tender kiss to Grace's lips and she didn't even notice her nose. Grinning hurt worse when Rick took the phone from her.

"Mrs. Evans. Hi. It's Rick," he said. "Grace and I have lots of things to work out, like any couple does, but without a doubt, we are together. Which is fantastic, because she's the best thing that ever happened to me."

"Richard Fleming, you'd better take good care of my daughter," Grace's mom insisted. "She deserves the best, you know."

Rick replied, "I completely agree with you, and you don't need to worry. It will be my pleasure to take care of Grace for the rest of my life."

When he hung up the phone, he took Grace's hand in his and kissed her fingers, the sparkle in his eyes telling her that he meant every word.

Acknowledgements

I'm always so humbled by those who give of their time to help an author take a rough idea to a finished manuscript. I couldn't write without them.

My thanks to all of my readers, especially Lori Standring, Teddi Bokovoy, and Nick Svolos (yes, men make great readers and tough critics). A hug for my granddaughter, Isabell, who apparently has conversations with floors. A special thanks to my editor, John Briggs. And of course, since Murphy hides in my right-hand pocket most of the time, I'm very grateful for my sweet husband, Richard, my knight in shining armor, who always champions my cause, no matter how many times I trip, fall down, or break something.

We all have our moments that seem to lack grace. I treasure those who do their best to lift the downhearted and help us carry on.

About the Author

Susan was born and raised a Southern California girl but is grateful to have lived on the Oregon coast and in the Rocky Mountains of northern Utah. She's now enjoying living with her husband in the incomparable beauty of the Redwood forest, nestled against the rugged coast of Northern California.

Susan raised a tribe of children, making ends meet as a registered nurse and lactation consultant, and now her tribe members have tribes of their own and she doesn't get to see enough of them. She loves to travel and is thrilled with a good movie or a great book, but writing is her passion. She writes almost anything, especially epic fantasy and romance.

Susan would love to hear your comments. Please review her book at your favorite retailer or at Goodreads. Take a peek at her website, susantietjen.blogspot.com, and/ or drop her a note at: stietjen.author@gmail.com.

www.ingramcontent.com/pod-product-compliance
Lightning Source LLC
Chambersburg PA
CBHW071905220626
47052CB00002B/209